CINDERELLA UNDONE

NICOLE SNOW

ICE LIPS PRESS

I NEED A WIFE TO SAVE MY DAUGHTER. SHE NEEDS MY MAGIC.

I loved her like a sister forever ago.

Before life served us tragedy with a bitter cherry on top.

Before I learned love isn't a damn fairy tale.

Before I became a single dad.

Protecting my little girl is all I still care about. Kendra is my lifeline if she'll just play along.

Her job is easy.

Wear my ring. Turn my scowl into a family man's smile. Help save my daughter from a scorched earth custody fight.

She gets the Cinderella treatment in return. My money, my mansion, my reputation. I'll put the glass slippers she's slaving over on main street and bend the world to her designer genius.

Simple. Painless. Mutual.

If only she was the shy thing I remembered, and I

wasn't the same red-blooded maniac who wanted her under me years ago.

My wall of ice isn't working like it should. Not when we trade barbs that make me throb. Not when I grab her hair. Not when I can't decide if I want to push her away, or drink those lips in an unending kiss.

Complicated. Messy. Cruel.

That's our crazy truth.

This madness ends one way: Cinderella undone, or me in stitches.

I: PLEASE JUST STAY (KENDRA)

*O*nce upon a time, he was beautiful.

Not because he was my high school crush.

Not because he survived the world crashing down around him like a toxic storm.

Not even because of his rogue good looks, or his family's money – and he had *plenty* of both to go around.

I mean, how could I ever forget my best friend's strapping older brother the second I laid eyes on him? How could I ignore those shoulders, built wide as the Arizona sky? What about the hard blue eyes that cut through everyone? The chiseled jaw framing the world's warmest, sweetest, most mischievous smirk?

How can I pretend I didn't squeeze my thighs together the first time he walked into the room a man, wearing his crisp new uniform, a proud Marine ready for duty? He turned every woman's cheeks in the neighborhood a subtle red. His special gift, and he knew exactly how to use it to get his way.

He was dangerous, scary, and still divine in his heresy.

He kept his charms close, and his secrets closer.

But even when he was a tease, a frustration, and a damn enigma all at once, he was gorgeous.

As long as I live, I'll never see Knox Carlisle as anything less than a striking, brilliant, beautiful beast.

Not even after the night he left, and came home ugly.

* * *

Four Years Ago

"KNOX, you don't have to do this. Don't go. A man can only take so much...listen to me!"

Of course, he doesn't. Not until I beg.

"I can't stand to see you hurt. Stay, Knox. Please."

When he spins around and looks at me, I'm expecting scorn. But what do I know, really?

I'm barely eighteen, a year into college. I haven't lived a fraction of his hell, only imagined it.

"No more, Kendra. You want to help? I asked for good karma and a little help making sure Jamers treats my baby girl right. It's long past time for me to fucking go."

I hear the adorable infant upstairs let out a cry. Then Jamie's voice, soothing her little niece, just six weeks old and already losing both her parents. One to business in one of the world's darkest corners, and another to God only knows what.

No one's seen her mom since the week she left the hospital. We don't know where Sam went, or what happened to her. It's got to be eating him alive, but he never shows his pain. There's nothing in his eyes except a tender love for his daughter, Lizzie, his sweetest creation.

Born to tragedy like a typical Carlisle, through and through.

His face is turned toward her innocent cries. The noise stops him with his hand on the garage door. He looks down for a brief second, before he turns his face up, hitting me with a strained spark in his eyes.

I see my chance.

"You hear that?" I say, walking up to him, reaching for his shoulders. I have to stand on my tip-toes to touch him when he towers over me. "Don't leave her. Lizzie needs you."

So do I. That's the part I don't say, but I know he picks it up subconsciously because his strong face softens. He's listening – I hope.

"Look, I get it. You didn't ask for my advice, but I can't help it. You're not the same man who left the military and came home. This job, the stress, chasing that stupid, reckless woman...it's *killing* you. I've read about that place you're going, the chaos and danger. I'm worried, Knox. Scared you'll make a mistake over there, and maybe you won't come home."

"Let me do the worrying, Sunflower. It's not your place. I'll live. And I'll find her when I get back from this gig. There'll be hell to pay when I do, walking out on me and my little girl like that."

My heart sinks, thinking he's done. Then he grabs my wrist, shoves me against the wall, and holds us there, locked in a gaze beyond words.

He wants me to understand. He wants me to believe he'll be okay. He wants me to think it's business as usual.

3

But I don't. I'm doubt incarnate.

Having his hands on me doesn't help. Every fiber in my being wishes he'd do more than a friendly touch, but I have to remember my place, who I am in his eyes.

I'm his annoying little sister's friend. Practically a surrogate sis.

To him, I'm Sunflower. Too young, too precocious, and too clueless to ever be anything more than a stormy night's sick fantasy.

"What if you make a mistake over there?" I whisper, trying not to shudder when I imagine how dangerous his work can be. He's told Jamie before about the friends who never came home. Chasing diamonds is a dirty business, and always has been. It's as brutal, dangerous, and risky as everything he survived in Afghanistan – sometimes more so. "You're a father now, Knox. And that little girl up there doesn't have a mother."

"Sam *is* coming back," he growls, his eyebrows furrowed. "I'll drag her irresponsible ass home and force her to sign over custody when I finally get a fucking break. Can't believe she screwed me over and ran. First chance I get, I'm tracking her down. We both know that can't happen until I've done my business over there. Enough worry, Kendra. Please. I'll be back in Phoenix in a few weeks."

It hurts when he tears himself away from me. I know it's my stupid, careless crush talking, but I also hate seeing my friend in so much pain.

If only I could keep my mouth shut, stop pouring salt in his wounds...but if I'm wishing for impractical things, I'd might as well wish he never knocked up the spoiled brat who left without a trace after their baby was born.

"I'm not asking for me, Knox," I whisper, lying through my teeth. "Just...please...think about Lizzie."

"She's all I think about, Sunflower. She's the reason I'm doing this. You think I'd give a damn about money if it weren't for her? She's the last piece of the world I have left that hasn't gone to shit. She deserves a piece of my company and the family name far more than I do." His voice is hard, but there's no malice. Just raw determination, devotion, plus a warmth I'll never forget.

"Come here," he says, pulling me closer. It's the firmest embrace I've ever had in those arms that used to pick me up, throw me around, and make me laugh to tears. "Wait for me. Focus on school. Find a decent guy. Keep my little sis in line – God only knows she'd get into a lot more trouble without you. You're a good friend, Sunflower. You *will* see me again. Mark my words and cross the fucking T."

Except I'm not a good friend. My mind spins with the painful truths I'm trying to hide. *I'm selfish. I'm young, heart-stung, and stupid. You're everything I shouldn't want...and all I've wanted since at least fifteen.*

"Whatever. Just...come home safe." I try to let the resignation in my voice hide the turmoil, the want, the fear.

"Oh, I will. There are worse places than where I'm going. Comes with the territory when this family's done gems since my great grandpa. We didn't get where we're at being stupid."

"Duh! I know...I'm not an idiot." It slips out in a whine.

His eyes narrow, big and bright full of sympathy. Everything I don't want from him, still looking at me like a child.

Then, before I know what's happening, my face sits on

5

his palm. His warmth cradles it while his thumb traces soft lines up my cheek.

I can't see through the sadness anymore. I'm terrified this is the last time I'll *ever* lay eyes on this walking contradiction caught in my heart like a rusty hook.

"You've been good to me, Sunflower. Sometimes I think you're the only true friend I've got left in this town. My own boys from the service don't say shit anymore, not since I wouldn't – couldn't – join them for another tour. Keep your heart as pure as your pretty little face, woman. You'd better have a good goddamned boyfriend by the time I get home, too. You're in college now. Too grown up to keep pining after what we might've been in another world, one where you're a few years older, and I'm a better man without an axe over my head. I'll send you a postcard. They're every-where over there when the internet runs like molasses."

Just like that, he tears himself away.

Just like that, I'm flat against the wall and sliding down it while the door slams shut, and I hear his truck's engine become a distant growl as he pulls down the driveway, heading for near-certain death.

Just like that, I'm barely breathing. Too weak in the knees to stand up in time, and run after him, screaming *don't go, don't go, please don't go.*

I do it anyway, and I'm far too late. I run until my knees burn, screaming myself hoarse like a crazy woman, chasing his non-existent truck halfway down the block.

It's hopeless. Defeat sinks through me swifter than the fire in my lungs, knowing I'll never catch him.

Somehow, I get it together, take a few deep breaths, and walk back to his mother's place. I plop down on the sofa with Jamers again. I'm careful to keep my face turned toward the massive TV mounted to the wall so she won't see my red eyes.

"Ugh, did he even say anything about the thirty bucks he still owes me for pizza last week?" Jamie looks up from filing her nails, casting a glance toward the little crib in the corner before she looks my way.

"Nah, his brain was already overseas, I think. Remember how he always got before he went back to active duty?" I turn slowly, and we share a look. Jamie's face is twisted in a sour frown that says she's only concerned with what a big asshole her older brother can be. She'll never understand the bruises spreading in my heart.

"Pig! He's so predictable," she says, shaking her head. "Well, I've got a couple weeks to be a badass aunt, at least, and make sure Lizzie grows up right. Hope he comes home in one piece, and becomes the awesome father he says he'll be."

"He will, Jamers," I say. That, I'm sure.

He has to. Time slows to a crawl.

I keep counting my breaths, watching his baby daughter every few seconds, the closest thing I have to seeing his face. I'm thankful the little girl has so much of him in her. None of the wild, cold bitch who incubated her.

It's a miracle Lizzie's tests were clean after she was born. Amazingly, her mom laid off the drugs while she was pregnant – more than I'd ever give that woman credit for.

Maybe miracles are real.

I still don't understand how Knox had a single hookup with her.

But I don't need to. My brain is too full of fog over the next six weeks.

Life goes on. I pass my mid-terms. Straight As, keeping a flawless 4.0 my first semester at Arizona U.

My design professor keeps inviting me out for drinks, says he wants to talk about scholarships and intro galleries next year. He says he's never seen such grace and ingenuity in my first big project, an elegant evening dress with enough glitter around the cleavage line to make Cleopatra blush from the grave. I try to bask in the praise, but that never comes naturally.

I share fake smiles with my bestie, and real ones when I see Lizzie's little face light up with the cluster of toys her doting grandma fattens weekly.

Six weeks are an eternity. I try not to ask about Knox, and the few times I do, Jamers tells me he's 'surviving over there. Just the usual.'

He's sent their mother a few letters. They're brief, dull, and straight to the point.

Everything I'm sure his reality over there isn't.

When I hear he's finally coming home, safe and sound, I'm stunned. I can't breathe until I see him, overjoyed because normalcy is finally coming back, and all my instincts were wrong.

Except there's nothing normal when he comes through that door, walks right past me without so much as a smile, and scoops Lizzie up in his arms.

He's a changed man.

I watch him kiss his mother on the cheek and take his daughter home without so much as a hello. He barely acknowledges Jamie either. I can't believe my own eyes.

Sure, he has the same good looks, the familiar flame in his blue halo eyes, and a rage against the world. That part stays the same.

The rest has grown colder, somehow. Different. Ugly.

He's as gorgeous as ever, and dead inside.

My instincts were right. My worst fears came true.

Whatever happened over there *killed* him, and sent him home a shell.

* * *

Present Day

TWO AND A HALF years is sometimes an eternity.

In the blink of an eye, I'm grown up. Finished with school, working my first post-grad internship, and thinking about a longer one in Paris next year.

But eternity wouldn't sting if certain parts of life weren't eternal and unchanging.

Jamers comes shuffling down the hallway wiping her brow, slick from the summer sweat of a sunny Phoenix day. Her mother's place is elegant, cool, and cozy in Arizona's toughest season.

"Another glass, Kendra?" she asks, standing by the fridge.

"Please. Just don't spike it this time – I'm trying to concentrate."

She pours us iced tea and flops on the huge sectional

next to me, adjusting her shorts. I'm nose deep in my laptop, focusing on a new pair of glass heels I need to perfect.

They're the reason *the* Eric Gannon tapped me for his internship. One look at my proposal and he skipped the oral interview. For a couple weeks, I was on cloud nine, but now comes the hard part.

The master designer I'm working under wants these babies on the market this fall. That means my name hitched to his brand, and a lot of money.

But only *if* I can actually finish what I've set out to do. I'm trying to keep the bitchy questions to myself, wondering why my best friend isn't hitting her home-work. Again.

Even the quiet doesn't help. She's slumped next to me for a minute before she lets out the world's biggest yawn.

It's infectious. I cover my mouth, and then slap myself on the cheek, shooting her the evil eye. "Do you mind? My day isn't over."

"Sorry. It's brutal out there. Think I'm more toasted and tuckered out than the kiddo," Jamers says, nodding toward the room down the hall. She sips her tea. Toasted is right, it's loaded with so much vodka I can smell it several feet away. "She'll sleep like a charm through the night, guaranteed."

"Sandy will be glad," I say, nodding, never looking up from my screen. "I know she loves being grandma, but everybody deserves a break sometimes."

What do I know about kids? Not much, honestly, but I don't think Mrs. Carlisle could ask for a better grand-daughter than the sleepy little angel in the other room.

Jamers bats her eyes, her lips turned sourly. I don't like it one bit.

"What?"

"Actually, girl...Knox is picking up Lizzie tonight. He's back in town. Just wrapping up business with Mr. Wright before he heads over."

Every muscle in my body stiffens. I keep my eyes glued to the screen, typing gibberish to make myself look busy.

Remember how I said two years can change everything, and nothing whatsoever?

That's Knox. He's the same gorgeous shell with the ugly heart.

The man who decided *just leave me the hell alone* was far too easy when I tried to be his friend.

His ugly heart took a sledgehammer to mine, and didn't stop ramming his message home until he'd demolished my teenage crush.

What happened that night at Danny's party, just a few months after he settled into his life as a single dad...I can't understand it, but it doesn't matter.

I read him loud and clear.

No confusion. No tenderness. No mercy.

It's the past. I can't forgive, forget, or let him get to me a second time.

The asshole rarely speaks to me anymore since that night, except when he decides to acknowledge my presence in the Carlisle mansion with a snide remark or two for appearances. Thankfully, that's rare.

I try to avoid him. Usually, it works. He only sticks his head in to pick up his daughter.

Reality ruined him. It hit after Africa, and wherever the hell he went to look for Sam.

He's realized he'll be a single dad forever, and the wild child mistake responsible for half of Lizzie's genes is never coming home.

Nobody on the planet can find her. I think even he's given up, and it's widened the void in his heart.

"He won't be around long, I'm sure," Jamers says, stuffing a stick of gum in her mouth. "Seriously, don't be afraid of my brother. He doesn't have time these days for more tricks."

Tricks? Not the word I'd use for the poison dart he lodged in my heart. But I haven't told her what he did to me, and I'm not planning to after sitting on it for so long.

"I'm *not* afraid. He's different, is all." I suck in a hurried breath, hoping it'll calm the fire in my blood. "His attitude isn't my problem. I'm just glad he isn't so gruff with Lizzie. It's the only time we see him smile, showing a crack in his armor that says he might still be human."

"He's been through a lot, Kay. Not that it's any excuse."

"Correction: he never *got* through it." I look up, seeing the empathy and sadness lighting up her eyes. She shares a softer version of the same baby blues every Carlisle man, woman, and child seems to inherit.

"What's the latest news? Nothing?" It's been months since I asked.

My friend shakes her head slowly. She sits up straight and sniffs, playing with her long black hair. "I think he hired another detective a few weeks ago. Saw him talking to an older man a few times at his place, when ma and me came by to pick up a few heaps of clothes he didn't need for Lizzie anymore. She outgrows the old stuff so fast. We're all about donations for the tax write off."

I snort. It's impossible to believe a few old outfits make

much difference in this family of multi-millionaires. Then again, her mother has always done things differently since losing her husband. Humility and generosity win her a lot of respect, including mine.

"Really, there's nothing new," Jamie says with a sigh. "Just more chasing ghosts. I don't know how he handles it, working with Sam's father everyday. Their relationship isn't the best. Knocking up your boss' daughter will do that. Kind of a miracle Lizzie's turning out as great as she is –"

She stops mid-sentence. "Hey, creep-o, don't you ever knock?"

I do a slow turn, and a double take when I see the tall figure standing near the wall. Knox is immaculate, untouched as ever by today's hundred and fifteen degree weather. His crisp grey suit matches the storm on his face, blue eyes focused on us like pins.

"Not when it's this house. Where's my baby girl?" He casts a demanding glance Jamie's way.

"In her room sleeping. Where else?" My best friend sticks her tongue out. "In case you hadn't noticed, normal people get baked in this sun."

"Baked. I'm sure you know plenty about that, Jamers. I'll let you nap while Sunflower does your homework."

I bristle when he calls me that name. Even after half a dozen encounters where he used it over the years, it hurts. "Hello to you, too, ass."

The delicious chills Sunflower used to bring are gone, replaced by honest, cruel ice.

"I haven't written so much as an outline for her this semester, if you want to know the truth," I say, turning back to my screen. I'm so over him, and yet he somehow makes me blush.

It's a conditioned response. It isn't real. Not anymore.

I've learned to hide the redness when it kisses my cheeks.

It's hard to believe he ever called me a friend, two years and a lifetime ago.

"I don't care. Long as you're letting my sis sink or swim. It's her degree. I'm sure you're busy, putting yours to work on making Dorothy a new pair of ruby slippers." He turns, aiming a quick glance at the heels on my screen.

"Dorothy? You'd have better luck with Cinderella because these shoes are glass," I say smugly. I've heard both names plenty of times. Always one or the other when he wants to insult my career, everything I've poured my heart and soul into.

"I'm too old for fairy tales." It's all he says before I hear his polished shoes hit the tile floor as he walks away, refusing to meet Jamie's sympathetic eyes.

I stare after him even when he's gone, anger burning in my eyes so full it physically hurts.

"Good reminder I'd better get on my crap tonight now that there's an evening without mom and Lizzie," she says, reaching for her backpack on the floor.

I don't say anything, just look at my screen, typing a few more notes. Knox returns a few minutes later, cradling a sleepy little girl in his arms. He stops near the door leading to the garage, the same exit he walked out of years ago as the man I used to worship.

Don't look at him.

It's as bad as eyeing a solar eclipse, and of course, I do

it anyway. There's a different man in my screen's reflection, a mirror darkly reflecting someone else.

"Come on, peewee. We're going home," he tells Lizzie, stopping to plant a gentle kiss on her forehead.

I watch their ghostly outlines. It's just enough to tug on my heartstrings, making me wonder for the thousandth time how much of him is left behind his smirking mask. If there's anything, he saves it for his daughter. She's the only one allowed to reach inside the ice chest holding his heart.

He murmurs a few more words to her, soft baby things I can't hear. Alien to my ears, coming from his savage lips.

Then the door creaks open and falls shut with a dull *thud.* Knox never says goodbye.

When I look over, my friend is holding her accounting textbook, probably feigning interest in her classes for my benefit.

"I'm sorry, Kendra. Something's been eating him this last week. More than usual, I mean."

"Really? I couldn't tell. He's just as big a dick as he was three months ago." I'm serious, and more than a little hurt.

I should be numb to it by now. I shouldn't care. I should believe the little words in my head I started telling myself years ago, when I knew he'd never be the same, and I'd damn well better get over it.

But we were good to each other, once. That's what makes this hard.

I remember when we were friends, even if we were never meant to be lovers. I just can't fathom why he's hardened himself to every human being on the planet who isn't his little girl.

15

Or why he shut me down so coldly when I offered him my warmth.

Why do the worst mysteries always go unsolved?

"More tea?" Jamers stands, grabbing my glass off the end table next to me, forcing a smile. "It's the least I can do. I've talked to him before about his rude fucking temper. I'm sorry nothing's changed. Someday, if we hold out long enough, maybe he'll be normal again."

"Jamers, please. Don't bother. That thing I had for your brother was a *long* time ago. It isn't like he's hurting my feelings." *Yeah, right.* "I've accepted who he is, even if I don't understand why. It's not like we're best friends or anything."

"Yeah, yeah, you're a big girl. You don't need my help. Just sayin'," Jamie says as she trots off toward the kitchen.

It's true. Knox and I aren't friends. Not anymore.

Nothing good lasts forever, or so they say. And if some things are too amazing to be true, or to last, then the ideal I built up was so vivid it killed me when truth threw its first punch.

I have no illusions. The older, massive, otherworldly Adonis I came dangerously close to loving isn't there anymore.

New Knox isn't the man who used to fill my head full of dreams every night, who drove me around town in his first car, or who hugged me so tight it hurt when I threw my arms around him every time he'd lace up his boots and straighten his desert camo fatigues, before he climbed aboard another military plane for the unknown.

I don't know what's eating him, assuming Jamie is even right and it's more than usual.

Frankly, I don't care.

He isn't my problem anymore, and I was never his.

If he ever really cared – truly, deeply, madly – if our friendship wasn't just a fad or a twisted act, then he never would've slammed his soul shut. He never would've become a pillar of lifeless, self-loathing stone before my eyes.

He certainly never would've given me those vicious glances bent on making my heart more like his than I'll ever admit.

II: SPLIT ROCK (KNOX)

"*Y*ou want *more*, Victor? Christ. Men broke their backs to bring inventory back here, expecting it to last for years. What happened to the precision cuts? The labs? You told me you had plans, you underhanded son of a –"

Fuck. I take a deep breath, stopping the insult when it's too little, too late. Everyone heard. They're already cowering.

The tension is so thick in this board room, it's like being underwater. The career beaks staring at me are all overpaid brains. They stayed behind, crunching numbers and painting fancy graphics on screens, getting on their knees for the tax man. They never busted their asses in those God forsaken places that seem to get darker and uglier every time I visit – and they never risked their lives, and lost, like the three men in my crew last time.

They never saw the kids, the pain, or touched pure evil.

Neither did their boss. The animal in the prim suit in

front of me never shows any outward emotion. He stares through his stone cold mask, his nostrils flaring once, before he says the words I'd stake my fortune on predicting. "Everybody out, please. I need a moment alone with Mr. Carlisle."

I'm able to put a cork in my rage, for the company's sake, while they clear the room. Then, as soon as the door shuts behind the last man, I'm done. *Pop goes the fucking weasel.* "Mr. Carlisle was my father, asshole. You can start calling me Knox, and remembering we're family."

"Please, don't bring our personal issues here. This is business, pure and simple. As you'll recall, I never made any strict guarantees about how inventory would be divided. I made inquiries with the labs in question, and had a whole team studying the latest growth and precision cutting techniques, but diamonds aren't people, *Knox.* You can't just make them appear from nothing."

"Now, who's getting personal?" I ball my fists under the table, eyes fixed on him like an eagle as he sighs, reaches into his pocket for a royal purple handkerchief, and wipes the sweat beading on his brow.

No sympathy. He still thinks I'm a murderer, or at least an accessory, and *he's* the one who's sweating?

"You told me you'd stretch our resources. Invest in new technologies. Spare us from more of these goddamn missions. I don't see you doing anything except pissing money away, gearing up to risk more blood. I *told* you about the kids."

"Ah, yes, the infamous debriefing. I read the summary, but not the details. This isn't an emotional business, man."

"It's more than hearts and minds when you put boots on the ground. It's people's lives." I want to add *prick* to the end of my sentence. So bad I bite down on my tongue, tasting blood.

"Yes, yes, and that's where you come in," he says, folding his hands neatly in front of him. "Nobody leads better acquisitions than you. We'd have a lot more men to replace if it weren't for your very specific talents learned in the service."

I don't say anything. I can't believe my own ears. This self-righteous fuck is sucking up to me *now?* Pretending I don't see right through his flimsy gratitude, his little pep talk about my 'unique place' in this business? That's the phrase he's used since I filled my old man's seat at this table.

"I don't think I'm asking the world, Knox. You're serving this company as best you're able, putting your special talents to work. You weren't ready for a place in this board room years ago. But neither of us could've planned for Martin's untimely passing, the shakeups that came after, or your...rather earnest interest in overseeing high level strategy for Black Rhino."

"I've earned my place here, so you can stop trying to cut me down. You deal with me, not my father." I try not to let the asshole get to me. I catch myself before I freeze up sometimes, thinking about my twenty-first birthday, when dad had a heart attack in front of us.

He hit the floor without so much as a goodbye. The paramedics never had a chance. I bawled my eyes out like a kid half my age for the next week.

That day, I learned mortality. A week later, I swore I'd never be like that fucking liar. Not after I found the letters in his office. Each sealed and addressed to a woman I'd never heard of.

Judy. A name as anonymous as it is infuriating, and I have zero desire to change it.

Dad left behind a secret mistress and a fake life. That was his legacy.

If only he'd left better lessons. I wish the rat bastard taught me sooner that sitting at the table with Victor Wright is bad news, and I should have treated his screwed up, missing daughter like kryptonite from day one.

"Careful, boy. You've earned an executive position, yes, but you're not a full partner," Victor reminds me. "Per the terms of your father's trust and our charter, that doesn't happen for a few more years. Not until you've proven your worth to this company. So, as you'll recall, that means I have to sit here and listen to your input on how we should trim our diamonds to nubs and hike our prices. My obligations *end* with listening, Knox. As the final, sole, and senior decision maker in this company, I think I'll let you flail around in your pathetic rage, while I make the hard decisions about what's best for the organization."

"My share's late again, too. Should've gotten my deposit weeks ago." My hands go together under the table, bulging. *Where the fuck is it?* I want to say, but I've already shown him he still has a disgusting amount of power over me.

Eight million dollars doesn't fall down a black hole, except when I have to beg this man like a dog.

"Ah, so that's what this is about." Victor smiles, his high end dental implants almost as white as his hair. "Your chief concern is always with yourself, isn't it? If I didn't have to tolerate your presence on the board, I'd keep you delegated to acquisitions and mail your check without any need for these lovely chats. That's where you belong, boy. We both know. Down in the dirt. Building fresh callouses on your hands. You're *not* your father. He gave you an open road to a good school and a sensible way up the ladder."

He pauses, smiling. "Shall we remember what happened next?"

"Go ahead," I snarl, swallowing the lump of black hate stuck in my throat. "Then we can take another trip down memory lane, and remember how your whore of a daughter never did a damn thing for Lizzie except serve as her incubator."

His smile is gone. I'm not done. "You heard me. I've been waiting a long time to say it to your face. I'd spend whole days here cursing her fucking name in front of you, if only we didn't have to drain the bad blood between us once or twice a year, long enough for a family photo. If you weren't my little girl's grandfather, I'd –"

No. Stop. I have to, before making any threats he could use against me in a court of law.

Damn, if it isn't hard to shut up.

"Tell me, Knox. I'd love to know precisely what you have in mind." He reaches up, adjusting his tie, a monstrous smirk hanging on his lips. "Would you like to go out back and take care of this right now? Perhaps I'll let you have your way, push my face into the dirt, knock my teeth out like the pea-brained barbarian you always were. And to think, Martin used to drink himself stupid some evenings after hours, worrying himself to an early grave over your teenage hijinks. Say..."

I've never hated the slow, tense drawl in a man's voice so much. I'm not going to like what this heartless fuck has to say next. I *know* it'll take everything I've got not to take the bait into punching him out right here.

"Sometimes, just between us, I wonder if all that worry for you is what caused his heart attack? A man of his class can only take so much with a son like you."

I bolt up, sending the chair flying behind me on its wheels. It crashes against the wall, something that slows my descent on him just long enough to wonder why he's pressing my buttons so blatantly.

It should rub me worse than it does. But he doesn't know dad left me sick with his secrets, and I'll stop just short of ruining my life defending his name.

"Name what you really want, asshole? This isn't working."

Victor leans back in his overstuffed chair, the nasty glint in his eye growing. They're a rich hazel color, almost gold. So different from the eyes my little girl got from me, it's hard to believe this bastard is related. "Frankly, I'd like you to learn your place. You're a charity case, Knox. A leather boot very good at kicking up dust and diamonds when we need fresh inventory, and less whining. If you're telling me you won't do what you're best at – wheeling and dealing with third world scum who'd love to slit your throat – then I'd *love* for you to drop the pretenses. Realize you're no equal. Take your measly seven figures, make me a buyout offer, and get the hell out. Become a real dad to our Lizzie without screwing her up. Stay out of my boardroom, begging for scraps you don't deserve."

"Scraps?" I take a step closer, but no further. I'm not giving this prick any reason to call security. Not that I think they'd stop me from having my way, considering who mentors them. "My family *earned* our place at this goddamn company for seventy years. I've done it, too, shoving my hands places you've never laid a precious finger on. I'm not your dog, Victor. I know, *know,* you'd rather be rid of me. Then you can hire more brutal, stupid roughnecks who won't mind the kids with their missing limbs over there, or how many casualties our own teams take. As long as you've got a few more diamonds to spin to gold, who the hell cares?"

His wicked smile wilts. He sucks his bottom lip in, and then with a sigh, reaches under the table for his briefcase. I'm standing there like a hand grenade, trying not to go off, wondering what the hell he's doing.

Victor pushes his case further down the table a second later, holding up a thin stack of papers. *Now, what?*

"You know, we'll never call a truce, not after everything that's happened...but I really hoped it wouldn't come to this. I don't do this lightly." There's a frigid sadness in his expression unlike anything I've ever seen. Since when does this bastard show heart over anything? "The truth is, Black Rhino is moving on, into the new century, with or without your cooperation, Knox. I won't be around forever. We need a better image, a family friendly one. Maybe Lizzie will pull it off someday, as soon as my trust makes it to her, and should she desire to carry on the family tradition here. In the meantime, I want you gone."

He can't be serious. Does he realize one of us won't be walking out of here alive if he's threatening me?

"Fuck you. I'm ten times the family man you'll *ever* be. You haven't even shown up for her birthday two years in a row." Placing my hands on the table, I feel the coolness on the wooden surface soothing my rage, just enough to lean over, looking him dead in the eye. "I'll never leave.

Give me my fucking share, old man, and stop playing games. Respect what I've earned. There's nothing you can do."

"Actually, Knox, that's where you're wrong. Humor me for a second and *read* what's in front of you. I know it's hard for you. You do bullets, not words." He pushes the papers toward me.

Gritting my teeth, I look down, my eyes scanning the dense text covering the first page. I see a judge's name, a court's address, then a lawyer's name next to Victor's. My heart doesn't start to pound until I see the references to Elizabeth C. Carlisle, and multiple mentions of custody arrangements.

No. Anything but this.

Not Lizzie.

You fucking sadist.

Words like unfit, irresponsible, and psychologically disturbed surround my name like a water stain seeping through the wall.

Now, I get why he isn't smiling. He doesn't need to. He's hit me so square in the balls they're in my throat.

He's threatening my family. My daughter. Vying for custody, ripping away the only thing my heart still beats for in the morning since my life became a wreck, since I shut everyone else who ever mattered out.

Ma. Jamie. Kendra.

Fuck, that last one hurt the most. Still gets to me like a dagger through the ribs when we're in the same room.

So many bridges burned for their good, and mine. All so I could save the last shell shocked piece of my heart for my little girl.

"I trust you're able to see the seriousness of the situation?" Victor's whisper oozes through my ears like a hushed roar.

I have a sudden flashback from Sierra Leone. A rival miner, some dispute with the man we bought our gems from. Ended with the maniac pulling his gun on my men. He pulled the trigger less than an inch from my face, and then we were on the ground, hands locked around each other's throat. I choked him out first.

Never thought I'd ever want to feel another human being's life fade beneath my bare hands again. Never, until now, when I look at Victor, and it takes every ounce of strength not to murder him where he sits.

"Knox, one more time, take my offer, or go. It doesn't have to come to this. I'll be sure you get help, the best money therapy can buy for your very serious, untreated anger issues. You can stay with Lizzie and do this the civilized way, like men, on *my* terms. Or you can throw away what little you have left. Your choice."

Choice. He's giving me one right now, but it's not in the words coming from his mouth.

Something stinks about the way he's egging me on. I look away from his monstrous face, turning toward the TV mounted in the corner. It's on mute, the day's news displayed, a talking head blabbing on while a financial ticker streams across the bottom with stock prices. I see the little black bulge plugged into the USB port, the one that wasn't there last week.

This whole conversation is bugged.

Fuck.

It's a setup, shoving this heinous shit in my face. He *wants* me to go crazy, break his jaw, turn his conference room upside down...all so he can march straight to the courts with the silver bullet on the table, and enough proof chambered to end me by ripping my little girl away from me forever.

One word starts pounding in my head, louder than my own heartbeat: *go*.

I don't do anything on my way out. I don't even stop by my missing seat to grab my laptop in its case off the floor. I just walk.

"Wait, where are you –"

Victor is on his feet, a scowl on his face. I don't look back even once as I rip open the door, and run.

My knees are numb. My blood runs cold. I don't even breathe until I'm in my car, engine started, making a direct course for the gate surrounding Black Rhino Jewelry's world headquarters. Victor hasn't had the time or will to make the security at the gate hold me over, thank God.

It's a long, hard ride home. First, I swing by mom's place to pick up my little girl.

No Kendra today. Just Jamie, who gives me her usual tongue lashing when I walk straight past her and scoop up my kid, waking her on the bed with a soft hand through her dark hair. There's so little of that crazy, disappearing bitch in her, and even less of Victor. I'm more grateful than ever today.

I slip Jamie a hundred bucks before I leave, pay for babysitting, something to blow at the bar when she's done pretending to study her accounting books.

"No Kendra today?" I say, unsure whether I'm relieved or wounded she isn't around.

"Like you care, idiot," Jamie says, rolling her eyes. "She has a life beyond waiting for your stupid jokes about her very successful career, Knox. Just wait. One of these days, she'll leave Phoenix, and you'll need to find yourself a new punching bag."

"Her loss." There's no time for this. I walk out, Lizzie in my arms.

Honestly, her absence would be my gain. I'd finally be free from the sour crap I've never been able to keep in check when she's around.

Kendra is a walking, talking, evil memory in the flesh. I sweat poison when we're in the same room.

I had to cut her off. I had to close the door on us. After Sam, and the business overseas, I knew full well I'd only bring her sorrow if I ever let her get as close as she wanted when I still knew how to smile, and she was still just that plucky little girl.

It's tough as hell to smile when I've got her buckled in, handing her a juice box I picked up on the ride here. Don't have a clue what I'll make for dinner. Something good, something healthy, because I *never* let my daughter eat crap. Even with all the work, so much gone wrong, I haven't buckled down and hired a chef for the condo yet.

I don't just want her eating right. I want her sitting down with family, sharing the smile on her little face that lights up the room, whether that's with me, or ma, or even Jamie – as annoying as my sister is.

When I'm stopped at the light a couple blocks from home, I see Lizzie in the rear view mirror, giving me a tired smile as she sucks her juice box's straw. "Daddy?"

"Yeah, baby girl? What's up?" I don't know how she's able to make me smile, and mean it, but she does. There's a reason I love the evenings.

"Why're you so mean to Ms. Kendra?"

I keep my smile, but my hands tense on the wheel.

"She and I have...a history. You'll understand someday. Know what?" I turn, before the light goes green, and reach for her little hand, giving it a squeeze. "You've just given daddy a very good reminder how important it is to be nice. I haven't done the best job with that lately, Lizzie. I'm sorry. I'll do better. For you, and for Kendra, too."

Shit, if only it were so easy. I've done everything in my power to torch the biggest love-hate quandary of my life, and bury our history forever. Short of pulling up stakes in Arizona, abandoning the family biz, and taking Lizzie somewhere else away from our family, I haven't found a way to make it permanent.

Most days, I spend wondering when all this went wrong. Why it's so easy to treat the girl who used to mean the world like she's less than nothing, just another splinter in my life worth ripping out with soft curses between my teeth.

It's easy to pinpoint other times my life went off the rails.

I can do it with Africa.

I can do it with my stupid, drunken one-night stand with Sam Wright.

But I can't do it with her.

Not with Kendra. Whenever I let myself step inside our darkest memories, I only remember everything that used to be right.

* * *

Five Years Ago

29

I THROW down my shitty flip phone and sit on the alabaster steps at my buddy's place, fingers trembling as I reach for a smoke.

By now, several years in the Marines, I thought I'd seen it all. Death, explosions, blood on the streets, villages brought to ruins. All the ravages war brings and a steaming cup of misery on the side.

Yet, no wartime horror ever shook me up half as bad as the words Sam just said over the phone.

I'm pregnant, Knox. Fifteen weeks. You'd better get your ass out of the military and help me before daddy finds out. It's time to grow up.

Forget her powerful daddy. What she really means is, *before I have to give up parties, booze, ecstasy abuse, and fucking a new sucker every week.*

None worse than me. I'm officially the biggest chump of all by screwing the psycho daughter of my old man's business partner.

I'm not stupid. Knew it was a mistake the morning after it happened. The pussy I'd had hit me through my hangover fog like a semi doing eighty.

But I never thought the universe had a sense of humor this sick. Never thought my dealings with Samantha Wright would be one more awkward regret.

I'd shrug, forget her, and move onto happier hunting grounds. Not wind up shackled to the apocalypse.

I don't know what the fuck just happened after that call. It's surprisingly hard to fathom this new reality, where I'm responsible for another human being's existence.

Jesus.

I sit down with a smoke tucked between my lips,

drawing a long drag. Sweet relief fills my lungs. It's a bad habit I've had the last few years, one I swear I'm giving up the day I'm discharged. It's easy to pick up in Afghanistan, when there's nothing to do at the isolated outposts except smoke and crack dirty jokes – right up until the moment some Taliban assholes start lobbing mortars at your head.

I'm still sitting there, face in my palm, when I hear the door to the house fly open and bang shut behind me.

"You look like *hell*, Knox. Hangover already?" I'd love to wipe the nasty little smirk off my little sister's lips. "You know, we can take some of that beer you brought off your hands, if it's hurting you so much..."

She's standing there with a towel wrapped around her, hair slick from swimming. Her shadow's there, too, next to her.

Kendra Sawyer. Bashful, hot, and way too young for me. They're both friends with my pal's youngest sister, another girl named Mandy. Seems like everybody's here today to break in the new swimming pool Danny's parents just put in.

"Fuck off, Jamers. I am *not* giving you booze. Don't even try to sneak one past me, or I'll throw you in my truck and drive you straight home to ma. You're not too old for a whoopin'."

"She wouldn't dare! You're just trying to scare me." Sis sticks her tongue out, crossing her bratty arms. Kendra pulls her towel closer, careful to look away, as if I don't notice the schoolgirl crush she's had on me for years.

Damn, do I wish Sunflower was older sometimes. Maybe then I'd have stuck it in her instead of crazy a couple months ago, and saved myself some major grief.

"Seriously, Jamie. Go. Leave me the fuck alone and

stay out of trouble. I'm in the middle of sobering up anyway, seeing how I'm your ride home."

"Okay, okay. Ass!" She pouts, pulling on Kendra's arm. "Come on. Let's go find some fun before Mr. Uptight tucks us in for curfew."

"You go on, Jamers. I need some fresh air." Kendra sits down next to me as her friend shrugs, and scampers off to find more mischief. "How're you hanging in there? This must seem boring, or very weird, after all the time spent over there. I can't imagine coming home, after everything..."

I smile. She's curious what I do in uniform, but she's too damn shy to stop dancing around it and ask. Her innocence is frustrating and adorable.

"Sunflower, this is heaven. Trust me. I've got every reason in the world to smile each day I'm out of some crazy asshole's sniper sights. Same goes when I can drive around town without worrying about rolling over an IED. Only thing *weird* around here is why you're not letting my sis get you into trouble with some boy."

Her face goes red, and she looks away. "I'm in the middle of finals. Can't have that kind of distraction."

"Get over yourself, darling. Someday, you'll be good and ready. Wait for college. Every wide-eyed, amped up shithead with a functional dick will want a piece of the girl who's smart enough to skip into Arizona U a sopho- more. Watch out. Their kind hops on innocence like a dog slobbers on a bone. And if any of them give you trouble, call me."

She laughs, studying the serious look on my face. I'm not joking.

I don't know why, but picturing her with a gaggle of

twig boy jocks watching her every move gets my blood hot.

She's too good to be fucked with. That's what it is. Kendra's too sweet to wind up deflowered by the average beer chugging, emoji flirting pissant from the frat houses.

"I'm almost grown. Can't have you fighting my battles forever, Knox, but thank you." She gives me a knowing look, and we share the last time I saved her from high school tears. "What's eating you? I thought you'd be out back longer, screwing around with Danny's new diving board. It's so fun!"

I look at her glumly. So far, I think I'm the only other person on the planet who knows the big secret Sam just dumped over the phone. I've never liked bottling my venom and hiding it.

What's so wrong with letting her have a sip? She's always been tight-lipped, and never spills her secrets, much less anybody else's.

"How about a dirty little secret? Mine," I say, waiting for curiosity to light up her pretty green eyes. Kendra leans in. "I'm having a kid. Just found out. This lame fucking late night hookup I had when I was in Scottsdale on leave last time had consequences. I'm a father, Sunflower, and one more broken condom statistic."

I wish like hell that shredded rubber was worth it. Only thing I remember about that coupling is how dim her eyes looked when I brought her over the edge, and let my balls throb loose when I'd had my fill of mediocre pussy.

It wasn't even good. I've had a dozen lays better than Sam. Disappointing for a crazy one, especially. Even the ones who think Elvis is President get wild, leaving a man with stroke fodder for weeks.

Not Sam. I got a chore fuck and an orgasm more like a sneeze than a proper release.

But the universe doesn't give two shits what I bought. It was enough to make a baby.

I've never seen the little angel in front of me so red. Kendra's heartbeat burns in her face, lightning her up like a Valentine. For a second, I wonder if I've fucked up, laying something this heavy on her. So far, it isn't much relief.

Then, next thing I know, she's got her little hands around me. She crashes into my chest, swinging herself around my neck, grasping me with all her might.

"Oh, Knox. Don't worry! Everything'll be okay. You'll be *great* at this stuff, a total natural. I know you'll be an amazing father." How she says it without a hint of irony or doubt in her tone, I'll never know.

Okay, damn it. So, I'm touched.

I reach up, squeezing her arm, running one hand softly and swiftly down her face. I make it fast. A second longer, and it'd be on the edge of something more than a man embracing a good friend.

"I'm not worried. I'll live," I tell her, after she pulls away, noticing the fog in her eyes.

"Why me?" she whispers, clinging to my bicep with one hand. "I'm glad you said something – no one's meant to carry feelings so heavy around – but why me over your friends?"

"Because you won't squeal to anybody. Not even Jamers." I smile, my busted up heart rattling once in my chest when I release her, and stand, throwing my half-burned smoke down on the driveway. My boot smothers it. "I can't rat off to Danny and the boys, and not my army buddies neither. Not yet. This one's between you and me, woman. Our little secret."

"If you ever need anything...I'm here. It's the least I can do after last year, at prom, when you –" her voice goes flat.

Christ, almost a year later, and she's still choked up about it. I remember like it was yesterday, and I smile, grasping her hand between mine one more time. It's so small, so fragile, so fucking innocent to be pinned right between my dirty fingers.

"Forget it, Sunflower. Told you before, it was nothing. Least I could do after that little jerkoff left you high and dry, without a date at the last minute. I'd still like to wring his neck." I don't get kids today. Kendra's boy skipped out just a day before her Junior prom, when she had her dress picked out and everything, all so he could buckle down for another night of Mountain Dew and Call of Duty with his idiot friends.

"Yeah, well, it was almost a bad night. Would've been a whole lot worse if you hadn't barged in on Jamie, pulled me away from the girls, and took me out to that drive-in place. I haven't been back to Camelback since. It was our place that night, Knox. Just you and me."

I've never heard a woman I haven't laid talk so much about a place we went, and mean so much.

So, there's more than one secret between us. More than one moment, sponsored by this strange, magnetic, fate-crafted pull between us. I'll never understand it, honest to God.

When I'm over there, thousands of miles from

everyone I know and love, or a good burrito joint, I remember that night. Made my time off worth it, hiking up Camelback Mountain with her, plopping down in front of the crystal starry sky.

Started out in an attempt to cheer her up. Ended with both of us smiling, happy, finding our peace.

We ate our burgers and malts on the mountaintop in dead, heavy silence, whispering a few times each hour about the moon, the constellations, the rock formations surrounding Phoenix's halo white lights below.

Leaves me wondering if the universe keeps bringing us together for a chance to make up bad karma.

I always try. Grabbing her hand one more time, I squeeze, trying not to let my mind wander to all the things these fingers would do if she were just a little older, and not my sister's sidekick.

"Get the hell out of here, Sunflower. I'm serious. Find some fun with Jamie, but reign her in for me."

"You know I will," she says.

It's hard to walk away when I know her eyes follow me, big as the summer sun, wishing one day I'll crack, turn back, throw her over my shoulder, and then into my car. I remember how those stupid, reckless teenage fantasies used to be because I had plenty.

Sometimes I feel like shit for leading her on, intentional or not. There's lines I've crossed in my life – too many to count since boot camp – but doing anything with Kendra Sawyer involving no clothes and a sting on her heart is a gate to hell I simply won't open.

Not if I want to keep what's left of my soul. And once this baby comes into the world, looking up to me because

I know it won't get much from its ma, I'll need my humanity.

I get in my truck and go, leaving Kendra to the care-free mischief every kid deserves at eighteen, and me to my worries.

Chances are it'll be the last time in a good, long while I lay my shit so thick on another human being.

If war has taught me anything, it's to keep my mouth shut. Words never help. A spine of steel does when we're facing life, death, or just shitty morale. I don't know much about parenting, but I'm sure this lesson goes double.

Lucky for me, I've always been a quick learner.

III: PRETTY DESIGNER MEMORIES
(KENDRA)

*W*as it really six years ago this month?

It was, and I was just a kid. I shouldn't even think of it, much less dwell.

I'm smart, mature, and knee deep in building my career. Everything that *should* matter infinitely more than the stupid, physically uneventful night that made Knox Carlisle my young adult idol.

Of course, it doesn't.

I can't get away. The man who's never truly far from my thoughts comes bounding back in when I've left our memories too little, too long. Like it or not, I'm reminded how he turned the worst night of my life into magic, and how big a fool I am for holding onto it when he's been nothing except a ginormous asshole for years.

It doesn't help that my laptop's background has rotated through its seasonal selection of Camelback Mountain pics. A nightscape comes on my screen. I see a familiar star-dashed sky.

It's too much. It hurts to look, and staring is just torture.

But it's even worse looking away.

When I take a few seconds to rest my eyes, when I step away from my computer and come back with a glass of water and an artisan chocolate bar, I hallucinate. I see more than what's there for an agonizing fraction of a second.

I swear on all that's holy I'm able to make out two tiny figures sitting at the mountain's zenith, their legs slung over the winding rocks, eyes fixed on the yawning heavens above.

That's when I hear his words.

Screw him, darling. Chicken-necked immature fuckboys are everywhere. Give it a little time. You're pretty, put together, and sharp as the edge of the moon.

One fine day, you'll find yourself a man. Then we'll laugh our asses off when I do the toast at your wedding, telling your future husband how we spent your prom night like two astronomy nerds fixed on the skies.

Yeah, *screw him.*

Except, years later, I can't even remember the name of the little idiot who stood me up. It's not him I'm cursing, or laughing about.

It's the best friend I've lost.

It's worse than Knox just disappearing, taking off, fading while he clutches a piece of my heart. I have to see the walking shell he's become, a constant risk each time I stay too long at Jamie's place.

It haunts me, and it shouldn't. I hate him for it, honestly, for keeping me tethered to a past I've tried *so hard* to bury.

Straight As, stellar networking, and a work-a-holic obsession go far. They just haven't brought me the right opportunity that comes with a one-way ticket out of Phoenix forever.

Not yet. *Someday.*

And someday seems a little more out of reach when I hear a heavy fist banging on our front door, rattling me out of the Photoshop adjustments I'm making to the latest pair of heels on my screen. I'm sitting with my laptop on our back porch, mom reading next to me. The noise surprises her, too, and she jumps up and heads for the door before I move a muscle, flashing a *let me handle this* smile.

I try to go back to work. I don't get far when I hear my name in a deep, gruff, achingly familiar voice.

"Mrs. Sawyer," he growls respectfully. "Is Kendra home?"

"Knox Carlisle, it's been years! Where the heck have you been keeping yourself – and with such a delightful little girl?! Come in."

I can't make out the small talk as they head my way. My heart is already in my throat, strumming a hundred miles a second. When mom brings him to the breakfast bar I'm using as a desk, a disbelieving smile on her face, I'm on my feet.

Glaring.

Too bad I can't stay mad when he walks in with Lizzie in his arms, the remains of an orange push-up in one hand, an orange ring around her cherub smile.

"Honey, look who I found on the porch! Surely, you remember –"

"I see him all the time, mom." It comes out sharper

than I intend, and my annoyance comes back when I see her happy smile drop. "Knox, what's up?"

He turns, casting a wry smile at my mother. "I'm sorry, but we need a word alone. It's nothing too serious, just business. Would you mind watching my daughter for a few, Mrs. Sawyer?"

Business?! I hate what he calls it, I do, but it's not the worst part. If he's here to deal with the very messy, hole-through-the-heart unfinished *business* between us the last several years, then I'm game.

But I know instinctively that's too good to be true. *What the hell does he want?*

"Oh, of course. And it's Sandy, Knox. No need for this Mrs. Sawyer stuff here," mom murmurs, stepping aside. "Can I bring you two some lemonade? Water?"

"Nothing for me, sunshine. Thanks." He passes the little girl into mom's waiting arms. Her smile and his words raise her smile faintly again. I hate it. "Kendra?"

"I'm coming," I say, turning around quickly to shut my computer, before I walk past, leading him down the hall to my room without another word.

When we're inside, I shut the door quickly, then flatten myself against the wall. My eyes blink a little too long. My lungs are drowning in cement. *Breathe.*

"Tell me what you really want." It's not a question. I need an answer, and then I need him to get the hell *out.*

Too bad that's impossible. Knox does a typically Knox thing: pacing my room, prowling uncomfortably close to my belongings. Really, just having him here at all is deeply uncomfortable, considering mom's house and the little room I use as a home office is nothing like the palace he grew up in.

"Big dreams," he says, picking up a shoe in the corner, next to my bed. "I'm sure every flashy fuck in Old Town Scottsdale will want one. How much is the going price?"

It's another experimental set for Gannon, stiletto heels with black bumblebee stripes and little flourishes like wings on the toes. 'The world's most elegant sting,' the artist calls them, and he wants me to help fine tune his vision.

"Well, that's up to my boss and the marketing team. I just handle design," I say, scowling. "Put it down, Knox. Please."

He casts a vicious look. "So, the answer is, not enough. Do you even get paid interning for that troll?"

"It's great experience. Not everything's about money. A woman can't get anywhere without contacts. Names. Reputations."

"Whatever. Eventually, you'll need money, too," he says, coming closer again, slowing my pulse as every inch between us disappears. "What happens when you're through with unpaid training, Sunflower? When you're done playing Cinderella all day, working your sweet ass off for someone else's dream, instead of finding a Prince who can help you realize your own?"

My dreams haven't been your business for years, ass, I think to myself, inwardly cringing when my brain flashes back to our night on Camelback. "I don't have time for this. Get to the point, or take Lizzie home. I know putting up with a certain amount of your crap comes with the territory when I'm at your mom's place. But this is my parents' house, Knox. *My* space. It isn't happening here."

He's not cornering me in my own freaking childhood room. Stepping up to him, I extend my fingers along my hip, ready at a moment's notice for a strategic slap of last resort.

"You're right. I've wasted enough time, so let's cut to it: I'm your shortcut to those dreams. Fancy shoes, dresses, the next black card soirée at the Eiffel-fucking-tower. You name it, and it's yours. I'll help finance it all, hook you up with the right people, wherever you'd like to go, and when. My gift to you. An all-expense-paid shortcut to an opportunity I'm certain the other ninety-nine percent less talented designers your age would kill for."

My hand goes limp. His mouth is still moving, but my pounding heartbeat drowns out everything. The floor drops out under me, and I stagger back a step or two.

It's a trick. Some kind of sick little game.

There's no other explanation.

"Wow. And to think, you'll only want me on my knees, wrapped around your finger." I flash my most sardonic grin. His cold stare wipes it off my face a second later. "I'm not stupid, Knox. I know this illustrious opportunity doesn't come cheap."

"Obviously. I need a favor," he says, closing the distance between us again. I swallow a gasp at the last possible second when he grabs my hand, rekindling the electricity that's always there.

How? Why? I hate it more than ever.

I can't believe what happens next. My heart skips more beats than I can count while he stuffs his other hand in his pocket, drawing out a little burgundy box. His thumb flicks it open with a *pop* and I'm staring at a lost crown jewel from England.

At least, that's where I think the biggest diamond I've ever seen came from, this huge rock he shoves in my face.

It's a halo of sparkling beauty, baguettes and platinum mesmerizing my eyes in its emerald cut perfection.

Then the words that turn this immaculate treasure into one more anonymous rock kicked up from the desert. "Marry me, Cinderella," he says, showing me the first spark in his eyes I've seen for years.

Holy shit. What?

What. Is. Happening?

Whatever twist I expected, wedding *proposal* was 999,999 places down the list.

"Calm down. I don't mean for real," he says, his voice rumbling to a low whisper. His fingers lace mine tighter, a balmy warmth that's just enough to keep me from passing out from the shock. "I need your help, and I don't want a bunch of questions. Work with me. Wear this ring for a few months. Tell the world how incredible it feels being Mrs. Knox Carlisle. Do it, Kendra, and I'll make every last dream rolling around in your pretty pink come true. Talking about your brain, darling, in case you're stuck on something else."

Dear God. The more offended I look, the wider he's smirking.

"I'm serious. Do me a solid, and I'll wave my magic wand. Make your designs gold. Teleport you from Phoenix to New York fucking Fashion Week. Marry me. That's it."

"Marry you!" It comes out like a hiss. I'm still trying to catch my breath. "Why...why in God's name would I ever do *that?*"

"Image. Marketing. You told me that's where you're clueless, so let me put it this way: I'm taking over Black Rhino. Wright won't last forever. When he dies, or steps aside, it's my company. And I need a family friendly image if I'm ever getting top job."

I study his face. It's tense, wrought lines crossing his forehead, which somehow makes him wickedly sexier. "I don't believe you," I say quietly.

There's more to it. There has to be.

"Don't care, Sunflower. I'm telling you the truth. Nothing less. Help me, and I'll help you do impossible things. I'll throw the whole damn world down at your feet."

I'm tempted. If only for a second, I bite my bottom lip, trying to resist his breath on my throat as he towers over me, pressing me into the wall as far as I can go.

Then I remember who I'm dealing with. My eyes narrow, and I stare into his, insult overriding fear. "You can't make me. Frankly, I can't believe you're asking for *this* kind of favor, Knox. After our history the past few years..."

"Look," he growls, reaching for my face. He cups my chin, digging his fingers gently into my tender flesh. "Forget what happened at Danny's place. Put your feelings, and your ego aside. It's business. That's all this is. One chance for two people fighting like hell to get ahead, two people who once shared their dreams like kids trade bubblegum. Are you really telling me you've forgotten –"

"Stop." I sigh, cutting him off, pulling away from his grip. "You're the one who made it *painfully* clear things are different. I haven't forgotten anything. I never will, not after what you did to me when I walked in and saw you –"

"No. We don't need to go there." His voice matches his eyes.

Blue diamonds stare through me, fanning the

shameful heat beneath my skin. I'm light-headed, way behind on work, and sick to *death* of this strange new twist to our cat and mouse game. The very same game I've tried to stop playing a thousand times.

I wish I knew what he's hiding.

We haven't been this close for years, but I know Knox Carlisle, and I also smell when he's lying. Lies hang off him like whiskey perfume, dark and powerful. Intoxicating.

Stretching my fingers, I form a wall with my palm, wondering if I'll have to deploy my strategic slap after all. But before Knox is able to bury me deeper in his stark, demanding gaze, we hear Lizzie's laugh closing in with mom's footsteps. They're coming down the hall.

We've been at it too long. It's probably much too quiet for her liking.

"Don't answer me today," he says, brushing past, heading for the door. "Take some time. Twenty-four hours, Sunflower. I'm confident you'll find a way to swallow your feelings, and do what's right for both of us. Never let emotion chew your career up. Not if you want to get anywhere this lifetime."

Before I can say another word, he rips open my door. I watch him break into the world's biggest grin when he sees his daughter, snug in mom's arms. "Daddy!"

"There you are, pee wee!" Lizzie laughs in his hands as he hoists her up, holds her toward the ceiling, before he pulls her little face securely to his shoulder.

Great. I can't possibly stay hurt. Can't keep the angry cloud on my face while I've got a perfect view of this innocent little thing who somehow came from the biggest bastard in Phoenix.

"She's a treasure, Knox. Really. Did you two need anything?" Mom smiles, hiding the concern in her eyes as she casts a look toward me. Even when she's worried, she never stops playing gracious host.

"We were just wrapping up. Truly appreciate your hospitality, Sandy. Kendra, I think you've still got my number, yeah?" He looks at me, his face lit with a wry, artificial smile. I nod. "Fantastic. We'll talk soon, I'm sure."

"Bye, Lizzie." I hold up my hand, waving it, totally ignoring the asshole holding her until he turns his eyes.

I don't say goodbye to Knox, which gets a dirty look from mom. I don't even follow as she shows them out.

I'm at my desk, pretending to work, but honestly struggling to un-fuck my head after our bizarre encounter when my door bursts open. "Kendra Elliot, I'm *very* surprised at you! How could you be so cold to that nice man and his little girl? I thought you two were friends?"

"That was a long time ago, mom. He just wants a favor."

I'm well aware I sound like an enormous bitch right now.

But she doesn't know our history. She doesn't know what he did.

She doesn't know how he crushed my heart and rubbed the wreckage in my face like a bouquet of dead roses.

She doesn't understand how a man who used to be my teenage idol became the closest living thing to Lucifer himself.

My what-if. My disappointment. My torment.

Marry him? In this lifetime? Hell to the *no*.

"Well, hun, when you're in this house, you'll treat our guests with the respect and dignity your father and I raised you with. Dinner in a few."

"Got it, mom. Thanks." I add the last part sarcastically as she flashes me one more disapproving glare, and then bows out.

As soon as my door closes, my face is in my hands. Nobody gets it.

Sure, I'll mull his offer, but just as a formality. I've never needed anyone's help. Shortcuts haven't gotten me where I'm at now, and I don't think they're a magic bullet to the dream career dangling up ahead.

In my heart, I already know there's no way, no how, I'll *ever* marry Knox. But there's no need to tell him as much just yet. I'll wait, purely so he'll taste a tiny sip of my pain.

After his self-destruction, his heartache, his games, it's the least he deserves.

I don't want him to suffer. I just want him to bow the hell out of my life, and disappear.

Fade, like the ugly phantom he's become, no more than a crude resemblance to the gorgeous man I almost loved.

I don't want his money or his connections. I want peace, an end to the agony every time I look his way, these bitter memories throbbing deep in my soul like a hidden tumor.

He can still give me the greatest gift of all.

If we move on. If we forget. If we stop chasing shadows that aren't even part of us anymore, and pretend we never had a clumsy, half-lit thing that went sour.

IV: SELL ME (KNOX)

I spend the next twenty-four hours walking a damn tight-rope. Kendra hasn't sent me a single text by the following afternoon, well after our deadline expired.

I bow out of work early, hoping I'll find her with my little sis.

Heading to ma's place, I find a lounging Jamers desperately trying to make up three weeks worth of missed papers. That alone tells me Kendra won't be by today.

There's only one place she can be: the posh, downtown office where her twitchy boss does his work surrounded by custom granite, manicured palm trees, and soft low lights.

I visited the public gallery attached to his studio once. Had to take Lizzie and ma out for the day, last year, during the anniversary of my old man's death. Always hits my ma the worst when it rolls around. She won't even step into the dining room where he keeled over in front of us for a good month leading up to it.

Art takes her mind off the reaper. If I can bring her to distraction heaven, I will, always keeping the bitter truth about dad's secret letters to myself.

Deep down, I still care about what happens to my family, including my lazy brat of a sister.

I park my truck in a garage across the street and step into the building. Inside, a receptionist with pink highlights in her short cropped hair looks up from texting on her phone. "Yes?" She chomps her gum like I just screwed her out of finishing her favorite show.

"I need to see Kendra Sawyer right now," I say, flattening my hands on the countertop.

"Oh, the intern? She's with Mr. Gannon. You'll have to wait."

Normally, I'd bribe my way in faster. Pull a Benjamin or two from my wallet, and lay it in her hand. But I don't like the stink-eye this reptile is giving me, so I just start moving, walking straight down the long hallway toward the studio.

"Hey, wait! You can't go back there without –"

Slouch. She yells, but she doesn't chase. I'm ripping open the sleek French doors a second later. It wins me appalled looks from Kendra and the portly, silver haired little man in the sweater vest who can only be Eric Gannon in all his pretentious glory.

"What's the meaning of this? Who are you and what the hell are you doing in *my* studio?" Gannon angrily pushes aside the mannequin they'd been working on, dressed to the nines in an ensemble too decadent for a royal, much less a dummy.

"Courtesy call. I'm here for Kendra." I smile, loving her mortified expression more than I should.

Shame it doesn't last long. She's stepping past her livid boss, heading toward me with a scowl and a speed in her step I've only seen before on a mountain lion outside Sedona.

"Knox, *don't*." It flies off her tongue like a bullet as soon as she's in my face. "This is my job. You can't bring this crap here."

"Told you I needed an answer yesterday. You're late. I'm not leaving until I get one."

I don't break from the storm in her eyes until a furious Gannon grabs my arm. His plum shaped face is turning red, and I briefly wonder if I'm doing her a favor, pulling her away from his temper. "I'm not sure what's happening here, but I'll give you until the count of three. Then, if you're not off my property and out of my intern's face, I'll call the police. Press charges. I'll leave a permanent black mark on whatever record you –"

"Does this guy always start with big threats?"

Kendra opens her mouth, but the words never come. It's a deafening slap that echoes through the room instead. Her palm slams into my cheek, leaves it red and steaming.

I smile like a fucking fool. "Tell him you need five or ten. Let's go," I say, totally undaunted by the blister she's left on my face.

Gannon stares in horror, and then reaches for his phone, stabbing his fishstick fingers at the screen while I drag Kendra outside. Practically have to throw her over my shoulder so she stops fighting me. I figure I've bought myself five minutes tops before the Phoenix police are able to get here through the rush hour traffic.

Fortunately, the receptionist with the pink hedgehog hair is back on her phone, blind to what's happening in front of her.

"Knox, please. Please!" She repeats it like a mantra by the time we're outside, the hot evening sun blasting onto the pavement next to us. Dangerous words to my dick. Even more dangerous tone.

I let her leave my grip for the shade, so the sun doesn't hide the hateful spark in her emerald green eyes. "Jesus. What the *hell* is wrong with you?"

"I'm serious about that offer, Sunflower. I didn't get an answer. Wouldn't have had to come here and make a scene if you'd called me up last night like I'd asked."

"I don't owe you a thing. If you haven't figured out it's a resounding *no* by now, then you really must have a screw loose after all. I'm going inside. Wait here, maybe the police will be able to get you the help you *seriously* need."

My heart bangs in my chest. Obviously, I knew she'd be upset, but I didn't know it'd be like this. I thought I'd sweet talk her after the initial shock, and now it looks like I won't get a chance.

I can't let it end like this.

Time to get serious. I step up, grab her arm, and feel her nails rake my skin as her patience cracks. "Asshole, I told you a million times – *stop!*"

"They're taking Lizzie away from me if you don't help."

The fury on her face melts into shock. "Wait, what?"

"It's Wright. Her grandfather, my heartless fuck of a business partner. He's threatening to drive me out of the company, and he'll take my little girl to have his way." I release her, throwing myself against the khaki colored wall, lowering my eyes. "I'm sorry I didn't tell you from the start. I'm backed into a corner, Kendra. Wouldn't be here otherwise, begging for a damn bone."

"Jesus, Knox. I had no idea." Funny how seeing sympathy curdling her expression makes me feel even more like shit. "I still don't follow. Why use Lizzie as leverage? Is he really so psycho?"

"Because it's all he's got on me. She's my weakness. Bastard can't just force me out without a full approval from the board he'll never get. It's in the agreement outlined before dad died. I'm supposed to receive his share of the profits, his stake in the decisions, and someday equal seniority. Last part hasn't happened yet. We've knocked heads for years, but lately, it's claws and teeth. He's done fighting. Asshole's brought out a steel toed boot aimed at my balls."

It's torture on her face. The truth doesn't ease this tension. Doesn't smooth anything over.

Wish she'd taken the offer. Then I wouldn't have to stand here like a jackass, watching the conflict written all over her.

I wanted to get her into this with the carrot, damn it, and not the fucking stick. Not even an emotionally manipulative one.

Sirens pierce the evening traffic, heading this way. Kendra steps up to me, puts her hand out like she wants to touch me, and then thinks better of it. "I'd better get back inside and call off Gannon before he has you arrested. Let me handle that part...and then I'll think about the rest. We'll talk soon."

Soon? Unless it's in the next five seconds, it isn't quick enough to suck the poison out of me.

Even when I'm trying to do right, keep my little girl, my family intact, I can't stop hurting people.

It's a stake through my heart to see the war on Kendra's face. It's been too many years since I screwed her up so bad. Not since the night I set her up to end her puppy love fixation on me.

I pushed her away for good reason. Because I'm bad, tainted by too many stupid decisions, too many fucked up circumstances. There's only space in my heart for Lizzie, and nobody else. I don't have a universe in my soul to give anymore, just one world, and it's all for my little girl.

Not after Sam's disappearance.

Not after I inherited a fortune with strings attached to a ruthless son of a bitch.

Certainly, not after I reached inside myself, found the little flame I still had lit for that sweet, innocent young thing, and rubbed it out with my boot the worst way I could.

I SPEND another night wondering if my life caving in is inevitable. It's around noon the next day when I get the call, two soft words whispered with a blush I can sense across the city.

"Sell me," she says, confusion in her tone. "I want to do this...I want to help...but, Knox, I just don't know."

"Yeah, you do. If you're trying to make up your mind, it means you're still making this about you and me. That's where you're hung up, and you shouldn't be"

"Well, technically, it kind of is about us."

"You know what I mean," I rumble, pushing my mouth closer to the phone. "Victor Wright *will* take Lizzie away if I don't find a wife. The courts frown on loner dads with my kind of history, and he'll have the lawyers to make the perfect argument. He'd be hell for her to grow up under, too. Bastard shit missed her birthday two years in a row, and I know he'd be all too happy to have her raised by hired help. Just as long as she's away from me."

"Knox, I know," she cuts in, oozing sadness. "I've heard plenty from Jamers. He's trouble, and I'll admit the idea of that sweet little girl with him makes me deeply uncomfortable."

"Help me, then. Please." My voice is low, more worry than I'd like slipping in. "I need you, Kendra. Only for a few months. Pretend it's real, wear my ring, fool the dogs Victor sends after us, and you'll have my undying thanks along with the expensive, dreamy shit I promised."

I'm deadly serious.

I'm also not used to weakness. Being vulnerable. Especially not with this woman who's been a ghostly tease since I slammed the door shut in the crudest way possible, five years and counting.

"Fine. I'll do it." Kendra's voice makes my lips twitch in an attempted smile. "Not for you, Knox. This is for Lizzie. You're a good dad, whatever else you are. She shouldn't go to that man."

"Glad you came to your senses. I'll be by later to pick you up. Got to move you in quick if we're going to pull this off."

"Whoa, hold up. I'm old enough to pack my own stuff, thank you very much. I don't need –"

"I'll see you this evening," I say again. Then I cut the call before she says another word.

It's hell muddling through the next few hours at Black Rhino, pouring over expense reports for accounting, and sketchy background checks on the new guys Victor wants for security and acquisitions.

He's taken a dump on my turf. I despise it, and I can't wait to march my Sunflower in, throw the ring on her hand in his face, and let him know he's no longer got a leg to stand on, legal or otherwise, when it comes to his 'family image' bullshit.

My life is becoming one big picture perfect lie. I've got the luxury house with its well manicured strips of grass and carefully trimmed orange trees. I've got the money – less than I deserve, but plenty nonetheless. I've got the little girl, who I'd surrender everything else for in a heartbeat. And now, I've got the woman who's going to pull my sorry ass out of the fire before it gets singed.

It's like a distorted mirror image of everything I thought I wanted when I was young.

Too bad I don't have time to worry about the morals. Keeping Lizzie safe is at the top and bottom of my To Do list.

I finish my day at the company and blow past Victor's vacant office. The asshole must've left early for the day to hobnob with his rich friends downtown, or maybe an evening trip to Vegas in that black and gold private chopper he flies around, spectacular enough to accommodate a Sheikh.

He's only a few tiers wealthier than me, and someday, I'll do him better. But I don't care about his flashy, self-serving crap. I care about bringing him down, and to see it happen, I need the woman holding the keys to his ruin.

* * *

IT'S JUST past six o'clock and I'm outside her place, fighting every urge to launch my fists at her door. I use the doorbell instead like a civilized person, remembering her folks are so nice they deserve better than my usual.

Her little hand practically jerks the door off its hinges a few seconds later. "That was fast," she says, shooting me a feisty look as I barge in.

I walk right past her, heading toward the cramped bedroom we made our battleground just days ago. "Jeez, slow down, Knox. I'm almost packed!"

Throwing the door open, I see a mess of sketch books, shoes, and fashion magazines strewn across her bed. "These are coming with, I take it?"

"Duh. Can't exactly do all my work at the studio. I hope there's somewhere in your place I can concentrate when I need to buckle down and –"

"There are six guest rooms. Turn them all into Leonardo's fucking workshop for all I care," I growl, unfazed when she blinks back surprise. It's easy for her to forget I'm exceedingly rich, successful, and old money by Phoenix standards. "You finish packing the art junk. I'll do your clothes."

"Hey!" She gets out one word before I snatch the other suitcase off her little desk, and start rifling through her dresser.

She's still glaring as I grab fistfuls of socks, panties, hurling them inside. Her wardrobe is basic. Simple, single-colored cotton bottoms and matching bras. No lace, no frills, not even a pair of fishnets.

Why does that make my dick so hard? I keep my back turned, hiding the wood that's getting more petrified by the second. She's finally gotten over herself by the time I move to the closet, sighing every so often as she gathers her work stuff.

"You'll have to work with me if it's going to work at all, you know." She gives me the evil eye when I rip three more dresses off their hangers, and stuff them into the bag.

"You're helping me keep my little girl. I'm giving you a shot at life. Don't remember talking etiquette." I dig deeper, snatching shirts and tank tops, whatever looks casual for lounging around in the stifling summer sun. My hand slides against the top shelf and something drops, bouncing lightly near my foot.

The object is long and solid. Cool to the touch. It only catches the light once before I pick it up, fighting not to grin like an idiot. I stuff it into my pocket without saying anything.

When I've cleared out half her closet, I turn, staring straight through her as she meets my eyes, arms folded. "What? You've got at least ten day's worth here. Anything else you need for a formal occasion, it's coming out of my pocket. Quit worrying."

"That's *not* why I'm concerned."

"Oh? Didn't know your parents were home. You figured out what you're going to tell them when they see you with this rock?" I reach into my pocket, pop the ring box, and walk over. "Need you to start wearing it today, Sunflower. People *will* talk when the announcement hits the papers and blogs. Legal formality, really, media evidence so Wright can't argue this is a hoax. Sooner you get used to being fake married, the – "

"Better? No way. I didn't agree to be your slave, Knox. Surely, this isn't how you're treating me in front of Lizzie?"

I stare her down long and hard. Don't make another move until she plucks the ring from its box, pushes it onto her finger, and holds it up to the light. "You never answered my question. I'm *trying* to do this. I really am."

"Yeah, and I appreciate it. Forget your folks, on second thought. Tell them whatever the fuck you want. I'm planning on telling Lizzie you're staying with us this summer for rent, maybe a little housekeeping."

She quirks an eyebrow. I don't understand why she looks almost...hurt?

"Really? It's not like we're strangers, Knox. I've practically seen her growing up as much as Jamers did over the years. You won't even tell her we're close friends?"

Hope swells eternal in her throat. I have the black heart to do a lot of things these days, but not make her feel even more like shit than she already does.

"I'll tell her you're help." Technically, it's the truth. It's everything I can offer without introducing my little girl to a new mother she'll only have for a few months. Sunflower glares anyway, clearly unsatisfied. "That's more than fair, Kendra. What would you have me say? She's four years old. Too young to understand how often we have to get our hands dirty. Too young to remember this, too, once it's over."

"That's something, I guess." She turns away, doing a poor job at hiding her hurt. "Lucky her."

"You ready yet, or what? We'll work on the details later." Her back is turned and I'm standing there, waiting for her to face me again. She doesn't move.

Fuck.

Suppressing a sigh, I drop the suitcase, gently grabbing her shoulders. "Look, I promise it won't be this hard forever. You'll get good money. Once you're moved in and set, you won't have to see much of me at all. Not outside the mandatory act to keep up appearances."

"I'm *not* an actress," she whips around, green eyes on fire. "I've never been good at lying, Knox, and I think you know it. Why bother with me? Why not get someone else for the job?"

Yes, why? I'm able to seriously contemplate it until I stare into her eyes a second later. Our raw history floods my veins, old impressions carved on my soul.

Because you're the only woman who haunts me. I want to say it, but I don't. *Because even after years gone by, even after I've pushed you the fuck away, you're the only girl on the planet I see myself pretending to love.*

Obviously, I can't tell her that. I open my mouth and blander words fall out.

"Because you're right for the job, Sunflower. You know me like nobody else. My imperfections, my faults, my low threshold for bullshit. Plus you know Lizzie, and you've always been kind to her. She won't be shy or afraid around you." It's softening her, but it isn't clearing the ice. Not yet. I clear my throat, coming in closer, staring deep into her eyes. "You really want to know? I need you because there's no fucking chance we'll screw this up. We see the lines. They're clear between us, impossible to blur. Only thing that'll screw this up outside Wright's lawyers are feelings, Kendra. We keep a lid on those, and we've got nothing else to worry over."

"You're right. There's *zero* chance anything would ever happen between you and me. Not after..." She breaks my gaze with a huff, turns to the bed, and starts struggling with her zipper. She won't say it, and that's fine by me.

I move in behind her, ignoring how she trembles when I pin her arms with mine, catching her hands and the zipper. Thank fuck this argument snuffed out the hard-on I had a few seconds ago. My stronger grip unsticks it, moves it in a solid line, seals it shut. "When do we leave? I want to turn in early. I need to be at the studio in the morning. Still helping Gannon catch up on his projects after the little delay you caused yesterday."

"Right now, if you're ready. Need to swing by ma's place to pick up Lizzie. Then we'll grab something for dinner and try to sit down like a normal family...assuming you're game to join us tonight." I can't expect too much. Keep remembering I need to ease her into this insanity.

"Of course. I have to eat sometime, and Lizzie's a total angel for company." No mention of me.

That's okay. I manage a smile she doesn't see when her back is turned as we head out to my truck, loading up her luggage.

She needs time to cool off, to adapt to the storm I'm pulling her into headfirst. I'll save the dirty little secret I knocked off her shelf and hid away for another night.

* * *

IT's the best part of the day. Half the time, I wake my little girl up at ma's place with a kiss on the forehead while she's resting in the guest room. Today, she's got the devil's energy, and she leaps into my arms before I'm even through the door.

I carry her back out to the vehicle, still running the A.C. on full blast. Kendra stays put. We haven't figured out how we're hiding this from Jamie. Already told her we'll figure something out. My nosy sis doesn't need to know a damn thing about our fake engagement, and neither does ma.

They aren't big on watching the local news. Chances are, they'll miss the announcement when it goes out. And if they don't, there's plan B: tell them it's a twisted prank.

We stop at a new Italian street food place on the way home. It's simple, tasty, and refreshing food for a hot day. Kendra and I get wraps with small pasta sides. Lizzie gets a kid's meal, grilled veggies with mac and cheese.

Later, at home, I help my daughter clean up while Kendra offers to set the table. I let her, taking her help while I clean the dried paint off Lizzie's hands. "What's the good word today, sweet pea?"

"Aunt Jamie helped us paint! Daddy, look. Oopsie." She turns to the counter, splashing me as she dries her little hands. I laugh, pushing the towel through her fingers.

So good. So innocent. So plucky.

Unbelievable, really. Hard to believe she came out of a psycho mom who abandoned her plus my own bad judgment.

"Look, look!" she says again, bouncing. I reach for the thick piece of paper rolled up on the counter. Taking off the rubber band, I unfurl it, and notice a big gray blob with a massive hugest grin under its...arm?

"Elephants, daddy. See?" Lizzie clarifies, pointing at the trunk.

"You nailed it," I tell her, stepping over to the fridge to hang her latest masterpiece. It's the first time in years I've managed to smile at any picture of the big, gentle beasts with tusks. When it's pinned down with magnets, I turn, scooping her up in my arms and lifting her high. "Kendra's quite the artist, you know. She'll be staying with us for awhile, just like I said. You two should talk. Probably find a lot in common."

The words just come. Maybe because I'm busy trying to see the childish innocence in her art, and not another fucked up memory.

There's no point. I shouldn't waste time remembering the elephants I saw in the flesh, chained up and miserable. No use thinking how many sick fucks we dealt with for acquisitions also had an extra hand in the poaching business.

Once, my crew drove our armored jeep over the flimsy barbed wire fence holding in five leathery beasts. It was late at night and totally intentional, before we took off for the airstrip in the jungle brush to bring us home. We let them go. Didn't have time to hang around and risk the local warlord's wrath before we continued on down the gravel road.

I hope like hell they made it. I'd love to believe those animals left and found their second chance, but I'll never know.

"It's ready." Kendra pokes her head in the kitchen from around the corner, hanging on the wall.

I look up, bouncing Lizzie in my arms, trying to stay

anchored in the moment before my memory pulls me deeper down its sinkhole. "Hear that? Supper time."

Sunflower blushes, smiling when I plant one more little kiss on my daughter's head, and then walk her into the dining room. Once she's in her booster seat, we sit down.

My gut rumbles so hard I think it shakes the house. Glad I got the extra pasta.

It's quiet as we dig in, devouring big bites, enjoying the near silence. Only the radio pipes classic rock through the speakers installed in my house.

"You wanna help with my art, Ms. Kendra?" Lizzie looks up from her food, eyes aglow. It'll be strawberries instead of ice cream for dessert tonight, or she'll never sleep.

"I'd love to, sweetie," Kendra says. It's the first time I've seen her look genuinely happy since I dragged her here. "Any evening. You tell me if you want paint, pencils, or clay, and I'll have it all set up. No better way to pass the time."

Sunflower looks at me when I hear the last part. Damn if I'm not thinking of a few much more adult ways to pass our time together, and it makes me check myself.

No. That's not what she's here for. Get your dick wet else-where. Practically anywhere else.

If only it hadn't been so long. I'm ashamed to admit it's been a long, hard dry spell, and it's likely responsible for making my balls suck fire every time I look at her. I've lost track of how many months it's been since I got out, one of the times ma and Jamie had Lizzie overnight, and fucked some club girl stupid whose name I can't remember.

"Just be sure she does her learning exercises first," I say, swallowing a big gulp from my water. "Always time for fun later."

"Oh, daddy, can't I paint tomorrow first? Just this once?" Lizzie looks up, huge and imploring.

"Yes, *daddy*. Please?" Kendra folds her hands in front of her, perhaps the most dangerous word she could utter on her tongue.

Great. She's been here for less than an hour, and she's already corrupting my little girl.

And trying to corrupt me.

"Fine. Only this time." I smile, watching my baby girl clap her hands. This isn't the ego clash, the attraction, the love-hate thunderhead invisibly building between me and Ms. Persistent. I do it because I want to make this as easy as possible on the two women at the table next to me.

My daughter doesn't deserve to suffer any more confusion than she's bound to walk away with after this is over. Kendra doesn't deserve more heartbreak, or to bang her head against the wall I've told myself I'm keeping up. If I can just lighten the load, keep my Lizzie with minimal damage, then it's a best case scenario.

I give them time for small talk while I head into the kitchen, taking their plates.

It takes me a few more minutes to throw together small bowls of strawberries and cream. Sweet, centered, and totally organic. Nothing but the best for everyone under my roof.

When I step back into the dining room and slide the bowls over, I find Lizzie laughing so hard she's clutching her stomach. "What joke did I miss?"

"Your doggie, daddy! Knight...skateboard..." The red

faced cherub in the booster seat can barely speak through her giggles.

"Really, Sunflower?" I narrow my eyes, watching her blush and lose it, too.

Apparently, there are some secrets I can't control while she's here.

"Come on, Knox. It's a funny story. Jamie still tells it sometimes when you're not around. Cracks me up. I'll never forget that day..."

"Yeah, almost a hundred and thirty. Hot as blazes. Think it was the heat that kept him calm on my board." It's been forever since I thought about my old dog. "We rode through every sprinkler we could. Dog had his tongue out, tail wagging, loving every drop."

It was his last good year before old age caught up to Knight. I'd grown up with that shy little beagle for years, and he never showed more interest following me off the property than he did that day.

I was sixteen, big into skateboarding, the best way then for young money and good looks to optimize pulling pussy. The dog whimpered until I let him on my skateboard, and we took off slow, winding onto the sidewalk with him riding along.

"He didn't want to give it up! Must've went several blocks for like an hour."

"Ten blocks," I correct her. "Took him to the gas station and back for a sip of my Slurpee before he tired out. Every car we passed slowed down to get a good look."

Kendra wipes her eyes, shaking off more laughs. "Yeah, what I'd have given for a good phone then! Could've captured every moment. Uploaded it to YouTube for posterity."

"You were ten. Same age as Jamie," I remind her. "Don't think your folks would've appreciated the data suck from snapping footage of me skateboarding with my dog."

"Oh, you'd be surprised." She narrows her eyes, leans over to Lizzie, and whispers loud enough for me to hear. "Make sure you take *every* opportunity to have some fun when you're older. It's easier than ever with all the gizmos today."

Shit, like I need a reminder. The teen years seem like a million miles away. They can stay there, as far as I'm concerned, until I'm good and ready.

Lizzie stops laughing. She's wearing her ice-melting smile when she turns her little face toward me, pink strawberry cream on the corners of her mouth. The expanding list of dreaded phrases gets another entry the second she opens her mouth. "Daddy...can we have a doggie too someday?"

"Someday." I don't even hesitate. It's also not her I'm looking at when I stab at my bowl, pop a bite of the dessert into my mouth, and chew so hard my temples hurt.

I don't want to see *someday* unless she's at my side, where she belongs. Not unless my daughter stays with me.

Fooling Victor Wright with this fake engagement might not be the hardest part.

Sunflower gives me a look that tells me why. Surviving the grinning angel across the table from me, who somehow stays playful despite our friction, just might drive me insane.

V: FOR NOW (KENDRA)

"**A**nother adjustment?" I ask, mustering my sweetest voice, staring at the latest marvelous creation in Eric Gannon's studio. They're my glass pumps, specially reinforced, designed to hoist beauty high and catch every prism of light.

They're not perfect yet, but we're getting there. It's like seeing something you've only dreamed about make its way into the real world.

"Another coffee, Kendra. It's exceedingly difficult to hear myself think." Gannon pushes his spectacles up his sweaty nose, dismissing me with a wave of his hand.

Glorious. It's seven o'clock in the morning, and I'm already seeing his 'tortured artist' side.

I hate being his personal doormat. But no one in fashion ever got anywhere without a certain price in suffering.

I storm out the studio, suddenly happy to have a few seconds away from my sour boss. Gannon abhors delays, any tiny break in his routine. The grenade hurled into his creative genius by Knox's unexpected appearance triggered all his darker qualities.

I walk past Lydia, the useless receptionist with the pink hair. It's incredible how much easier she has it, actually being on the payroll, but then again I'm the one working for 'experience.'

Honestly, as much as I hate it sometimes, I'm privileged to intern for the world renowned designer. He offers an eccentric world class connection and a resume credit I'm not sure even Knox's money can buy.

I'm at the espresso machine, working my best barista skills. Gannon takes his coffee seriously. He's thrown it on the floor more than once if it isn't just so. I don't want another situation where I have to choose my own pride or his egotistical flogging.

My phone goes off. I press it to my ear, heart in my throat as soon as I see his number.

"Hello?"

"You got a minute, Sunflower?" Knox's deep voice rolls in my ears. It's smoking charcoal and monarch butterflies simultaneously.

"Two, maybe three. Hurry up," I say, watching Gannon's coffee steam.

"That's plenty. Give me a second, and listen up." For a second, I think he's disconnected the call. I hear the phone ringing, and then another voice.

"Carlisle? What in God's name are you doing calling my satellite phone? I'm on my way home to Phoenix right now."

"Important news, Victor. You have that thing for emergencies, right? This is one."

My teeth graze my tongue. I don't move, even when

the timer goes off for the espresso. I'm not sure if this is a three-way call, or if I'm just a passive listener.

"I don't have time for your games, Knox. Unless Black Rhino distribution has caught on fire, or men in suits are shoving a lawsuit in your face from a high-powered firm —"

"Shut up and listen. This is about that family friendly thing."

Oh, God. The second of dead silence between them swells forever with my pulse pounding in my ears.

"You've decided to come to your senses before I initiate a custody hearing? Good. I'll just need your full resignation in my Inbox by the end of the day." Another long pause. At last, Wright sighs "Just spit it out, boy."

"I'm getting married, Victor. I've found the perfect woman. We'll be hitched in a matter of weeks. Faster than you'll be able to recover your retainer from the jackals you've lined up to chew me to pieces in court."

"Married? Impossible!" A *thump* accompanies Victor's gasp. It's easy to visualize a fist slamming into a dull surface next to him.

"Hardly. Pull up your local feed from Phoenix and you'll see the announcement." Knox makes a sound through Victor's soft curse. I can't tell if he's suppressing laughter or just savoring his vicious triumph. "Yeah, I thought you'd need time to cool down. Have at it. Then let's sit down like civilized men and talk through what's best for the company. Oh, and just so we're clear – Lizzie won't be needing your once in a blue moon pat on the head from grandpa. Don't worry about the holidays this year. She has all the love she needs with me and Kendra now. I'll still sign a Christmas card and say it's from you."

"You think this is the end, you arrogant prick?" Murder seethes in Victor's voice. "This won't last. I'll find a way to get her away from you. Nullify every damned share of Black Rhino you think you're entitled to –"

I lean against the wall. That espresso will need a re-do by the time this is over, but I don't think I could tear myself away from the nightmare in my ear for a million dollars.

"Wrong. This really is the end, Victor." There isn't a shred of doubt in Knox's voice. "Look for a letter from my attorney next week, outlining everything. I want my share before we sit down, too."

There's a clicking sound. I never know which man disconnects first.

"Sunflower?" His tone changes so dramatically I jump.

"What the hell *was* that?" I ask, trying not to tremble. My spine curves against the wall like it's still trying to exit my body.

"God himself laying down the law," he growls. "Couldn't have done it without you. Thanks for helping me out. See you tonight. You're doing fine. Put in the effort to keep up the act, and maybe we'll both walk away with better memories than the fucked up drag on us."

"Hey, wait –" Two hollow words. That's everything I get before he's gone, my phone flashing with the call ended.

"Asshole," I whisper, closing my eyes.

It takes a few more minutes to calm my nerves. I contemplate bringing Gannon the cold espresso, but in the end I make his stupid drink again.

* * *

It's incredible how mundane this is to him.

If life on the edge is his creed, then maneuvering around powerful, scary men and outsmarting them – or at least thinking he has – is his religion.

I try to make it through dinner with a straight face. Lizzie makes it easier to smile, thankfully, chirping on about her evening with Jamie and grandma. Apparently, my best friend just showed her Chinese Checkers.

While I'm all for the little girl having fun and games, I make a mental note to ask Jamers later about her accounting. It's been hard to talk much at all since I started wearing this diamond on my finger, icy in its elegance.

I keep it on in public, just like he asks. I can't see a day when it'll ever feel natural.

We feast on a tasty rosemary beef stew he threw together. Cooking is one more skill I didn't know Knox had. Afterward, I work on the heels for a couple hours. It's later when I head down to his office. He should have just put Lizzie to bed for the night.

It's a routine he takes seriously, a ritual. I wonder if he adores her so much in the evenings because there's guilt over missing the other twelve hours of the day.

It's a cool summer night. A brilliant view of the valley glows outside his estate, sprawling across God only knows how many acres, a gorgeous and high maintenance garden lining the outdoor shortcut to the other end of the house. I take it slowly, gathering my words.

They never come easy with this man. Not even when my senses are on overdrive, sharpened by the fragrant citrus perfume in the air. I stop just outside the French doors attached to his office, close my eyes, and breathe.

You're here for answers. Don't let him intimidate you.

There's a light on inside. I knock, watching the lamp's yellow glow fade beneath the door, melding into his shadow as he gets up, approaches, and opens the entrance to his private sanctum.

"What's wrong?" his blue eyes intensify the second he sticks his head out, as if he's got a built-in Geiger counter for detecting my radioactive worry.

"Nothing urgent, really. I just came by to talk," I lie, pulling my cardigan tight around me. Under his eyes, it's flimsy. I feel as exposed as if I just stepped before him in my underwear.

"I thought we were clearer than ever after today." His voice matches his eyes. Low, commanding, mysterious.

"You're seriously calling *that* clear? Keeping me on the horn while you eviscerated your business partner and Lizzie's grandfather?" I can't stop. It just trickles out.

"Kendra..." He hesitates, and for a second I worry he'll simply throw me out. Then he sighs, his huge shoulders rolling, and he motions to the leather chair across from his desk. "Have a seat. Let me pour you a drink."

Drinks are good, I tell myself. A surefire signal he's about to open up, give me answers, maybe even take my concerns seriously for once since he snuffed out my innocence. I slide into the seat across from him, surprised how the cold leather makes me shudder. He pulls out a bottle of expensive scotch from behind his desk with two crystal glasses.

"Too strong?" he whispers, pushing more than a single shot toward me.

"No. It's just...it's been awhile. Not since graduation. Dad shares your taste in ritzy booze strong enough to choke a pack of javelina, so I'm no stranger." Smiling, I tip the glass to my lips.

I don't tell him I could pound one round with my father and Jamie before I switched to mojitos for the rest of the night.

Smooth fire hits my belly a second later. By some miracle I don't choke and make an even bigger fool of myself, pretending I'm used to this.

"You understand there's no fixing things with Victor, yeah? It's not your place to ask, anyway, but I'd like you to know we're far past any bullshit family therapy will fix. He understands force. Nothing else. Now, I've got his arm pinned behind his back, and you'd better believe I'm not letting up until I hear the scream."

His about-face to business throws me. Those infinite blue eyes glow a little brighter as he sips his drink slowly, savoring it, a wicked contrast to how I took mine like a sorority girl trying to prove her worth.

Why the *hell* does he still do this to me?

There's no earthly reason. But then the day hearts start running on logic is the first day of the apocalypse.

"Obviously, I'm not trying to get up in your business, Knox. I want what's best for you and Lizzie, no question. But I'd also love to know exactly what I've stepped into by wearing this." I lift my hand slightly, wiggling my ring finger. He doesn't say anything. The scotch leaves a shadow burn on my throat, making words even harder. "You hit him *hard*. Do you think he'll finally roll over and leave you alone?"

"Fuck no," he says, so swift and blunt I blink. "We're in the 'watch your back' phase. Keep your wits and look out for daggers, Sunflower, because there will be *plenty*."

My heart drops in my stomach. Thank God for the hearty stew, or I'm certain I'd be physically ill.

"What kind of 'daggers' do you mean?"

"All of them. Sabotage, spies, diversions, real cloak and dagger fuckery. That's his way. Victor doesn't come at anybody straight – crooked is as crooked does. He'll keep his hands clean and let his minions drown in the mud. He'll never stop trying to take Lizzie hostage while I'm a threat to his grip on the company." He pauses for another shot of liquid gold in his glass before he looks at me head-on. "Buckle up, darling. I'm telling you now, there will be turbulence. Victor Wright will try his damnedest to deliver a whole new level of misery you've never imagined."

I break his gaze, staring at my hands. The light captured in my ring's oversized stones is almost blinding.

"You're worried?" he asks, like it's even a question. "Nothing will happen, Kendra. I won't let it. You're not the real target, and neither is my little girl. His vendetta revolves around me. Always remember. If the day comes when he decides to hurt you to get to me, it'll be his last. I promise."

"I'll survive, Knox. If we're not talking physical harm, I'm ready for anything. I'm an adult. Demanding, petty men are a fixture in fashion. I've never let them put me on a leash."

Although I've come awfully close with Eric Gannon's disgusting attitude. I don't mention that.

"I believe you. You're being compensated well beyond your grade to pull this off and deal with any minor infractions."

"Oh? Does fake fiancée have a pay grade now?"

His eyes narrow to royal blue lasers. "Regardless, I've told you how it goes. Why are you here at all if you're not seeking assurance?"

"Answers, Knox. Curiosity. I want to know why you're in a blood war with higher stakes than anyone should ever face. Does this all go back to her? Is it because of –"

"Don't even say it." His voice slips to a growl when he warns me.

I'm persistent by nature. "Why not? What really happened to Sam? Does he still blame you for her falling off the face of the earth?"

"I'll always be the devil incarnate to that man. The reasons aren't important. Frankly, that's all you need to know."

"You do know I'm trying to help, right? Not make this harder." I'm almost resigned to the violent resistance tightening his handsome face. Resigned, but disappointed.

"You really want to help, Sunflower?" He eases to a whisper, leaning forward, his big hands folded.

"Please." I'm tempted to reach out, to feel a human connection for the first time in years.

For a second, I hallucinate. I see the sweet young man who once held my heart in his spartan hands. He's there, wishing we could have the connection we had that night on Camelback again, swimming in the soft blue pools of his eyes.

"Do exactly what we agreed to. Stop asking so many fucking questions. If I had answers to even half your needling, they'd change *nothing*. Sam's gone. I'm fucked if I don't do this. Only two facts that matter. You're wasting time hunting ghosts, and I've chased enough for both our lifetimes."

The trap swings shut. My old crush – really, my illu-sion – dies a second time, drowning in angry, unsettled blue.

"I'd better go," I say, looking away as I bolt out of my seat, hiding the hurt in my eyes.

"Finally, a good idea."

Asshole doesn't bother standing to show me the door, or escort me back into his cavernous house. When I'm halfway down the hall with its mission-style lantern lights and alabaster marble floors, I regret not closing it behind me.

His eyes never leave me before I turn the corner. I'll never cease being amazed at his magic. How stupid, small, and undone he's able to make me with a few precise words and a withering glance.

It's never been harder to resist grabbing my keys, leaving this prison ring on his counter, and walking out.

* * *

IT'S after one o'clock in the morning and I'm too angry to sleep. I sit in one of the many dark, ample alcoves built into his house's hand-crafted nooks.

I think I'm imagining it at first when I hear voices. They're low, just a short distance upstairs, coming from Lizzie's room, which is at the other end of the hall, several doors down from my guest room.

I'm confused, and then I'm concerned.

I need to move, to shake off the venom he's left in my heart. This seems like the perfect opportunity to creep lightly upstairs for a better listen, pretending I'm walking on light, happy feet.

"And then what happened, daddy?" Lizzie's innocent voice pierces the stillness. She must have woken up like little girls sometimes do on long nights with lots of bad juju swirling around them.

"Then Cinderella turned the corner, clutching her glass slippers. Her Prince was nowhere to be found, exiled to the Land of Not by the witch's spell. She took a deep breath. And then, in the corner from where the Big Bad Wolf was hiding, a growl." He pauses from the fairy tale mash up he's reading, and makes a thoughtful murmur. "Hmm. It's very late, peewee, and I think this next part is too scary for a Phoenix night when you need to rest."

"Daddy, nooo! Wanna find out the rest."

"You will, sweetheart, just as soon as you're rested."

I lean into the wall, biting my lip, trying to make this make sense. No matter how hard I try, I can't do it. It's impossible to reconcile the cold-hearted bastard everyone sees with the guardian angel who sits up with his daughter half the night, reading her bedtime stories. A yawn reminds me how good his calm, measured reading voice is at calling everyone to dreamland except this rambunctious girl.

"Give me a second. I'll be back with warm milk and a splash of honey." He ignores her last little protest, and I hear an audible kiss on the forehead.

I have to scramble toward my room, ducking next to a portrait of the Grand Canyon and hoping I'm out of sight. But Lizzie buys me more time with another question, one which stops him in his tracks when he's halfway left her room.

"Milk just like grandma makes, daddy? I like it!"

"Actually, she got it from somebody else. My old man

used to do it for your aunt and me when we were your age. Always put us out like kittens. Count to thirty, baby girl, and daddy will be right back."

There's an edge in his voice when he talks about his dead father, a longing and a regret too subtle for a four year old to understand.

Damn. It can only mean the asshole is still human in there somewhere, besides being an amazing dad.

If he'd stop living the Count Dracula stereotype – rich as sin, nocturnal, and moody – he'd probably win my sympathies despite being a total prick. Tonight, I suppose he has.

I wait until I hear him in Lizzie's room again before I race down the hall, gently push my door shut, and flop into bed.

For now, I'm in this.

Rattled emotions are no excuse for savaging a happy family. And although it shouldn't be possible after the psychic lashing he just gave me, I keep hoping he'll show a fraction of the humanity reserved for his little girl.

If I could just see him smile once, or talk to me again like the last four years never happened, it might make this worth it.

It takes forever to fall asleep. When I do, my dreams are pure longing. Scenes from a dead past I should have stopped mourning.

* * *

Five Years Ago

IT's after our star gazing trip to Camelback when I finally break down.

There I am, struck by the teen rage fueled meltdown I've been trying to contain all night. Every tear is rattlesnake venom.

I'm not alone. For some unholy reason, I'm with a man who's older, wiser, and far kinder than I think I deserve in this state.

He's gone miles beyond anything I expected to cheer me up, and it still isn't enough.

It *hurts* to miss prom. Rejection stabs deep. I can't believe I've been tossed aside by a gamer idiot like a piece of trash. I'm not worth a night away from fighting imaginary wars on a screen.

My self-esteem is hanging by a thread, and the only reason it hasn't snapped is the huge Marine in the driver's seat next to me.

Knox keeps his eyes on the road, waiting for me to talk when I'm ready. I don't know that I ever will be. We're halfway home and I'm drying my tears.

I don't notice he's pulling over until I wipe my eyes for the dozenth time, blinking away enough crud to see. "I...I'm really sorry, Knox. You've been good to me. It's just so...so disappointing. Still. It hurts real bad."

"Let it out," he tells me, his voice low, laying a brotherly hand on my shoulder. "You want to cry half the night, do it. I'll be here. We'll pretend it never happened. Keeping secrets is all I've ever been good at."

His words are balm. Even when they're gross exaggerations. His chiseled physique and rebellious wisdom tells me he's good at plenty besides just playing therapist.

His reassurance is my anchor. I grab on and it settles

me so I can look at him feeling halfway human. The immense warmth in his eyes, full of empathy and moonlight, nearly sets me off a second time.

"Walk with me," he says, flicking the switch for the locks.

"What? Out here?" It's almost eleven o'clock.

"Yeah, five minutes. Promise. I'll have you home before curfew, before your folks decide to carve you up for an early jack o'lantern."

I smile at his dorky joke. "You're ridiculous. I'm *not* turning into anybody's pumpkin."

It's remarkable Afghanistan hasn't destroyed that side of him, or the bawdy military humor men become accustomed to when they're far from home and fighting for their lives. If it were anyone except Knox Carlisle out here with me, I'd never put a pinky outside our vehicle in this place, this time of night.

We're parked near a desolate strip of Camelback not far from the exclusive Scottsdale resorts tourists and big money love to pile into. Our feet crunch desert rocks. We step into the grey zone between desert and civilization, where the sparse growth enjoys more color and life, courtesy of plants escaping the resorts.

I guess I *do* feel a little better moving around, but I'm still not sure why we're out here among the saguaros. Not that I mind the view, considering it's Knox's tight-end and hulking shoulders rippling in front of me. The very tips of what I think are new tattoos peak above his collar.

"So, uh, as much as I love to look at cacti and all, are we almost there? I don't want to step on a scorpion in these sandals."

Knox stops, and does a slow turn. He's wearing an expression like hot death. "Okay, Princess. If you insist."

Surprise rips out of my throat as he picks me up. I'm laughing, overwhelmed by being so high in the night, so suddenly.

I'm not looking up at his warrior shoulders anymore. I'm on top of them. Safe and secure, hoisted up high by my own personal bodyguard like something from a fairy tale.

He moves faster without me slowing him down. Laughter brings happy tears, replacing the anguish mere minutes ago. We run deeper into the desert, careful to avoid bigger rocks, until we're so close to one of the three story resort casitas we're able to see tiny shadows moving in the window lights.

"Right here," he says, coming to a sudden stop. "Takes forever to find them sometimes, but when you do, they're all over."

He isn't kidding. A cluster of tall saguaro cacti shield a tangled, secret oasis ahead. Desert flowers pulse vibrant color into the night. White desert stars, purple willows, red-violet blooms at the ends of each cactus.

Each kind is beautiful and breathtaking. They're also close to drowned out by the yellow sea nearby.

Desert sunflowers explode in a large, crowded ring. I'm in awe. If he wanted mother nature to do the hard part putting away my childish problems, he's succeeded.

"Congrats, Kendra. You're a perfect match," he says, lifting me off his shoulders, gently to the ground. He points at my tank top, a perfect and brilliant mirror of the same color splashed across the desert ground. "Mean it in the best way, woman. I've hiked these trails a thousand times, every God forsaken nook and cranny in the valley. Always found a few big blooms this time of year, usually tucked around these resort kennels for rich people."

He says it without so much as a self-conscious smirk. He was born in money, and then dipped in whatever polish makes a human Adonis. "It's beautiful, Knox."

I turn to face him slowly. We hug. Our eyes lock when I look up, my arms around his waist, and for a moment, I'm lost in the moment, in him, in something I can't even understand well enough to put into words. "Thanks for bringing me out here. I do feel better."

"Don't thank me yet. You still don't get it," he says, reaching up and patting my cheek. "Didn't just stumble over rocks in the night for the view, darling, as gorgeous as it is. I want to teach you a lesson."

If I rearrange those words in my head, it's easy to imagine he's talking about me. Just for a second, I do, closing my eyes a little too long. "Oh?"

"*You* are this place, Sunflower. Good and tough as every flower strewn all over the desert in front of us. They don't mind the heat when it comes, or the monsoon, or even the fucking bugs who swarm in and try to chew them up. They're back every year. Stronger, brighter, more beautiful." I can't break the spell in his face. His eyes have never tried harder to hook my soul. "Chin up, darling. Never take shit from any man, any group, anybody trying to make you less."

"Okay," I say softly, trying not to let my seventeen year old feels stop my heart. "Understood."

"Yeah, I hope so," he says, turning around, beginning our slow, rambling walk to the road. "Because I'll keep reminding you anyway, Sunflower. Every time we hang out, you'll remember who the hell you really are. That's my job now."

Outstanding advice.

No, amazing. Heartfelt. Touching.

Like nothing no one's ever given me before.

I drift on behind him in the quiet night as the desert echoes with its own subtle music.

Seventeen year old me found her way home with a smile on her face after what should have been the biggest disaster of her short life.

She never once imagined the man who piled on the hurt and degradation the most over the years would be the one who said never take it.

VI: INTRUSIONS (KNOX)

I don't see much of her the next week. That's intentional.

It's harder than I imagined sharing dinner night after night, watching her make my little girl smile, weaving herself into my life like she was meant to be its fabric.

Worse than my nightmares every time I catch her when she isn't looking. Every time I step close enough to see the emerald in her eyes, catch her scent in my house, my truck, clinging to my fucking shirts. Her perfume is a delicate lunacy, and I'm exactly ten more sniffs from needing a damn straitjacket.

Lengthening my hours at work is all I've got to keep my mind clean.

Not like it's hard, either, with more tension than ever at Black Rhino. Its poison filters through our teams.

They sense the hate between me and Victor, partners in name-only. It hasn't been a secret the last few years. Now, it's open war, and I haven't caught a glimpse of the bastard in the flesh since the day he threatened my family.

I have to hold a conference call with security and acquisitions, my departments, just to tell them to buckle down and do their work without any drama. My beef is personal. If we want this company to survive, that's where it needs to end. Can't have personal loyalty turning my death fight into a tornado that wrecks careers and profits.

What we've built is family, too. It gives me a direct line to my grandfathers. I own this jewelry mill with all its flaws, its imperfections, its taint from men who are far from perfect – including yours truly.

After the heart-to-heart with my team, I realize I've had it. I can't stay glued to the office playing babysitter. Also can't stand going more than a few days without bringing my little girl out for a solid meal, soaking in her innocent aura until it's time to tuck her in for a bed time story.

Yes, I fucking love to read. Calms me like nothing else. Probably puts me to sleep easier than it does her, or at least keeps me from spending all night in the home office, brooding over mysteries I've tried like hell to solve, and never will.

When it's evening and I swing by ma's place, I find my sis and my make believe fiancée slouching on the sectional. Lizzie's out too, napping with her head in Kendra's lap.

If this were a normal relationship, if I had the good grace to get sentimental, it'd be the sort of shit I'd share on my personal Facebook feed.

But this is as fake as the endless counterfeit diamond suppliers who try to con the company every day. I haven't had a Facebook account in years. And what little grace I ever had died with Sam fading into the ether, my constant arguments with Wright, plus several bloody supply trips to Africa.

Kendra stands, greets me with a guarded nod, and walks over before she whispers a few words about dinner. "Take out again tonight, or should we make something at home?"

"We're going out. I like to introduce my girl to flavors I don't know how to make every so often, and there's a few new places in Scottsdale I've had my eye on."

"Lovely. I'll grab my things." Kendra walks over to the chair across the room to pack up the mess of laptop, notebooks, and fashion mags she's probably hauled around all day.

"You guys are going out and you're not taking me?" Jamie yawns, stretching like a scorned cat on the sofa. I also don't like the sudden question in her eyes when she's awake.

"You've got homework. Just because dad left us loaded doesn't mean you piss your tuition down the drain, Jamie." It's harsher than I intend. But I need to do something to get her the hell off our trail.

"Relax, maestro. I'm on track for solid Cs and Bs this semester, believe it or not."

Kendra spins around, inadvertently waking Lizzie. "Jamers, that's great! Seriously proud here."

I take the lull in girl talk to pick my little girl up, letting her wake in my arms with a smile. "Hey, peewee. Time to clean up and go home."

"Wait a sec," Jamie says, suddenly on her feet. Her arms are crossed and she's glaring, more suspicious than ever. "You two have been spending *a lot* of time together lately. Are you dating, or something?"

Red-a-fucking-lert. I don't need more complications when this situation is bursting with them.

I look her in the eyes, ignoring the shock on Sunflower's face, and tell the most important lie ever. "No. I've taken her on to help with Lizzie in the evenings, if you want to know the truth. We're also doing an art project."

Jamie snorts. "You? Like what, Knox? Naked modeling?"

Kendra's cheeks go red. I walk over and pass Lizzie into her waiting arms. Anything to get her mind off freezing when it counts.

Play along, I tell her, hoping the darkness in my eyes gets the point across.

"I'm doing you and ma a solid, sis. Our mother needs a break, and you need to keep earning those Cs and Bs to get your damn degree." I aim my smirk right at the sour twitch in her lips. "The company's going through some major crap right now on top of it. Kendra and me cut a deal. She helps with the kid in the evenings while I pull extra hours, steering the ship back on course. She does dinners, movie time, and laundry. I help her at the studio. It's business. Nothing more. Run along with whatever nasty little fantasies you're filling your head with."

"Whatever, guys. I'm meeting Lorraine at the bar tonight anyway." She shrugs, momentarily deflected. I don't let my guard down until she gives Kendra her good-bye, enthusiastically kisses her niece on the head, and pads toward her bedroom upstairs.

Sunflower saves her breath for the truck. Once we're down the long, winding driveway leading out of Scottsdale's most exclusive gated community, she lets out the sigh clinging to her lungs. "Jesus. That was *close.*"

"It's history. Forget it. Nothing happened, and we did everything by the book."

She squints, fixing her eyes on me. "You're not worried about next time?"

There won't be a fucking next time if we play this right, I want to tell her, but I need a second to figure out how I'm going to soften it in front of Lizzie.

"Daddy, what's for dinner?" Peewee takes the initiative before I say a word.

I look into the rear view mirror at her and smile, before I shoot Kendra a sideways glance. "Onto more important things. I think I know just the place."

* * *

DINNER at a luscious Latin-Asian fusion cuts the tension. Kendra makes small talk with Lizzie while my daughter tucks into her sweet chili pork, clapping happily as her mouth sings with new flavors for the very first time.

It's like any other evening when I get to tune out the bullshit and play family man. I'm happy.

I also can't stop eyeballing the woman next to me. Sunflower looks like sex in a creamsicle today. That orange dress with the white stripes running through it teases my cock when I need it to behave.

Doesn't mean I don't stare down her slip of cleavage every chance I get.

Everybody knows some sorry unrequited love case. Is unrequited lust a thing too? I really wonder, imagining the sugar I'd taste at the ends of her tits if they slipped into my mouth, and that makes me think other things I really ought not to.

Like the times I pulled myself off to her over the years. Too many times. Far too frequent to count.

Don't know if it's her aging like a fine wine that causes the ferocious need to have her in my head when I blow my load. Maybe it's just the added, twisted attraction – knowing how easily I could've had her once upon a time, and how brutally wrong it would be now.

You can't fuck your little sister's best friend, I keep telling myself.

Not even if she's my fiancée.

Not even if she's babysitting my kid.

Not fucking even if there's still a vulnerable spark in her eyes I'm sure I could rekindle with a few harsh, close breaths against her throat, a hand caressing up her thigh, or one bold kiss when she's up against the wall, asking me if I've lost my mind.

Hell, maybe I have. Because the hundreds of innocent questions Lizzie asks and a shot of straight whiskey can't switch my brain off scheming ways to erase Sunflower's dress.

"Still early," I say, checking my watch while I settle the check. "How about a walk?"

"Only if it's to sell the Rolex, grandpa. I can't believe people wear those things in the digital age."

Sweet merciful fuck. She doesn't know the sort of fire she's playing with today using *that* mouth, words as sassy as the playful smile hanging on her lips. I send up a silent prayer asking for the universe to give me strength.

Slowly, I start undoing my watch, passing it over when it's off my wrist. Lizzie watches quietly in her booster seat, so bored by our little exchange she goes back to coloring.

"Take a good, hard look, Sunflower, and then tell me again how big a snob you think I am just because I like having platinum on my skin."

She blinks at me before holding it up. "Jeez, learn to take a joke. If I'd known it were such a sensitive subject I wouldn't have – oh. What's this?" She turns her head, mouthing the seven names captured in a thin, almost invisible script engraved on the inside.

"Martin Carlisle, 2009." She looks up as soon as my father's name is on her tongue. Heavy as this is, the red heat blossoming on her cheeks does nothing to kill the hunger stirring in my balls. "Sorry, Knox. I mean it this time. If this belonged to your father, then I really do apologize for –"

"Bought it at an upscale place here in town just a few years back. I've taken it in a few times since to add more names since the first time it came back customized. Guessing you've got no clue who the others are?" I wait for her to shake her head, her temples bulging slightly. She's clenching her teeth, knowing the answer is bound to make her feel like an even bigger ass. "Two guys from my old Special Operations battalion. Blown to kingdom come when we went after a terrorist asshole in Tora Bora."

"God." A breath so raw slips out her throat it seizes her body. I hold in a smile, enjoying how her breasts move when she's upset. Goddamn, do they bring questions. Filthy, nasty, cock-teasing questions. "I'm sorry. And the rest?"

"Africa. All part of my crew who never made it home. Needless deaths. Blood for Victor's pride. He insists we keep doing acquisitions the old, dirty way. I want to start growing our rocks in a lab. Let the state of the art machines and eggheads do the heavy lifting. Not warlords and risk assessment bean counters."

"Jesus. So, that's the disagreement then?" She leans in, whispering, her eyes wide with questions. The ones she's hanging onto cause her bottom lip to pull against her teeth, setting the pulse in my cock to full jackhammer.

"Yeah, at least the bad blood in recent history. The rest comes from Sam." I hold up a finger, pushing it against her lips, before this goes too far. "Leave it right there. No point in ruining a nice night out with any bullshit I shouldn't be saying, and Lizzie's too young to hear."

"Daddy, look!" My baby girl perks up as soon as she hears her name. Kendra and me both whip around, staring at her nervous face as she slides the coloring book on the table toward us. "I did a thing for you and Kendra."

"Another masterpiece, peewee? I think you've got all the Ninja Turtles beat making art – or were those renaissance Italians?"

Kendra laughs. Lizzie just looks at me confused, too young for the Turtles reference. I'm an eighties kid through and through, but there's more than silly nostalgia flowing into my heart when I see what's on the page.

It's...fuck, I don't even know what to feel. I hold it up for Kendra to see, and watch the nervous twitch in her smile.

"You like it, daddy? It's our fun tonight!"

It's that, and so much more. On the surface, I ought to be grateful it proves I have a perfectly happy, spunky little girl. But damn, if she was even five years older, she might realize the kind of fucked up message it's sending to see my stick figure self towering over a smaller one with blonde hair and green eyes, and then an even smaller figure with my matching blue eyes that can only be the artiste herself.

Everyone is smiling in the picture. Even the house behind us, the big orange sun, and the puppy next to what looks like one big happy family.

In her four year old world, it really is that simple. In ours, it never is with the backstabbing, the secrets, the hearts hardened over several ruthless decades.

"Who's the dog?" I say, giving peewee my warmest eyes, trying to deflect the awkward moment from sinking too deep in Sunflower's head.

"Knight Two! Don't you know?" She stabs her tiny little finger on the paper, as if it's clear as day to the entire universe. "Your doggie, daddy. I want a beagle someday."

It's then I notice the dog is riding a skateboard. I'm the first to stand up, and Kendra follows my lead, gently tucking my little girl's new masterpiece in her purse. It'll find a home later on my fridge's shrinking real estate.

"You'll get one, kiddo," I say, rifling my fingers through her hair. There's so much of myself in her before I got corrupted. Makes me proud and heartsick all at once sometimes. "Someday."

* * *

WE TAKE a long walk through the arcade-style section full of upscale shopping. Old Scottsdale turns its charm on most at night, the Old West mingling with rich couples eager to impress their dates. Tourists stop in the middle of the road to ogle the soft string lights hanging over the streets and parking areas.

Lizzie loves staying up past her bedtime. Also loves the ice cream we pick up an hour after dinner. Kendra ducks through the clothing stores and kitsch shops open in the evening. I watch her and Lizzie from a few paces away when they're not at my side, smiling at the illusion.

It's no more real than the grinning stick figures my little girl just put down on paper, but damn if it doesn't feel like there's a family. Double damn it's bothering me less the longer I indulge in the delusion.

Who am I becoming? This isn't Knox Carlisle.

I've lived the last four years of my life protecting two precious things: my little girl and my company. There's no room for a third. I can't keep looking at Kendra like she's another possession, one more gold vein attached to my withered heart.

It's a slow, creeping madness. *Stop fucking brooding and enjoy yourself,* the edgy voice in the back of my brain says.

I try to take its advice for once. When I do, I'm stunned.

I'd forgotten what it's like to be comfortable. Somehow, I'm having a decent time, holding out my arm to escort my fake girlfriend through the narrow alleys while Lizzie laughs and twirls around us.

Kendra casts a sunshine smile my way when we slow, stepping over a puddle reflecting blue powder moonlight. I don't return the look because, fuck, I don't want this to end.

And it's bound to the second I slip and break the spell.

It can't last.

It's the first time Kendra and I have been out in public

since our deal. Her hand brushes mine, hundred thousand dollar rock on her finger and all.

I don't even hesitate.

One fluid move locks our fingers tight, telling her without a word I don't have the patience for timidness or second guesses. If she wants this, practicing our illusion, then we'd might as well do it right.

"Oh, my. Didn't think there'd still be one open." She slows, pressing her face close to the little boutique's glass, peering at a yellow jacket style dress, black ribbons curling through the balmy lemon. "Just my style. I'd *love* to try this on, if you don't mind. It's a good match for a shoe project I'm working on."

I look at her and crack a smile. "Run along. I'll wait with Lizzie inside while you load up my credit card. Can't hurt to expand your wardrobe for future outings."

She blushes, flashing me a grin, before she quicksteps ahead. What I told her is a lie.

I don't give a fuck what anyone from Black Rhino or the posh charity balls I sometimes attend in Phoenix will think about her attire. I want her in it now, because I know it'll make her curves hit my eyes like a merry go round.

I wait by the door, true to my word, passing Lizzie my phone so she can play a puzzle game. While both my girls are preoccupied I have a chance to look out the window, into the orange lit streets.

That's when I see the silhouette. It's a tall man, dark in his unassuming clothes, a grey ball cap pulled low over his eyes. He's too built to be a civilian, and his sideburns are just a little too uneven for the usual Scottsdale crowd.

He's so ordinary it's off.

In the blink of an eye, he's easy to miss, too. But my years in the military and mercenary trade have sharpened my senses.

A normal bystander wouldn't trip wires. In this area, on a summer night, the chances of seeing the same random face more than twice are slim to none. Odds are even longer he'd stop just across the street from us, whip out his phone, and subtly glance over it twice in the forty-five seconds I'm mentally counting since noticing him.

"Lizzie, get behind daddy, please," I say, gently helping her behind me.

She looks up briefly, a worried expression on her little face. Can't hide how my voice means business. I hold her tiny hand, leading her to the other corner of the store, where I pretend to sift through clearance shirts.

It's ten seconds later when I hear the door open. Don't need to stare at the glass next to me to see the man's reflection. He's here, scoping us out. A woman comes by, asking if he needs help, and he says he's just looking in a California accent.

Perfectly average.

Perfectly up to no fucking good.

I don't turn around until he's moving again. When I look toward him, he's heading for the dressing area. Deliberately.

I follow, Lizzie in tow, and stop outside the dressing room where I'm able to see Kendra's feet. She's singing softly to herself. I wait impatiently.

Our uninvited guest sees me. He turns his back after a few seconds, pulling a random suit jacket off the hanger on the wall. It's at least a couple sizes two small.

I give it thirty seconds. Just enough time for the wood

paneled door to swing open, and Sunflower comes strutting out, her eyes going wide when she sees me.

If this were a normal night, it'd be the other way around. The bee-sting dress clinging to her curves sends lightning to my cock. I have to ignore it, focusing on the fury entering my fists instead.

"Knox?" She calls my name, still doing a double take.

A split second later, I hoist Lizzie up, shoving her into Kendra's arms. "Take her and get back inside. Lock the door."

"What? Hey, wait!" Surprise clouds from her throat.

It's too late. Even that three second hesitation on my part gives the anonymous asshole a head start. His speed walk becomes a run when he reaches the door to the street.

I chase him like mad, giving every bone below my waist a burn it hasn't felt since Sierra Leone. I'm out the door, closing fast. He's quick, almost as fit as I am, but I have more endurance.

Four blocks away from the boutique, he slows when his heel hits a crack. I leap like a mountain lion, closing the gap, hurling my elbow around his neck as he goes down fighting.

Mr. Peeping Fuck doesn't last long.

No man has a chance once my hand grips his throat. We hit the ground together and roll. My knee goes in his back. An agonized groan is my reward.

No more games. I'm lucky there isn't a crowd out tonight.

"Who the hell sent you? Wright?" We're cutting straight to it.

I ease my grip just so he can nod. Next question.

"What are you? Some kind of PI?" I wrack my brain, considering the possibilities. He's cut too clean for a dirty merc after a tougher job.

Detective, then. Again, his head bobs up and down meekly.

"He's looking for a slip, isn't he? Sending goons to prowl around, capture my every move, bring him scraps that show I was *never* serious about this family thing?" The rest is easy to piece together.

It's too much, or he's recovered his wounded pride. Peeing Fuck doesn't answer. Not until my knee digs deeper into his spine, close to a satisfying crunch. "Talk, damn it. Also want your phone."

I don't wait for him to do me the courtesy. My free hand slips into his pocket, ripping out the black Android device I saw earlier in his hand. It's in a flimsy case, thankfully.

He groans. "Let go, Knox. Do it. Both know...you won't...do shit."

He's right. I can't leave lasting damage, or his boss will have all the evidence he ever wanted to steal my little girl. It's hard not to collapse this idiot's lungs.

I let him stand, awkwardly, before I slam him into the nearest wall. His split-second hesitation tells me he's waiting, thinking I'll actually apologize and give back his property.

"Move along, asshole," I growl. "If you're smart, we're finished here. You'll collect your hazard pay and go, without staying on his payroll. Because if this ever happens again, if I *ever* catch you sniffing around my people, we'll find a nice spot in the Sonoran desert for you, me, and a shovel. We both know you've done your homework. I know that you know how unholy I can and will fuck you up."

I pin him with one hand, skimming his pockets with the other, checking to make sure there isn't a secondary listening device. Then, I dispatch him with one last hateful look, watching as he takes off running.

It's a small miracle Sunflower hasn't caught up to me yet. My greatest fear after losing my daughter is her ever seeing this side of me.

They probably turned down the wrong street, if they're not waiting inside the boutique, expecting me to send a text. I count my blessings, seize every spare moment, and throw his phone on the sidewalk. It rattles like rotten wood underneath my boot, blown to smithereens by the impact.

When I'm confident there isn't a single circuit in that thing left un-warped, I draw out my own phone and fire off a message.

Meet me at the car. Hold your questions until we're home.

* * *

FOR ONCE, Kendra listens. Her sweet lips stay silent, as much for my benefit as Lizzie's, who's fallen asleep in the backseat. She doesn't even wake up as I grab her from the seat, carry her into the house, and lay her gently into bed. Always leave my nightly kiss on the forehead before I close her door, and tonight is no exception.

Some rituals, a man never breaks.

"Okay," she whispers, as soon as we're in the hallway. "Why the 007 stunt tonight? Who was he?"

I keep walking. Don't say anything until we're further

down the hall, closer to her room, where there's no chance my sleepy little girl will overhear us. "Loose change you don't need to worry about. Told you before, Sunflower, by doing this, we're stirring the pot all kinds of fucked up. Victor won't go easy."

"Yeah, but so quickly? Do I need to start checking under my bed?"

"That's a start." I watch with a flicker of amusement as her eyes pop wider, giving up their emerald perfection. "I'm kidding. Mostly."

"Idiot." She punches me in the arm, causing a smile like a reflex. I haven't heard her use that tone since we were both kids, or I was still nearer to the innocence she could relate to. "Seriously, where does this go from here? If he's got men like that following us around, watching our every move..."

"We take this more seriously than ever. It's the only way," I say quietly, cornering her against the wall, one arm over her head. "Listen to me, Kendra. Every word. Follow my lead. Believe in us. Trust the lie so much it starts seeming real, like we're truly something special, embarking on our long and happy lives."

She blinks a little too fast to be natural. "I don't know how to walk this line. You're asking me to up the ante, but you don't want Jamers and your mom finding out? Jesus. Such a tight rope."

"Better brush up on gymnastics then." I stare through her, cock rising in my jeans.

Throwing the nosy fuck on the ground hasn't given it amnesia. It remembers full well how cruelly delicious she looked tonight. "You looked hotter than the days I remember you bouncing around in those tights for dance squad your senior year."

"Ew, I barely lasted a year! And since when were you looking?"

"Since always." I stop right there, looking away. If I stare a second longer, that blood red splash gleaming on her cheeks is bound to tell me how she is to the touch. I can't put my hands on her, or they won't stop. "You were born tight. Destined to be eye candy for every immature fuckwit with his tongue hanging out in our old days, or were you blind to that too?"

"Obviously not. I just chose...not to explore my options."

"You were too good for them," I growl, letting my eyes roam her throat, everywhere my tongue aches to follow. "Just a hot, shy, puritan piece of ass too busy with her nose stuck in a book to give her first handjob to some hairless little chimp holding the winning numbers to your panties."

She's blazing quick. Her palm flies across my cheek, razor sharp against my stubble. *Goddamn, that feels good.*

"Thanks. Now, look at me like we're still in love," I say, boxing her face in with both my hands, back where they belong against the wall.

"Huh?"

"You're failing my test, Ms. Four-Point-Oh. If I don't believe you still want to be with me after that, how the hell will the creeps Victor has watching us every time we're outside this house? How will *anybody* else?"

"Knox, please."

"Sunflower..." I bring one hand softly across her face, lifting her by the chin. "I'm not playing games."

Oh, but I am.

"I can't lose my little girl." *I'm completely serious about that part.* "Show me the fire in your eyes even when I don't deserve an ember. Show me you get how serious this is, and you're willing to punish me for being a bastard later when I act up. Because we both know I fucking will be sometimes when it's all I'm good at. Show me, darling. Your mask, your game face, your best poker scowl. We're in this together, and the stakes could not be –"

Higher? That's where I'm flying the instant her lips reach for mine. Kendra grows a few inches on her tip-toes, more than a tentative little peck when our mouths collide.

Hot. Sweet. Surprising.

On second thought, screw the pep talk. I take what's mine, giving it back to her better than she gives, throwing her against the wall with my chest. Our lips dance with hunger, find their delights together, and skip to the moon on a ten second mote of x-rated fairy dust.

My hand is in her hair. Her moan is in my mouth. I'm pulling, sucking, and biting her all at once, manic like I haven't been for years with the need to mark a woman inside and out.

And I do, down to this flower's roots. She groans, soft and supple, when our hips grind once.

Then it hits me how far this is bound to go if I don't stop.

Stop, you bastard! I tear myself away, hoping a swallow of oxygen will ease with the withdrawal breaking away from her lips. It never has a chance.

Kendra looks at me, her eyes lidded, bright, and wanting. Takes everything I've got to hold her gaze without my hand between her legs, pushing them open, finishing where we just left off.

"I have to go. Early day tomorrow. Watch what you say when you're outside in the gardens if you decide to take a walk or whatever. Victor shouldn't have had the time to get this place bugged. It was clean the other day when I checked, and I'll do another sweep in the morning. But until then...you never know. Didn't expect him to send the dogs after me so fast, trailing us in town tonight. You wait for my all clear, understood?"

She nods, slow and messy. "Jesus, Knox. I –"

"If the next words out of your mouth aren't goodnight, then we've got nothing to discuss."

Anger flashes in her eyes. Then disappointment.

She doesn't get it. I have to shut her down cold, or we *will* fuck.

And if the lid comes off this sick attraction we've been nursing for years, I know I won't have nightmares knocking at my brain. I'll be living them.

"Whatever," she murmurs, barely under her breath. "Goodnight."

We share one last look before she backs into her door, walling off our tension when it closes.

That last look, I recognize. Not across the years, but in the present. It's in my blood, my bones, fogging up my mirror when I look into my own strange eyes.

It's fear. It's hatred. And it's love – the forbidden, impermissible, fucked up thing with a thousand consequences.

Every last one a new disaster.

* * *

I CAN'T SLEEP. When counting sheep and melatonin won't work, ritual does the trick.

My office has a secret in the bottom drawer that's gnawed at me since shortly after Lizzie was born. I sigh when I open it, pull out the little box, and wonder why I think I'll do anything except work myself into an exhausted frenzy.

There never are any answers. The FBI team dedicated to Sam Wright's missing person's case gave up and put it into cold storage years ago.

But there I am, three o'clock in the morning, sifting through everything I know about the last days on earth of a woman I despise.

She left me with something beautiful. Lizzie deserves closure about her mother someday, and that's half the reason I keep trying to break the enigma.

The rest is hoping I'll find something damning about Victor, blunting his threats forever. Even after all these years and not a shred of proof backing it, I think the chance he was involved in her vanishing is greater than zero.

My hands go to work, faster than my brain, flipping pages. Old photos, investigative field reports from the countless detectives I've hired, test results from a forensics lab I paid out the nose for.

Always the same damning artifacts.

Never any conclusions.

I see the name Jake Burton, the fucking bum who fed her addictions. We played pool a few times at the same watering hole attached to the back alley where my beautiful little girl was conceived. He opened his new place in LA to her when she blew Phoenix without any notice.

Supposedly, she stayed with him for under three weeks before disappearing forever. The beat up gas station across the street from Jake's place took her last photos on a crappy security cam.

Her eyes are too grainy, too dark to really see in those photos. But I've tried to stare, even hovered a magnifier over them.

I don't need a picture perfect view of her crazy eyes to know she looked like hell. I want to regret, worry, fear – emotions that might lead me *somewhere* on this maddening chase.

Wright made sure Jake was hauled in for questioning and held for months as the main suspect. Or at least he gave the appearance.

The bum had nothing. Just a half-cocked story about how she went out for beer one night and never came home. Too much corroborated it. He was released in under a month and moved upstate to Redding. Never had the opportunity to question him myself. Running dope for a rival gang on Grizzlies Motorcycle Club turf got him beat to death in a biker war roughly a year later.

My fingers move with an angrier energy the longer I flip through the pages. An hour passes, and I'm no closer to anything. Not even sleep.

When I hit the last page, I stop as I always do, my lips turned up in a vicious smile. My greatest mistake smiles up at me, the last decent picture she ever had taken, laughing with her drunken eyes. "Where the *fuck* did you go? Someday, you'll tell me."

I shove the pile off my desk and hear it clatter on the floor. I see the other box tucked under my desk while I'm cleaning the mess up I've created. By the time I've finished tucking everything back into its neat folder, I'm smiling for real.

Why suffer more agony tonight when I can have a little fun before sunrise?

I pour myself a scotch night cap and sip it slowly while I grab my finest stationary, plus the pen I only use for multimillion dollar deals. I scrawl a quick note on it, pop the container open, and tuck it inside.

Then I carry the box with Sunflower's dirty little secret upstairs, bend down next to her door, and leave it for her to find in the morning.

I can't decide whether imagining her reaction when she finds it makes me want to stroke my cock or laugh more. So I hit the sheets and sleep instead.

It's the first time in a good, long while I drift away without the steady darkness staining my soul.

VII: WRETCHED THIEF (KENDRA)

I'm awake and yawning, totally ready to shower, and maybe find a quick breakfast in town before I'm due at the studio. It's one of those mornings I sorely miss sleeping in. But Gannon doesn't give me that luxury when he starts work at six o'clock, punctual and demanding as ever.

I clean up and change in a hurry. The new bumblebee dress I bought in Scottsdale last night fits wonderfully. It's everything I like in one elegant black striped ensemble. Maybe part of me is still asking myself if it's a little tacky, but the fashion world demands a little classy eccentricity. That goes double at the public gallery I'm helping with tonight.

Time to go. Taking a deep breath, I leave my room, and nearly walk over the box sitting outside my door before I see it.

Now, what? I wonder, reaching down. Holding it up, I shake it gently.

Something dense and heavy rattles inside. It's a silver

box with a luxury name in men's cologne stamped on the front. Certainly not something I'd order. I duck back in my room, sliding a fingernail under the tape.

It pops open, revealing a lump tucked under a note on thick cream paper in his handwriting. As soon as I hold up the page to read it, I'm horrified.

My vibrator stares me in the face. It's one of the few I keep around to sate the urges that come without a good man in sight.

Just because I'm a virgin at twenty-three hardly means I'm pure.

"Ass," I mutter, unsure how I'm able to conjure the strength to read what he's left me, but I do.

Mornin' Sunflower. Never took you for a size queen until this rolled out when I was packing your bags. Thought I'd return it.

P.S. Good news: mine is bigger. Also a whole lot more fun to ride.

"Idiot!" I mutter, angrily slamming my vibrator into a dresser drawer. I head out, hoping to God he's still asleep, so I won't have to leave more mortified than I already am. Fortunately, he is. It'll be another hour before he wakes Lizzie and they're dressed, making breakfast, heading over to his mother's place to drop her off before he goes to the office.

After the morning ambush, Gannon's orders are actually a relief. They take my mind off the total privacy violation Knox just delivered, the last man on earth who should know *anything* about my masturbation habits.

We spend our time prepping for the public exhibition tonight. It's been thrown together quickly, ever since Gannon found out several big names from Europe were due in Phoenix. I guess they think there's some creative merit in experiencing a 'real Arizona summer.'

Well, they've picked a perfect time. I'm barely able to walk two blocks to my favorite Mexican grill for lunch.

These are the dog days, broken only by short nights and sudden monsoons. The pavement burns your toes when it's been in the hundred and twenty degree sun. The nicer places have their mist turned on, and I stop at an upscale French place next to the grill, catching the spritz pouring off their patio above.

My phone pings. It's amazing how fast the burn moves inside me, and I forget all about being comfortable when I see the name on the screen sending me the text.

KNOX: Still expecting a ride home tonight from the art shindig, or what?

I GRIT MY TEETH, tapping out a response, and really hoping this line starts moving because anger makes me hungry.

KENDRA: Don't bother. I'll Uber to your place whenever I'm done.

I DON'T WANT his help. Sure, he might have Lizzie in the

109

car with him, easing the awkward tension, but I don't know if I can see him today. Not after his nasty little 'good morning' shock.

KNOX: The offer stands. So does the chance to get something between your legs that doesn't run on batteries.

KENDRA: Not in this lifetime, or the next. You're crazy, crude, and a complete ass.

I FLICK MY SCREEN OFF, silence its tone, and plunk it in my purse before he has time for more torment. I'm able to eat my burrito in peace and work the rest of the evening, doing some final checks before the show tonight.

"Hey, we're shorthanded." Gannon taps me on the shoulder an hour before it's supposed to open. "See to the refreshments and snacks, please. Our esteemed guests have no tolerance for vending machines and fast food, Kendra, particularly Mrs. Brunwick."

Great. Not only am I pulling a double shift for this stupid internship, I'm now a glorified waitress too.

I also can't walk out on him and blow my experience. That would mean even *more* sucking up to Knox so he'll expedite the rewards he's promised for this insane fake engagement. And after this morning, I'm honestly afraid he'll want me to put my money where my mouth is when the time comes to cash in.

I flash my egomaniac employer a lovely smile, batting

my eyes, and tell him I'll make sure the caterers have everything picture perfect.

I'm still working on stocking drinks with the bartender when the gallery opens. Gannon greets his guests at the front door with our receptionist, Lydia, who has her pink hair covered by a hat from the artist's own collection. She does more work than I've seen for months. Maybe ever.

"Ladies and gentleman, I'm honored. Right this way." He smiles at the gaggle of guests, no more than a few dozen, all wearing more money than I think I've seen outside Knox's wardrobe.

The men look like penguins. The women like a menagerie of strange insects and birds, dressed so fashionably their exotic wear looks downright uncomfortable.

Prowling the tables, they mostly ignore the caviar, pate, and brioche brushed with veal broth, heading straight for the bar to whet their appetites. I listen to them chatter in at least four languages. Gannon's exaggerated laugh pierces the chaotic roar every few minutes.

Dealing with Knox's crap is becoming more attractive by the second. *When does this stupid thing end?*

We're nearly an hour in before he starts his speech. His guests crowd around, following him through the gallery. He's able to check his ego, at least for as long as he needs to rub elbows with world famous titans who can snap his reputation like a rotten twig.

I watch him, chewing my lip sourly. He leads them on through a mess of prototype dresses and men's shirts we've been working on for weeks. The sweat on his brow is visible under the hot bright lights, specially installed just for tonight.

The other designers aren't impressed by his jewelry, which he pinned his hopes on. I hear a man with an honest to God monocle lean over and whisper to the lady next to him in a thick German accent. "Pedestrian. *Where* is the life? Imagine wearing that droll medallion – like something out of a Gothic fantasy!"

Gannon clears his throat, and maneuvers them on toward the front, skipping the sequined 'black swan' dresses worn by the row of manikins, all in different shades of ebony and gold.

"Ladies and gentleman, if I may, I'd like to set you free to peruse at your leisure and wrap up our tour early. You've been very gracious. But first, allow me to introduce a little secret I've been slaving over between other projects. This, my friends, is the future. Radiance, clarity, and fairy tale whimsy."

Wow. He's staking a lot on this.

Gannon stops at the small table next to him, eyeing the ceramic black lid over the top. With a nervous flourish, he peels off the cover.

My heartbeat triples ahead of the crowd erupting in a fascinated rumble.

Gannon's royalty lift their drinks. Gesturing in awe, their hurried whispers double. They're absolutely delighted, and it's all thanks to *my* glass Cinderella slippers.

The same ones Gannon hasn't spent a second working on for weeks.

"You okay, Kendra? Looking a little flushed." Lydia flashes a knowing smile, amused by the sudden twist in tonight's drama.

I give her a killing look. "Did you know this was coming?"

She looks down at her nails, sipping a cocktail she's stolen, careless about drinking on the clock. "Oh, yes. He's been talking them up a lot lately. Thought he'd save them for the grand finale, but it seems he's bumped up his schedule. Be grateful, I suppose. You're *finally* getting some recognition."

The last vicious blow to my ego today hits like an uppercut. I turn, stomping off to the room in the back, covering my face before hot rage leaks out my eyes.

I've been robbed.

Pride? Shattered.

I've run out of people to trust.

How much can a woman take? How much *should* she, before something gives?

I don't know. But I've already decided I'm done being dissed.

My revenge won't wait for morning. I can't live with myself if I have to suffer one more deprecating smile for this wretched thief.

* * *

I WAIT for the steady chatter to fade before I make my move. The gallery is quieter now. People move more freely, half of them hanging close to Gannon. They all tsuna a chance to shake his hand, prostrating themselves to the new 'visionary' they've discovered in the unlikeliest place.

I hear 'dirty, backward, sun-choked' town more times than I can count. Apparently, even the lingering heat after

Phoenix's sunset is too much not to melt their tender sensibilities.

They have no idea. The fire I'm lighting will be infinitely worse.

The crowd slowly circles the gallery, trailing Gannon like puppies. I wait until the last few stragglers are done marveling at the slippers I designed. Then, I snatch them off their podium, place them on the floor and change my shoes.

Someone discarded a glass of wine after only a sip on the small bench nearby. I reach for it, too.

No one sees me coming. I have to walk through the narcissistic herd several times before their egos soften enough to notice what's on my feet.

The glass taps staccato notes on the gallery's cherry wood floor, creating a resonate echo that only grows as they quiet down, staring in horror. The bloviating idiot hasn't noticed the commotion yet.

"Ah, my muse? You wouldn't believe how it came to me. I've had the book sitting on my shelf for years, a gift from my grandmother, as fate would have it. They called it *The Little Glass Slipper* then. First edition. I hadn't read it since I was boy when I picked it up on a whim late one night. The moon splashed across its pages, and my eyes lingered on every word. I *felt* this in my bones. I sat down and began working like a maniac the very next day, throwing everything aside, devoting my life to –" Gannon stops mid-sentence.

It takes three heart-stopping seconds for him to process what's happening.

I'm coming toward him, mid-stride, still a couple feet away. His fawning guests lose their smiles as they notice me. There's a gasp, worried whispers rising, a stifled laugh in the corner that could only be Lydia's.

Oh, it's funny, all right. Like, ha-ha-oh-my-God-you-thieving-fucking-asshole hilarious.

Now for the punch line.

I don't say anything. Stopping a couple feet from Gannon, I watch the sweat soak through his collar. He clears his throat, putting his eyes anywhere but mine, blood rushing to his cheeks.

"Eric, forgive me, but what *is* the meaning of this?" An exasperated woman with guts steps in front of us, asking the collective question.

"Bravo, Ms. Sawyer." He begins to clap, anger slamming his hands together. "Please, everyone, join me in giving my lovely assistant a hand. It's performance art, you see. I simply couldn't let you admire them inanimate. My creation is meant to be worn, to dance on the body like the vibrant light it catches, and – wait, where are you going?"

If he didn't sound deranged, he might have pulled it off. But the crowd sees through it. The most sensitive ones are leaving in mass, peeling away.

I stand, a human fixture, hands on my hips, waiting for the room to clear. I never take my eyes off the ruined idiot who thought he'd get away with fraud. He misjudged me as a total pushover.

It's eerily quiet once everyone is gone. He looks past me, giving Lydia a death glare. She gets the message and scrams, running through the back door. It's so desolate we hear her car start a moment later.

"Have you lost your goddamned mind?" Gannon

speaks first, coming toward me, eyes hateful black stars behind his icy spectacles.

"Does gross humiliation make you psychic? Because I was about to ask you the same question."

He's shaking. Spit flies from his mouth, narrowly missing my face when the outburst continues. "Really, you little cur? That's what you say after trampling on my career?"

"Well, if you hadn't stolen *my* design..." I wiggle my toes, a gesture that's surprisingly elegant in these.

"Bitch, I will *ruin* you – you're insane! It's like you have no-self awareness, no common sense, no fucking clue who I really am."

"Wrong. It's easy to see, Gannon, and I'm kind of glad I could show the world tonight. You're a petty, burnt out, patronizing fraud and –"

He hits me across the face. *Hard.*

I go down, senses spinning, bringing my hands out before I hit the floor. It barely softens the blow. My ribcage shakes my entire body, but I wince the hardest when my ankle twists, causing the glass heel to bang the floor with a noticeable *thwack.*

Incredible. I'm more worried about the precious slippers on my feet shattering than a broken ankle.

I smile, tasting blood, wondering in my delirium if Knox will still tease me tonight when I drag myself home. *If* I get a chance to go home ever again.

Gannon breathes heavy. The brute looks around the room. He's either panicked because I'm not moving, or contemplating a way to finish me off.

Get up. Move. Try to get away, before he –

"You again!" Gannon freezes near the wall, his eyes

wide, hands on a bust resembling Prince in purple geodes. He created it last year to commemorate the musician's death. "No, go away! I'm telling you, fool, you're about to make a massive mistake if you –"

A huge shadow power slams him into the floor. Knox.

Gannon's scream chokes off after a second, the wind knocked out of him, too lost for words to continue begging for mercy or making idle threats.

I'm dizzy, but barely able to sit up on my hands. The ex-marine, the mercenary, the piece of my life I can't figure out shows his full power. *All* of it, or enough to change our lives forever. He shifts from slamming his knee into Gannon's ribs to clawing the back of his head, smashing his face into the floor.

"I give the orders now, prick. *Do. You. Understand?*"

"Knox..." I try calling his name, but it's happening so fast, and he's too determined to break the bastard who hurt me, if not murder him outright. "Knox!"

He stops and looks over, taking a five second breather from his savage retribution. "Let me handle this, Sunflower."

"Knox, no!" I'm standing up, wobbling on my feet, the full horror of the situation hitting me like a hangover. "Don't hurt him any more. Please. I *hate* what he did to me, but if you don't stop now, you're risking everything. Lizzie..."

Hearing his daughter's name tames the hateful flicker in his eyes. He's reluctant to stand up, ungluing himself from the creep groaning on the floor, but at least he's detaching. I walk over, throw my arms around him, and practically collapse. It's hard to walk in this cracked shoe with my head throbbing, the universe on a non-stop carousel spin.

"Call the police and get him an ambulance," I whisper. "Leave the explaining to me."

He grabs my chin, gentle and firm. "Darling, you're hurt. I'm taking you home. Fate gets to decide whether this piece of shit ever walks again."

I look over at Gannon. He's moving, breathing choppy, making painful sounds. He'll live, probably, if he doesn't have a serious concussion.

"At least let me call Lydia, and *promise* you'll file a police report. We need something on record, a statement, before he twists the truth."

"Five minutes, Sunflower. You make the call. That's all you get before we're leaving, even if I have to throw you over my shoulder and carry you to the truck. Count-down's already begun."

He's true to his word. I leave Lydia a frantic message, and wait for her to call back a minute later. She says she's still in the area, draining a stiff drink before she heads home for the night. I tell her to make sure Gannon has a ride to the hospital. I also make sure she knows I'm done, I'm keeping the shoes, and charges will be pressed if he dares to so much as talk to a lawyer about my fiancé's self-defense.

I hope it sinks in.

I'm even more hopeful I'll find some way to hold onto the anger over the stupid vibrator incident this morning, instead of staring into his eyes like I'm absorbing my personal hero. Knox lifts me up, carries me to the passenger seat, and hooks my belt for me.

He really cares. Asshole that he is sometimes, there's

no denying it. Makes it hard as hell to hold onto the crumbling ice barrier between us.

"Two takedowns in a week," I say, amazed it's barely been twenty-four hours since he ran off the spy Victor sent after us. "Is that like a new record?"

"Here in the States, maybe. Overseas nah. Can't say I like so much piling up on home turf."

"No Lizzie tonight?" I whisper, once he's in the driver's seat, guiding us out of the parking lot.

"She's sleeping over at grandma's. I figured we'd need some privacy to talk after my stunt this morning, after I chose to ignore you for shooting down my ride home. Didn't expect to find you half-knocked out by that fucking imbecile."

I cock my head, studying him slowly. "I'm glad you showed up."

"And I want you to know I'm sorry," he says, a low growl hanging in his throat.

"What? Look, if it's about this morning, I can forgive —"

"Sure is, but that's not why I'm apologizing. Truth is, I was wrong. Never should've waited until morning to fuck with you, Sunflower. If I'd had my wits last night, I'd have hid that thing in my pocket after we got home, and broke it out while you were wide awake. Should've put it to good use when I had you against the wall, never breaking that kiss. Should've let my lips bring you home."

Home. The tender, unexpected weight in one word cuts through my confusion. He takes my hand when I put it in his lap, a low rumble in his throat. He pushes it against his jeans.

His bulge is scary, exciting, enthralling all at once.

I don't even know what this is anymore, or where it's going. But I'm not afraid.

Nothing frightens me more than the thought this insanity could be temporary, and the ring on my finger might go up in smoke as easily as Gannon's career.

* * *

WHEN WE'RE HOME, he doesn't drop the caveman thing. I'm in his arms again once he parks the truck, thinking he's carrying me to my room.

It's an escort in the strongest arms I've ever had around me, all right, but the spacious guest room where I sleep isn't where we're going.

In all my time here, I've never seen Knox's room. His unmistakable masculine scent serenades my nostrils the second we're inside, and deepens when I quicken my breath, going gently down on his bed.

He lays me there softly and disappears. When he returns, he's carrying a glass of water and a couple aspirin, a thoughtful shortcut to soothe the dull throb behind my eyes.

It feels good laying here in the darkness. Even better when he climbs in, wraps his strong arms around my waist, and holds me like he's making up for the times he let go.

"Sleep, darling. I'll be here through morning. If you're up when I am, I'll make breakfast."

"Knox, you don't have to –"

His thick hand presses gently against my mouth. "You deserve a good meal after the bullshit tonight. Rest, and I'll have one ready in the morning."

My eyes are so heavy. I'm slipping deeper into the sweet nothing my body craves, a need that's only slightly more powerful tonight than the one he ignites when we're pressed this close.

It's miraculous, really. There I am, in his bed, snug against this beast who's taken me between heartbreak and heaven more times than I can count. I want to do more, but I don't know if I should, and the broken pieces rattling around inside me after Gannon's antics just make me more tired.

Sleep. That's what I'm after to de-fog my mind, and maybe once that's done there'll be more clarity for my bruised heart.

If Knox ever lets me go through the length and darkness, I never know it. I fall sleep in his arms, snug against his chest, bristling while his delicious heat envelopes me.

It's grace, it's strength, it's a calm I didn't know he even had. He shows a boundless patience for my pain. His chiseled biceps squeeze me tighter, whenever I stir in my sleep, as if to say, *you're safe, Sunflower, and I'll be fucked if I let you go anywhere there's suffering.*

My subconscious wants to go to a thousand dark places each time I bob toward waking, every time my eyelids flutter, and I'm forced to remember for a brief second how I got into his bed.

But the true, relentless darkness never comes. Knox is my shield and my flame.

He is fierce. Dogged. Omnipresent.

His protection blunts the chaos my life was just plunged into. His eyes shred it and banish the vicious pieces from stabbing my soul, at least for one gentle, silent night I'll never forget.

I'm amazed he doesn't take this further when my body is *so* damn ready against his.

When I wake, it's just after dawn, and he's gone. I swear his warmth lingers on my skin.

He's left me a fresh towel and a change of clothes, carried from my guest room. When I clean up, change, and pad down to the main floor, sizzling bacon scent wafts up my nose.

"Good timing, woman. Thought I'd put yours aside to warm up later." Knox stands by the glass stove top, holding two plates with crisp bacon, hash browns, and the biggest country omelets I've ever seen. "Have a seat."

He brings me a coffee and orange juice, sliding my plate over at the breakfast bar. I dig in, realizing how maddeningly hungry I am. It's also a wonderful distraction from re-living last night's sideshow.

"Need you to go by Ma's place and pick up Lizzie later, if you're free." It's sweet that he asks, even though we know full well I have nothing to do now that I'm Gannon's *former* intern.

"Of course. I'd like to get out of the house," I say, chewing more food. It's criminally rich, and if I wasn't impressed with him for his many other attributes, his cooking could bring any woman to her knees. "I'll ask around about last night. Find out if Gannon plans to press charges."

He holds a hand up, sipping off his huge slate gray mug. "Don't bother. He'll listen if he knows what's good for him. Every last word I coughed in that motherfucker's ear. They always hear me, Kendra, or they pay big."

There's a dark spot in his blue eyes warning me his threats are never idle. They run a chill up my spine.

Proud because he's using his rich, ass kicking, Neanderthal powers for *me.*

Scary because I wonder what'll ever happen if the worm turns, and someday I'm on the receiving end.

"It's over, Sunflower," he says again, sliding out of his chair with an empty plate. He rinses it in the sink and clasps the two top buttons he'd left undone during breakfast. "I'm going to the office. Remember Lizzie for me."

"Knox!" I'm on my feet, calling after him, right before he bolts past me.

He stops, lending a few precious seconds to cross over to him, and lay my lips on his cheek. The tiny hint of business-like scruff burns beneath my lips. He looks, smells, and feels as good as he tastes. "Thank you," I say, two little words holding a universe.

"Evening," he growls. "We'll talk more then. Or maybe we won't bother. That bed we shared can do a whole lot more than put us out under the right circumstances."

"Oh?" *Oh. My. God.* "I...honestly, I thought it was a one-time thing. Didn't know last night meant we were sharing it again."

He doesn't say anything. I'm breathless when his hand makes it to the back of my neck, clasps my skin tight, and pulls my lips into his. "Don't forget the rest of our deal. You *will* be rewarded, and you'll forget about that twitchy prick who ripped you off, Cinderella. That's how this Prince Charming crap works."

He's gone, shooting one last smoldering look over his shoulder.

I'm a smiling, weak-kneed mess. Until last night, it was hard to believe he had a charming bone left in his massive body.

Now? I'm not sure what to believe.

I just know I need the marble counter to help hold me up, before my racing heart takes the world out under me.

Everything is sped up. It's swift, it's fast, and it absolutely will leave me in Knox Carlisle's riptide if I don't get a grip very, very soon.

* * *

"OH MY GOD, peanut. You're going to get sick, and then I'll catch hell from daddy." Jamie swipes a moist, cool towelette across Lizzie's forehead.

Sweat beads off the little girl's skin. That makes three of us.

We chose a melting point day for the zoo, and now we're on the curb after several hours exploring, waiting for our driver. Just because Jamers does the low key student thing when she's out and about doesn't mean she doesn't use certain advantages, including her mother's chauffeur.

"Can you watch her while I fetch a couple waters? Saw a vending machine back there," Jamie says, heading off before I even answer.

I smile down at the little girl, who looks like she's about to pass out in the shade. Incredibly, she hasn't complained, and still wanted to linger by the lion pit while Jamers and me fanned ourselves. The magic and energy of a child is a force of nature.

We're standing under a palm tree reaching halfway to the sky, a small mercy on a summer day in Phoenix. I uncap my water bottle, holding out the last lukewarm swig to her, which she politely turns her nose up at.

"I take care-a-myself real good, ya know," she says matter-of-factly, ignoring the soft concern in my eyes. Looks like Knox's tough as nails approach to life is already rubbing off.

"I know, honey. You're handling this better than I am!" I wipe my brow, underscoring the point. "But we need to make sure you're healthy. Drink some more water, please. There might be a coconut smoothie later."

She's able to pretend my silly bribe won't work for all of ten seconds. Then she snatches my bottle away in her little hands, gulping the last sip. I smile, looking over my shoulder, sighing when I see the huge line Jamers is in.

It'll be awhile. I can't say I'm sorry for the wait, though, because as oppressive as the heat is, it's better out here than dwelling on everything at home. It's good being out. I don't need to feel bad about losing my internship with Gannon. And I also don't need to wonder, for the millionth time, what Knox means after he whispered the word *evening*.

As in this evening. Him. Me. And a bed.

It's butterfly season in my stomach just imagining the insane possibilities. And those butterflies multiply because even after all of his crap, there's a slim chance any of the scenarios involve me saying *no*.

"Drink, peewee? You look exhausted." An older man's gravely voice oozes into my ears.

I turn around and come face-to-face with my worst nightmare. Lizzie is running toward a stranger. He's an older, stern looking man in a tuxedo, hanging halfway out the back of an open black Mercedes, a shark-like smile on his lips and a bottle in his hand that looks like flavored water.

"Get away from her!" I'm screaming, running, ready to tear her away from him as all my instincts kick in.

Naturally, Jamers can't hear me over the crowd around us by the curve. She's staring at her phone, oblivious to her niece's peril.

By the time I catch up to them, the man has the bottle to Lizzie's mouth. He wraps her in one arm while he crouches. "What's the matter, young lady? Can't a man surprise his only granddaughter?"

I stop cold, just a couple feet away. So, it's him. *The* dangerous, unrelenting Victor Wright, a silver fox in a tycoon's suit, elegant in his evil.

"Let. Her. Go," I snarl between my teeth. His dark eyes take my gaze hostage.

I'm reaching for my phone, ready to leave a messy voicemail because I don't know what else to do.

"Nonsense. I think she's coming home with me for the evening." Wright looks down, his eyes big and full of hope, waiting for the little girl to back him up. "You remember me, don't you, sweetness? Last Thanksgiving? You adored the pecan roll ups my talented chef served us."

Lizzie stops drinking, shifting uncomfortably in his arms. She takes her mouth off the bottle and wipes it, then gives me a pleading look. "Wanna go home with daddy."

Wright's face sinks. I watch him look quickly to his left and right, scanning the crowd, mentally doing the math on how fast he'd be able to throw her in his car, and have the driver take off without risking a scene.

I'm ready to give the bastard one if he moves her so much as another inch toward the car. "Don't do this," I tell him, stepping closer. It's a fine line between getting him away, and not upsetting Lizzie, who already knows this situation is very wrong. "Just turn around and go. She doesn't want to be with you. Leave now, and maybe I won't have to tell Knox."

That's a bald lie. My finger lingers on my phone, ready to bring up the contacts any second, tell him he needs to drop everything and get here *now*.

Wright stands, dragging his arms off the little girl. "By all means, tell him everything. He should know I stopped by. Perhaps he'll realize I'm serious about gaining full custody over my granddaughter this summer. It's good we met, Kendra Sawyer." I stiffen when he says my name. "It seems our delightful little lady has other plans for the evening, so I'll leave her be. For now. Just know I'll be watching. Waiting. You will slip up, dear, and so will he. In fact, it seems – maybe – you already are."

Victor's gaze flicks to my hand. My heart skips a beat when it hits me how naked I am, the ring stripped off my finger, hidden to avoid any unsavory questions from Jamers. It's a small relief anyway to see him take his hands completely off the little girl, slink inside his car, and shut the door.

She breaks for me as soon as he lets go. Shoving my phone in my pocket, I sweep her into my arms. I embrace her like she might be blown away. God forbid, she *could* be.

I'm cradling her, trying not to tremble, my eyes closed. I don't even see Wright's car drive off. When another black sedan pulls up on the curve, I'm halfway out of my skin, wondering if he's returned with backup, this time to steal her away for good.

But the man I've seen a few times before during other outings with my best friend steps out of the driver's seat, a huge smile on his face pointed our way. It's the Carlisle's chauffeur, and we're heading home.

"Jesus H. Christ in a chicken basket, what a frigging zoo," Jamers says, pressing an ice cold water into the back of my arm. I jump, and wheel around, a dirty look on my face. *"Whaaat?"*

I'm not smiling. She realizes it a couple seconds later, when the frown stays plastered on my face. "Jeez, what'd I miss? Hey, and where the hell did you girls jack the melon water?"

"Get in," I say, climbing past her into the leather seat as our driver holds the door. "I'll explain on the way home."

VIII: HEAT LIGHTNING (KNOX)

I'm in a blinding rush when I get to ma's place, practically tearing the door off its hinge. "Daddy's here, peewee!"

No response. "Lizzie?" *Where the fuck is my daughter?*

I see her aunt step into the hall a second later, a sleeping little girl in her arms. Rushing up, I snatch her away, cradle her to my chest. Relief and fear cross swords in my heart, two competing masters bent on seeing their war through to the end.

"She's okay, brother. We got to her just in time, like I told you on the phone. Nothing even happened." Jamie gives me a look like I'm overreacting.

Bullshit. I could've lost her. Knowing it makes me clench her tight, giving my sister a look like ice, and ask the second most important question of the evening. "Where's Kendra?"

"Hiding, probably. Can't say I blame her. You look like you want to interrogate her."

Of course I fucking do.

I need to know everything. Need to be sure there's no sign Victor intends to resurface tonight, and thieve away my precious girl. I start moving, heading down the hall, hoping I'll find her in the big chair by the fireplace.

"Hold up, Thor. You *do* realize she's the one who stepped up and kept our peanut safe, right?" Jamie paces after me, but I'm not slowing down.

I find Kendra out on the patio next to the dining room, a hurried look in her eye when she sees me, bolts up, and tenses. I take the seat next to her, gently rubbing my little girl's head. She stirs softly in her sleep.

"What did he say to you?" I growl, blood running to lava when I think about the Heartless Fuck's arms on my baby.

"That he'd be back. That he thinks we'll slip up. That we'll –" she catches herself. "Jesus, Knox, I don't know. It was terrifying."

Her eyes stare through me. They're on Jamie, standing behind me, arms folded tight as her face looks while we're having our pow-wow. "Idiot, I'm so glad I heard you add 'thank you.'"

I turn around, pissed off, but careful not to wake my snoozing kid. "Don't you have margaritas to shake or something? Give us some damn privacy."

"Not so fast. I didn't hear a word out of creepo's mouth, but Kendra told me everything." My little sis looks at her friend, who's blushing and looking away, telling me she omitted the important parts. "What I can't understand is why he's so persistent, why he came after her, why he even knows who she is."

"You think a fucking billionaire can't hire a whole team to do the grunt work when it comes to finding out who's tied to me? Victor probably knows the name of the last scorpion I stepped on."

Jamie pouts, pursing her lips, quiet in thought. "I don't like this, guys. Not one bit. It's like there's something else going on here, something beyond wanting to screw Knox over, and have his revenge –"

"What don't you understand? Maniacs have no logic." I cut her off mid-sentence before she says Sam. "By the way, I put in for a leave of absence today."

Both my sister and my fake fiancée do a double take. Nodding, I continue. "It's for everybody's good. Tensions are so thick around Black Rhino it's dynamite. Teams can't work, can't plan, can't even fucking think when the two men at the top are at each other's throats."

"Jesus," Jamie whispers, letting her arms fall to the sides. "I'm just surprised. If dad were around to see this, he'd –"

"He'd get it. I'm not doing this because I need a giant dick waving contest with a bitter old man who thinks I killed his daughter. This is for our family. I'll settle Black Rhino's business as soon as I'm through with Wright."

I mean it in the worst way. If there were a way to put him behind bars or deep underground without any consequences, I'd do it in a heartbeat.

"I'm sorry, Knox," Kendra whispers.

I take a long, hard look at the woman who's done so much for me. Rattles my bones knowing she was the only thing between that snake and my daughter. If he'd decided to go through her...

Fuck. No, I can't think that way. It'll lead me dark places I've only begun to put behind me. Don't need a list of all the reasons I strangled her crush on me years ago, and intentionally made myself toxic.

I can't hurt you again, I think to myself, pain coming rough in my throat the longer I look at her.

"Knox, I'm telling ma." Jamie blinks as soon as I whip around, giving her a death glare. "We've kept her in the dark long enough. She deserves to know what's happening, even if we're short on details. She isn't stupid. I'm not lying to her face anymore, pretending this will all just go away. That man proved it won't when he tried to take our peanut away."

Kendra stands, crouches near me, gently runs her fingers down my arm. Fireworks hit my brain in sexy, bedazzling, furious lights. It's hard keeping my *don't you fucking dare* look aimed Jamie's way.

I get it. She's trying to soothe the animal clawing out of me. In the process, she's wicked close to blowing our cover, and I wonder if she's fucking trying to.

Not now, damn it. Don't you go losing your mind too, Sunflower.

"Tell me, Jamie, what do you think ma will wind up thinking about if she has to dwell on Victor Wright again?"

My sister chews her lips, her eyes softening once the realization set in. "She's a tough woman. She'll handle it, Knox. Obviously, the last thing I want to do is drag her through that again –"

"Wrong. From where I'm standing, it's the first thing you're willing to do, all so you can do – what, exactly? Remind her she's powerless? That she can't do anything to the feral weasel our old man shacked up with for business? He's holding the best hand until we call his fucking bluff."

Until I have my way, I mean. Sooner or later, with God as my witness, I will.

"Take her, Sunflower." I pass my baby girl to the woman next to me, caught between our thinly veiled attraction and this charade we're forced to play. "Ease off before you make a big goddamn mistake, Jamie. Let me handle this. Plans are in motion. I'll deal with Victor once I've laid my trap. Don't bring ma into this, and force her to re-live everything with dad again."

For a few short seconds, I'm teleported back in time to the thick of our family hell. The weeks after he died, trying to pretend I'd never found those damning letters. The heart attack killed his body. But my father's honor died when his dirty little secrets turned up, and I had to lie to my mom and sister about his family man legacy.

I remember Jamie and me sitting on the chaise, both of us on each side of our bawling mother. It was the same routine for weeks after the funeral. His end gutted her.

I swore I'd never let his double life finish the job.

Then his estate, the arguments with lawyers, Victor obeyed by the corporate trust, gave her 'just enough' to make our family comfortable per the legalese and Black Rhino's operating agreement. Dad left the door open for me to earn more. Used to believe I could do it honestly, if it weren't for that thing with Sam.

But Sam or no Sam, I was never dealing with an honest man. The illusions broke down years ago, revealing the python I'm dealing with, and now there's no choice but to put him under before he chokes the life out of me and everyone I care about.

"Kendra, let's go," I say, pulling gently at her blouse. She stands a second later, careful not to wake Lizzie. It's another reminder this little angel is the lynchpin holding our lives together in all its myriad parts: good, bad, beautiful, and ugly.

"Wait!" Jamie stamps her foot when we walk past. I stop and turn around. Her blue eyes have a familiar shimmer I've only seen in the mirror. "Okay, fine. I won't say anything. I'll wait. But Knox, I swear to God, if there are any more surprises, or this thing with Victor Wright gets worse, I'm not breaking the news to her. You are. And I'll kick you straight in the balls if you don't."

"Deal." I mean it, and it's the last word I say while we're in this house.

This needs to go down my way, even if I'm risking the family jewels.

* * *

WE'RE HOME, and I'm staring at Kendra again, holding a snoozing Lizzie in my arms. "You fed her?"

"Yeah. Mini-burgers and a salad after we got home. It was a really hot day and she saw all the animals."

"Arma...dillo..." Lizzie muses in her sleep, smacking her little lips, somewhere between planet earth and the zoo in her dreams. I smile, wondering for the thousandth time where the hell that sweetness goes when we grow up. I kiss her on the forehead, taking several steps toward the stairs.

"You coming up?" I give Kendra a look over my shoulder, wondering why she looks so damn surprised. "You saved her today. If you want to come up and help tuck her in, you're entitled."

She smiles, trailing after me. It's the least I can offer after she saved Lizzie's life, plus my sanity.

The nightly ritual puts me at peace. I pull my daughter's sheets over her, making sure they're snug, and place a sippy cup of water on the nightstand in case she wakes up thirsty.

I'm able to forget today while I'm going through the motions. The poison drains every second I'm watching my own lost innocence distilled into this little girl.

The thoughts I have when my eyes flick to Sunflower are anything but innocent. She sits next to me at the end of Lizzie's bed for several minutes. Then I take her hand, and I'm hard as canyon rock the second I hear her gasp.

"Knox?"

"Quiet." I lean in, lifting her up with me when I stand, leading us out of my little girl's room. I stop to shut off the light and close the door. "Couldn't keep your hands off me in front of my sister, could you?"

Her cheeks burn red, twin suns begging for my lips. "I should've, Knox. I'm sorry. It was just the moment, trying to calm you down, hoping we'd throw Jamie off before she got too close to –"

"Not our biggest worry anymore," I say, seizing her by the wrist and bringing that ivory hand to my mouth. Just having her skin on my lips tastes like perfection. It's the stars we had our lost night on Camelback. "I'm caring less by the day if she finds out. Wright's the real problem."

"You will," she says, coming closer, flattening her hands on my chest. "Give it time. You'll find your way, and he'll be a distant memory."

Something flashes outside the window next to us, catching my attention. The skyline over Phoenix and Tempe lights up in a quick blue burst.

"Heat lightning," I say, wrapping an arm around her waist. I pull her tight until I hear the satisfying hitch in her lungs. "Truth be told, I'm done with memories, Sunflower. You've got no clue how bad I want to live in the present, without these fucked up worries."

Lightning flashes again, bathing us in its intense blue glow, covering the red balm on her cheeks. She leans in, her voice a husky whisper, shaking when she pops the question. "So, why don't you? I'm right here in front of you."

If my eyes were beads trained on her before, they're two hungry dogs now, tracking every soft curve of her body. My hand slides lower, stopping at her hip, grasping the edge of her blouse in a sudden rough handful. "Christ, you're a tease. Reminds me some things never change."

"Me?" Kendra's pupils swell. So big, so needy, so fuckable I want to lose myself there forever. "Like you didn't string me along. Hell, you're still doing it, aren't you?"

Finally, the night's million dollar question. My cock stirs in my pants, angry and throbbing, ready to deal with a hundred consequences in the morning.

"I'm doing what you want," I say, stopping just short of a kiss, laying my forehead hard against hers. "Everything we've needed since the minute I let you back in my life, and shoved the ring on your hand that should be there constantly."

I lace my fingers through hers, feeling the bareness. She hasn't had the time or need to replace my ring since leaving my sister's place.

Damn if it doesn't bother me at some screwed up level I barely understand.

"What, and wear it in front of Jamie? Your mom? I thought we agreed –"

"Deals change all the time, darling. That's part of life on this rock. You said it yourself. I'm not worried about us anymore. Just Victor." Lightning flashes in the distance again, illuminating the mountains. I bring both my hands to her face and cup it, giving her head a gentle turn to the window. "You see that out there?"

She nods, breath quickening. Those palm-sized tits under her top press harder against me. I know if I take them in my hands right now, her nipples will be pebbles, aching to be sucked soft the instant I rip her shirt open. Or maybe they want to be pressed against my cock instead, while I show her a new way to torture me with that sharp little mouth.

"It's calling us, Kendra. Pure energy. Makes me want to lay you down and do reckless, scary shit you've never had with any man." I pause, grinding my hips against hers, loving how she tilts into me when my knee goes between her legs. "There, Sunflower. *There.* That's where I've always belonged. Everywhere I've been begging to be, even when I lied myself into thinking I wanted to be somewhere else. Real regret is not taking you years ago. We should've had it first, should've had it long ago, after Sam and Africa, before I shut you out and ran like a fucking coward –"

"It's not too late, Knox," It comes out of her in a hurried hiss. She clams up the second the words leave her mouth. "You can be the first."

My fingers tighten on her face, and my thumb digs

into her cheek. "What did you just say? Look at me," I growl, refusing to say another word until I see her eyes.

When she turns, lightning splashes us again, painting her eyes blue like mine for a split second. It's a surreal, beautiful catalyst for the want rising up inside me, beginning to scream in this strange, stormy night.

"I'm still a virgin," she says in a hushed whisper, ridden with angst. "I was too busy. I never got over you, not even after that night –"

"Don't fucking say it," I growl, silencing her with a kiss. She takes my mouth hard, muscles twitching in her cheeks. They juggle fear, regret, disbelief.

Everything I can't stand. My tongue brushes hers, tasting everything, needing more. "Leave the past behind us. Tonight, just *be*. Be in the here and now when you're calling out under me."

"Knox!" She whimpers my name, her breath turning shallow. Cradling her head in both hands, I kiss her again, this time harder.

I need to take what's mine, and it isn't going to wait.

My hands move instinctively, throwing her over my shoulder, carrying her to my room. By time we reach the door, knowing I'm about to take Sunflower's cherry makes me feel like a clueless virgin all over again. My cock can only take so much before it explodes, ideally deep inside her.

IX: RECONCILIATION (KENDRA)

*H*is hands are my ultimate undoing. It's hard to pin down just one when his lips, his gaze, and the handsome slab of muscle that's quintessentially Knox Carlisle are all over me, hotter and more demanding than they've ever been.

But if I had to choose, it's his hands lifting me to heaven when I'm on his bed, prone to his marvels. They roam my body, massaging my skin, sampling my breasts and my ass as he holds me against him, his mouth intent on smothering mine.

Every kiss is a new addiction.

I give him my teeth, sinking into his bottom lip. His delirious hands start pulling off my clothes. It's incredible how fast I'm undressed, stripped bare, buried underneath him while he works his shirt open with his free hand.

"Go ahead and look. Admire," he whispers, grabbing my hands and using them to slide his undone shirt off his shoulders, exposing his tight shield of a chest. "Touch me,

Sunflower. Put your little hands on my ink. Know you've always wanted to since the days we were kids."

He isn't wrong. I'm barely breathing as I reach out, closing my eyes. My fingers graze his tattoos like they're a priceless canvass. His lungs pump harder as I lay my hands on him.

He's raw, alive, and completely burning up. His half-naked body is living art.

My eyes open, drinking in the work and insanity that went into crafting the muscles underneath his dark tattoos. I see an eagle, USMC over it, his unit's number branded in him for life. Then I see the familiar Black Rhino logo, a dark horn with a diamond ring around it, and what looks like several neat lines beneath, as if he's keeping count.

"Men I lost," he answers, searching my eyes. "Just like the watch. They're a big part of the reason we didn't do this sooner. Losing half my crew in the dirtiest, darkest slums you can imagine chewed up a piece of my soul. Their sacrifice is the only reason I'm still breathing, gearing up to own every last inch of you tonight."

His voice drips cold emotion, calling goosebumps to my skin.

So heavy. So serious. So sweltering.

My fingers pivot, aiming my nails at his skin. He releases a low growl as they slide down, below his chest, across the ripped mountains in his abs, closer to his belt line. When the very edge of my hand touches him there, he grabs my wrist so quick I gasp.

"No. You get my cock after I see your eyes roll. Lay back." He doesn't have to push hard to topple me. I hit the mattress with a soft bounce, recoiling against Knox's huge body.

He hovers, reaches behind me, unhooking my bra. The clasp gives an audible *pop* and he lifts it away. Nervous heat flows free like magma, caressing me from the inside and out, re-igniting every doubt and insecurity I've ever had about my body.

Knox is blind to my imperfections. He gives a soft grunt, exhaling like he's tasted a fine wine. His hands palm my breasts while fresh lightning spills across the valley. His huge windows in this room are portals to the turmoil in the sky.

Except it's getting harder to tell if the storm is outside anymore, or in here with us.

"Always knew you hid an angel's body under those grandma tops and skirts, Sunflower. Can *not* believe I'm the first lucky SOB who gets to see it." I love how he says it with excitement flooding his voice.

Can. Not.

That makes two of us. I can't believe I'm here, melting into a sticky puddle while his hands stroke nirvana into me, his feral gaze on my skin every waking second.

My nipples throb, blooming between his fingers, twin helpless peaks at his mercy. His fingers close around them and I bite my lip.

And those fingers are just a prelude to his tongue. My eyes are half-closed, but he doesn't care when he brings his face down. His gaze intensifies while his tongue flicks over my right nipple, fueling the fireball in my hips.

"Knox…" I moan his name, a quiet plea, bracing for the second his smirking lips part to devour.

NICOLE SNOW

Nothing prepares me for the heat. Lips, tongue, and fire swarm my body. Lightning crackles again, a vision of the inferno conquering my nerves.

Another low, soft growl vibrates in his throat, and through me, when his tongue picks up. He's lashing one nipple, kneading my other breast, fingers and mouth moving in unison.

My pussy swells beneath the last scrap of clothing attached to my body. His knee splits my legs, driving against my clit, but holding back before pleasure over-whelms my senses.

Of course he has to tease. His every movement reminds me of that silly name I've had since our night in the desert, when I was just a baby, worshiping the ground he walked on.

Look at me now.

See her, Knox? The woman who always had your hand, walked with you through hell, even when you pushed her away?

See how her lips form a perfect ring when they stretch taught, moaning your name, teeth clenching when your teeth seize each nipple, and pull?

See how I try to grind while you hold me down, asserting your control, steering this mad, beautiful what-ever between us?

See how fucking sorry I am that I'm not wearing your ring tonight?

How bad I want to, and want it to be real?

How salaciously I lift my hips, wrap my legs around you, pleading with every word to have your naked body seething against mine?

Do you still see your Sunflower?

"Kendra, fuck!" He breaks away from skating his lips over my belly, like he needs his precious oxygen. "What the hell you doing to me, Sunflower? What, and how?"

I don't answer. Just kiss him harder, running my fingernails through his hair, opening my legs even though it's the last thing I want to do. What I really want is to close them around him and find the delicious friction that ends this heat, before he drives me completely insane.

Oh, but he has other delights in mind for tonight. So many, it's frightful.

I'm not a patient person. That goes tenfold when I'm minutes from saying goodbye to the shy virgin baggage chained to my life for the last six years.

Knox's fingers are on my panties. They dip inside, underneath the waistband, and I have a half second reminder I'm not wearing anything lacy or exciting.

He doesn't seem to care.

His sky blue eyes say I'm exquisite.

His clenched jaw says he wants what's in front of him like he's never wanted anything.

His hands say *now.*

I'm barely able to lift my butt before he pulls, stripping my panties.

They're gone.

A tremor runs through me when I realize how completely naked and vulnerable I am. His mouth soothes my worries, returning to my flesh, a heat and speed in his kiss leaving me breathless, joyous, dizzy.

Oh, hell. A new fire unlike anything I've had before curls my fingers and toes. He's at my inner thigh, licking and sucking, trying to soften me before he moves a few inches to the steaming, needful mess in the center.

"Knox, God!" I shake harder, whimpering, nerves trying to close my legs.

He holds them open with a growl, adding a delicious pressure with his thumb. His fingers sink into my skin, a prelude to the first stroke of his tongue across my pussy an instant later.

His lick is a full body quiver.

The landscape shifts inside me. I'm flat on my back, splayed open, grinding into the face of this manic animal taking me apart from the waist down. Knox brings his heat faster, splitting my labia with each taste, edging fierce, hypnotic circles around my swollen clit.

I can't hold on. I have to grip the sheets. I'm sweating and aching, dying for the man I've loved like my own brother, and hated for what he did to me.

I don't know what I'm doing in sex yet, but I understand emotion. It hits like fine whiskey and leaves me just as dazed, pleased, and addicted. The space between us closes in his quickening tongue-work.

My hips won't stay pinned to the bed anymore. They give themselves up, surrender to his mouth, pressed as tight as he'll allow, riding his face.

He's growling into me, hooking thumbs into my skin even harder, reminding me that sometimes the very best things have to hurt, if only a little.

The slight discomfort in his pinprick fingertips has nothing on the ecstasy descending.

My clit throbs as he fully takes it, stroking my bud in his lips. Then his face drifts up, his lips draw a little tighter, and the circles he brushes into my skin become inescapable.

"Knox, Knox, Knox..." I call his name, trying to count, trying to hang on before I'm pulled completely into him.

It's scary, but I want to be. And that's when I finally let go, his hands holding me open, face buried in my pussy, tongue in my folds.

Lightning flashes for the hundredth time. The sky rips, joins me, screaming thunder when I come undone.

Coming!

I'm paralyzed. The raw, throbbing shock rolls through me, seizing my muscles, turning me to granite. I'm a prisoner to his handsome face, a willing slave. His body controls mine and I adore it.

I come so sweetly, surrendering to his face.

His licks come rough, but he knows how delicate I am, too. When the breathless aftershocks finally let me lay still again, panting for dear life, he brings me home with a kiss.

"Goddamn, you come as good as you taste, Sunflower." He kisses me harder, making sure I taste my own scent on his lips. "Love that wetness wrapped around my tongue. Too bad there's another place aching for it more."

There's no mystery what he means when his cock presses into me, separated only by his trousers. He rears up, guiding my hands to his body, holding them at his sides while working off his belt. His zipper goes down a hair second before his bottoms.

Then the most magnificent flesh I've ever laid eyes on springs out, ready and alive.

"Wow." I feel like a total dork with my one liner. It isn't

even adequate for a single twitch of his flesh when he wraps it in his fist. Staring deep into my eyes, he rolls his hand down it, and I watch the pre-come trickling out in a steaming line to the sheets. "Holy hell," I whimper, everything that's about to happen hits me like another bolt rending the heavens.

"Not hell. Heaven, Sunflower. Once I'm inside you, there's only one place you're going. Just gave you a taste when you saw what my mouth can do. Now, we're done looking over the ledge," he whispers, shuffling his boxers and pants off behind him, before fisting my hand and bringing it straight to his hard-on.

It's hot. Quivering. Glorious. My toes curl against his calves, imagining the damage and the glory it'll do.

"Now, it's time to leap," he says, rolling back on his hips, bringing his cock's mast to full attention. I've never even seen one before, but it's no shock he's *huge*.

Knox does big like most men do good. And what he loses when he's less than concerned with being civil, he makes up in other attributes, like the glint in his eye when he tugs on his thick length, fist pressed to his balls, leaning forward.

"You ready, baby girl?"

Can't you tell? I've only been waiting for years.

"Please," I whisper back, tightening my fingers so hard around his I think they'll snap. "I want you in me."

The oceans in his eyes deepen when the lightning comes again, painting them an almost otherworldly blue. A low growl pools in his throat, giving thunder to the storm splitting the sky above his roof. "Show me how bad, Kendra. You get every inch when I hear it."

He grabs my hand, places it on his cock, and closes his

fist around it. I shut my eyes, wondering how I'm able to love and hate what he's making me do, stroking up and down. I want to keep going, but God I want him in me.

He wants me to show him I'm worthy, the ass. Or maybe he just wants to prolong the torture disguised as foreplay until I've soaked his sheets more than I already have.

"Harder, darling," he commands, jerking my hand faster, tighter, harder with his. "Just like you want me to fuck you."

Oh, God. More fire throbs between my legs. I pinch my thighs together, sucking my bottom lip, thoroughly addicted to the heat in his skin.

I pick up the pace, rolling him in my fingers harder. Every time he pulses in my hand, a new delight. Each time the low, masculine groan in his throat gets louder, pride. My heartbeat synchronizes to his rhythm, beating faster as his cock jerks, oozing more napalm across my fingers.

"Yeah, Sunflower, yeah...fuck!" His eyes are closed.

I'm braced for anything, wondering if he'll shower my body with his seed if he shoots off now.

But Knox seizes my hand at the last instant, yanks it off him, and brings it over my head. He pins me to the mattress, knocking my legs apart with his hips, positioning himself for the inevitable.

My eyes are wide, flickering with the lightning's reflection as they bore into his. He holds my gaze, my heart, my very soul. I wish they could stop time, too, leaving us both here to savor this unforgettable bridge between my soon-to-be-stripped virginity and God knows what comes after.

"Wish I had mirrors in my eyes," he says, kissing at my

throat, a strange statement that makes me do a double take. Typical Knox. He doesn't follow up until he's licked to my cleavage, nearly causing me to forget what he just said. "You've got no frigging clue how beautiful you are now, Sunflower. I love this look."

"What?" *The one where I'm the typical first-time fuck, shaking and clueless, core clenched so tight it's practically in my throat?* I only think the last part, holding it in while his fingers stroke circles on my wrist. "You mean the one where I'm hardly able to breathe because I'm waiting for Casanova to finally lay his claim?"

"No. Try the one where you pretend you're a good girl, completely innocent. Like you haven't been flicking your clit to the dreams where I deflower you for years."

Guilty. He knows it, and the shameful heat rushing to my face tells him that I know he knows.

"You on the pill?" he asks, teasing me when he rolls his swollen cock's tip between my lips.

I remember to nod. Barely.

"Good." His eyes don't match his words. It's almost like he wishes I'd said unprotected, and I'm scared because it actually excites me.

I want him skin-on-skin. I want him deep. I want all of him. My body cries out for his at a base biological level.

"Fuck, Sunflower," he growls, his blue eyes vanishing behind his lids for half a second. When they open again, piercing through me, they say play time is over.

So is time for talk. *It's on.*

Everything next happens so fast. His hips roll back in the blink of an eye, and he flicks his angry cock against me one more time, before it's plunged into my heat.

Blue lightning. White moan. Hot thunder.

Or is it the rumble in his throat as he sinks into me?

Knox thrusts slow and steady, taking the last parts of me my toys haven't reached. His size doesn't let my virgin body off so easy, though.

I'm still when he's in. Breathless. Counting my own heartbeat.

It takes all my focus not to cry out the first time he brings himself to the end of my womb. Then the thrusts begin, stern and powerful as the desert storm, leaving just as much chaos in its wake.

His cock pries me open each time he thrusts, snug around him, accommodating his thickness. It hurts, but it's the *good* kind, like running a marathon or swimming vigorous laps in a sports pool. I'll work for my reward.

"So. Fucking. Tight," he grunts, working himself in deeper, pacing his strokes. He stops when he sees my eyes pinched shut, runs his fingers through my hair, noticing my first-time discomfort. "You okay? Taste me, Sunflower. Focus on the kiss. Look at me."

Sweet words. Sweeter mouth. I twine my tongue with his, and before I fully realize it, I'm moaning.

Knox swallows my heat, pushing his hips firmer into mine. My legs fold tight around his muscular body, mirroring his movements. My legs trace his when he sinks into me, claiming what's his, marking it with deeper thrusts.

"Yeah, darling. Yeah, yeah, yeah." That same word comes rhythmically, almost like he's keeping beat.

It's infectious. Pleasure wells deep in my head, dragging me down.

My body, my mind, my senses bow to his sweet fuckery.

I'm entranced. Enthralled. Overwhelmed.

I'm coming!

Knox snarls when my breath hitches. He quickens his thrusts, raking his stubble against my throat. I feel his teeth go in my shoulder, a firm but gentle love bite, just as I'm swept away by orgasmic bliss.

The feels are a stampede. Right, wrong, so many multifaceted shades of emotion tearing through my soul.

My pussy clenches on his cock. He holds it in me, his groans deepening, while new lightning crashes through the window.

I hold on tight, raking his back, writhing underneath him. When I'm able to breathe and think again, I open my eyes, feeling his forehead's pressure on mine.

"Turn the fuck over," he whispers, helping me along when I'm too slow to comply.

Why don't you look at me? I want to see his eyes when he finishes, but Knox has other plans.

Once I'm on my hands and knees, he mounts me from behind, grabbing my ass. The question haunts me for a few more thrusts before my lust silences everything.

My second O comes faster. Harder, too.

It's freer than before, a quick moving fire reaching up from my legs to grab me by the throat. I throw my hips into him. Fucking with the fury building up inside me, the need to reconcile old longings and swift release.

Let go, Knox, I think to myself. *Let me feel you come undone, just this once.*

"Shit, Sunflower..." he whispers in the darkness, fingers

pinching my ass tighter, riding the bucking mess I've become. Colliding, thrashing, one wave of flesh, we bring our bodies together like pistons, the same engine driven by desire. "Kendra!"

I smile when his cock begins to swell. My name is the last word on his lips.

It's the last conscious decision I'm able to make before lightning fills my eyes, and sweet release finds us.

Then there's just convulsions. Pleasure and his fiery heat.

Knox spills himself inside me, hurling his seed deep, his ragged breath matching each jerk of his cock.

Lightning flashes one more time as our ecstasy peaks.

Once, outside the window. Once, inside us.

I don't regain consciousness until I'm in his arms, watching the fading blue lights from the sky dancing across his face. "That was...totally worth the wait." I hope it doesn't sound sappy, and if it does, maybe the kiss I plant on his lips takes the edge off.

"Yeah, Sunflower. Better catch your breath. Then we're marathoning the other nine hundred and ninety-nine times we missed over the years, all the nights I should've put you to bed after pure fucking fire."

* * *

I WANT TO FORGIVE HIM.

Somewhere, deep inside, I know the good man I grew up with never died. No pain, tragedy, or frustration could ever kill him.

The Knox I knew was always too strong for that – and

tonight he's shown me everything I suspected all along is true.

Forgiveness, though...that's the final bridge left to cross. Easily the hardest. Is it too far?

I don't know. Not yet. My brain works overtime while I'm tangled up in his bed, and makes me re-live the day he tore my heart to pieces.

* * *

Four Years Ago

IT's Danny's house again. I haven't been here for almost a year, not since the day Knox found out he was going to be a father.

It's insane what's happened since. Who knew how much it takes to actually be an adult?

I'm working myself to the wire between class and part-time jobs, always carving a little time for myself to let my mind play. Creativity flows best when I trade my laptop for an old fashioned sketchbook.

I also try to keep up with Jamers, who pays good bribes to write her term papers. I can't get her better than Cs in most subjects. She's on her own for finals, but at least she won't flunk everything this semester.

I need the money. College isn't cheap. Brainpower is. Especially when you're from a normal family, without my best friend's wealth and luxury.

And it's Jamie who's brought me to our friend's house

for the newest late night bash among Scottsdale's young money. They're having a bonfire in the huge stone fire pit now flanking the pool. Fires dance on ornately arranged desert stone, drawing my eyes.

Beers flow freely. Girls I've seen on campus look shocked to see me in *their* world. Jamie sneaks off early in the evening with a big lacrosse player who has pinstripe tattoos going down his arms. Then a skinnier, richer, clean shaven boy a few hours later.

I'm left alone, nursing my margarita, smiling and saying a few words to the drunk passers-by who have a boring minute to make idle chat with the new girl. Danny, our illustrious host, and kind of a douchebag dude-bro, leans in and grabs me in a way that's more than friendly when he comes by, mumbling a few words about how happy he is to see *Kayla* here.

Later, I'm grabbing a wine cooler, the last drink of the night my lightweight makeup can handle when I see the only person I'm interested in talking to.

Knox looks like hell. I mean, he's just as handsome outwardly as ever when he turns around, and looks me in the eye. But there's a darkness that wasn't there before, a pallor in his face. He tells Jamie it's just a side effect of some exotic disease he got in Africa, which he'll be over soon.

I think he's lying. He looks like a ghost because some-where over there, he lost his soul.

"Hey, Conrad. Fancy seeing you here," I smile, using the nickname I've given him ever since he returned from that trip to Sierra Leone. If there was ever a modern *Heart of Darkness* face, it's the mask he carries around everywhere, the one I keep hoping will one day crack, and reveal the man I'm missing more than ever.

"You're here late," he says, taking a pull of his beer. "Frat parties too dull for you?"

My brow furrows. I can't tell if he's teasing me, or if he really thinks I'm becoming some kind of snob. "Um, no. Jamer's idea," I insist. "Says she doesn't want to blow off the cobwebs if my social life gets more dusty than it already is."

"Fuck Jamie," he growls, lifting his beer to his lips. This time, he doesn't stop until the can clinks empty when he sets it down. "She doesn't understand. People *need* their peace and quiet sometimes. One fine day she'll get it, mark my words."

I sit next to him, cautiously bumping arms. He gives me a look of pure hell.

This is a mistake, I think. *Why can't you just leave him alone? Stop subjecting yourself to this torture.*

It's been months since he cracked a joke or smiled on the rare occasions we've seen each other. He'll listen when I talk about my classes, sure, but usually for all of ten seconds before he has to run off to...wherever the hell Knox Carlisle goes these days.

I can't figure him out, what he's turning into. I know a walking contradiction if there ever was one.

Diamond seeking warrior.

Ferocious single dad.

My lingering toxic crush.

Yes, I know it's dangerous. Unhealthy. Wrong. I should find someone younger on campus, without his baggage, who actually treats me like he's happy to see me.

But I can't let him go without finding out why he frowns all the time when his adorable daughter isn't around. He gave me time and heart, my confidant for teenage disasters that seem sillier in retrospect with every passing week.

Even if it doesn't make sense, I want to repay him. Doesn't he deserve an ear, a shoulder, a soul willing to help?

"No Lizzie?" I ask, noticing how slow and reluctant he moves when he turns toward me.

"At grandma's tonight. Damn good timing for once, too. I love my peewee to death, but I need a break once in a blue moon. This is the first I've had since the last acquisitions trip."

"Oh, yeah, Africa. How was it?"

I regret the question instantly when the bonfires reflecting in his eyes turn to ice. "Hell. The places we go, the things we do to keep our company's supply rolling in...makes me want to fucking puke. There's *got* to be a better way. There's a lot of talk about the stuff they're doing in labs. Growing stones like magic, duplicating rare earth elements left and right. Just need patience. I'll have the money and the pull someday. And then, I swear to Christ, I'll shove my squeaky clean diamonds down that Victor's dirty throat until he chokes."

I clear my throat uncomfortably, raising my bottle. Thank God for wine coolers.

"I'm sorry he's still giving you trouble," I say, staring at the fires reflecting in the glass pressed between my palms. It's less insufferable than the hate, sorrow, and confusion tarnishing his beautiful eyes. "Is it Sam...forgive me. Sorry. I shouldn't have asked."

Oh, God. He's glaring. "Knox, look, that came out wrong. I said I'm —"

"Sorry? Buzz off, Sunflower. What's happening with my missing baby mama is none of your goddamn business. Neither is anything else in my life." He stands, shooting me another vicious glare, or what looks like one at first. "If you're smart – and I know you've got a brain the size of the Grand Canyon between those ears – you'll forget whatever special glowy spark you think we have."

"Jesus, Knox. In case you hadn't noticed, I'm trying to help, like friends do. I had no clue you'd get this upset." I'm scowling, all I can do to build a box around the radioactive hurt in my heart. "And yeah, I *get* it. You're not particularly friendly, or much else anymore. I don't know what happened to you over there, or what's going on with Sam, and true, maybe it's none of my business. I just wish I could help. That's all. Really."

"There's no helping this shit, Kendra. None of it." He turns away, but not before swiping his empty can off the brick bench, crumpling it in his hand. "Leave me alone. Maybe you're not hearing the message, still, even though I've tried to be crystal clear. Maybe that's the problem..."

I don't know what he means. There isn't a chance to ask.

Before I can even blot my own tears, he's gone, leaving me to the fading reverie and laughter next to the fireside pool party. I've never been so miserable staring at so many happy people.

* * *

IT'S ROUGHLY HALF an hour later when I realize my purse

is missing. I notice it when my phone gets down to the last few percent left on its battery, and I really need the charger.

Of course, it's about time when I want to check in with Jamie, and see if she's up for leaving early. She probably isn't. That means I'll need another ride home. I don't know or trust any of the thoroughly boozed up acquaintances here enough to ask.

I'm walking the perimeter around the pool, passing the kerosene lanterns, half of them gone dark for the night. Trying to remember the places I could've put my bag.

I'm frantic. I still can't find it anywhere.

Stop and think. Where was the last place you saw it? You sat by the door, had a few drinks, chatted with these idiots. Then you grabbed a wine cooler and made your way over to –

Knox.

He must have taken it, or knocked it over in his angry stupor when he crunched that stupid beer can. I lift my phone to my face, ignoring the low battery life warning. I fire him a text, saying I need to go, and I can't find my purse anywhere – has he seen it?

I'm not seriously expecting an answer. But my phone pings a second later, docking another battery percent. I see the cryptic message on my screen.

KNOX: Up in Danny's guest room on the third floor. End of the hall. Busy. Come get it.

So, he has it, and he knows. I wait five more seconds for

NICOLE SNOW

an apology that never comes, then stuff my phone in my pocket, clenching my teeth as I race inside.

Danny has a total mess on his hands to clean up tomorrow, assuming he doesn't leave it for the cleaning service his parents hire out. I make my way through the big house, careful not to trip on beer cans or the kids passed out in the hallways, stinking like weed and used latex.

I wish I came from money. Almost as badly as I wish I didn't have to see Knox again tonight.

That's the thing about wishes, though. Sometimes you wish for ponies and get piranhas.

It takes another minute to get to the guest room. There are only four up here in this McMansion, and all of their doors are closed. I walk to the door at the end of the hall, just like he said.

My fist raps lightly at the door. "Knox?"

The first thing I hear is laughter. A woman's voice. Playfully annoyed.

I'm flushed, thinking I've got the wrong room, but then I hear his booming voice. "It's open. Get in here, little girl."

I'm holding my breath when I jiggle the knob, pushing inside. He's there, all right, and he's not alone.

Knox sits on the bed, his trousers around his ankles, reclining on the mattress with his hands propping him up. Not one, but two women look up from kissing his thighs, their hands tucked neatly around his...

Jesus. It's obscured by their faces when they turn toward me, but I catch a heartbreaking flash to leave no doubt what they were doing.

He looks me coldly in the eye. "It's on the desk,

darling. Thought I'd keep it safe up here and see if you want to join the fun."

The two drunken bimbos at his feet giggle. "Really? *Her?*"

"Talk about robbing the cradle!" the other one says.

A bitter rock catches in my throat. My knees move, breaking the numbness. I'm able to take the seven steps to the little desk, rip my purse off it by the strap, and start pacing toward the door.

The two women are laughing again. His killing blue eyes never leave me.

Finally, before I slam the door, I crack. "You're a fucking pig, you know!"

If he ever responds, I'm not there to hear it. The door crashes shut under its own weight. I'm running, stumbling to the driveway, where I wait to fetch a cab home.

It's a clear night, cooler now with summer's heat gone. There's no one around except the winking stars to see me cry.

In theory, they're the same stars I shared with Knox what seems like a lifetime ago, when we poured our hearts across Camelback. But they've changed. It's undeniable.

They're fainter, darker, and a thousand times more distant.

"Asshole. I *hate* you," I whisper.

And for the next four years, I do.

I stop chasing Knox, rarely so much as greeting him when he comes around Jamie's place, the only time we're ever in the same room together. His numb, lifeless looks don't bother me anymore.

I'm the one who shrugs him off when he acknowledges my presence with a derisive snort or a snide word. I'm the one who looks his way with a single question in my eyes.

I can't give him anything more until I finally have an answer.

Why?

Why did you have to be so fucking cruel?

X: UNDER THE DESERT
MOON (KNOX)

J wake up alone the next morning, my dick unfathomably hard. Must have emptied myself in her at least four times last night, and I'm still popping morning wood.

I grab my robe and head downstairs, making quick peace with my absence at Black Rhino. It's been years since I had any time off I truly enjoyed. Once I've swung my axe at Victor and ended this, I know I'll be back better than ever.

I peek in Lizzie's room on the way down. My little angel is still asleep. It's early, and she's got another hour or two before it's time to wake up.

When I step into the kitchen, I'm greeted by beauty itself. Kendra in her robe could make the sunrise itself jealous while it tip-toes across the valley. I walk toward her while she sips her steaming tea, wrap my arms around her waist, and think hard about dropping that burgundy cotton hiding her body.

"Morning, Sunflower." She tenses, managing a troubled smile as I lift her face to mine. My turn to frown. "What's wrong?"

"Nothing. It isn't important...or it shouldn't be."

"Tell me." I sink down next to her, clasping her hand. She's wearing my diamond.

Damn if they don't look right when the light glances over their edge. I'm holding her hand, almost in the position I should've been in if I'd ever asked her to marry me proper.

She's holding it in. It's a few more seconds, squeezing her hand tighter, before she'll look at me. "That night at Danny's party years ago..."

Fuck. I knew she'd want the truth sooner or later.

A man can't just have the best lay of his life, and then hide it. If there's anything I've learned about the past in recent years, it's that it doesn't stay buried forever.

"I didn't want to do it. You left me no choice." It's point-blank honest, almost too direct when it comes. *Is that my hand shaking?* I close my fist, pressing it into my thigh, hiding how hyper-aware I am that this little chat could blow my world to kingdom come when I'd just started fixing it.

"That's your defense? Sorry, I don't remember anyone holding a gun to your head, telling you to treat me like crap."

"I did, Kendra. I was holding the gun," I growl. Grabbing her wrist, I pull her hand to my chest, curl it softly, and wish I never had a reason to let go.

She has to believe me. I have to make her understand the pure hell boiling my brain in those days, plunging my heart into a tar pit I thought I'd never save it from.

"You're not making sense" she says, ripping her hand

away, turning her face. Her eyes refuse to look at me when the next part comes. "Maybe if you showed some regret, if you hadn't subjected me to seeing you with those disgusting bitches, I'd understand. What you're saying now, Knox – you're not sorry at all."

Christ. She really doesn't get it.

"Look at me, darling." I put my hands underneath her shoulders and lift. Need her to face me for this, look me fully in the eye, even though she twists like hell in my grip. It takes the better part of a minute to calm her, digging my gentlest tension into her skin until she relaxes. "Need you to hear this, without any confusion – nothing happened that night."

"Oh my God. I'm *not* stupid, Knox. I know what I saw!"

"You saw what *I* wanted you to, Sunflower. My optics. An illusion." My eyes drill hers, searching her pain, her skepticism, her disgust. I want to lance every fucking part of what's welling up in her and drain it from her soul.

"No!" Her little hands bang against my chest. She's too tired, confused. Too unsure of everything to hit me like I wish she would. "I saw you with your pants around your ankles. You were in their hands, up in their faces, the same part of you I made a terrible mistake with last night and –"

"Quiet," I whisper softly, running my hand over her face, tilting her up by the chin. I'm not joking when I say I *need* those eyes. "Nothing happened that night, Sunflower. Honest to God. Swear on my little girl's life. Here're my sins: I wanted you gone, wanted you to move on, wanted you to forget and live without being trapped in my fucked up shadow. I acted like an asshole to squash your little crush. I took your purse at that party and paid two drunken, squirrelly bitches for a tease. That's as far as it went, I swear."

Her eyes open like it takes enormous effort. "Oh, please. Look, if you're sorry, just say it. I don't need another lie to get over what –"

"Figured you wouldn't buy it. Hold on." I reach for the phone on the counter, and tap the button that dials Jamie's number.

"Knox, what the hell?" Kendra crosses her arms, eyeing me suspiciously.

"Yeah, sis, I've got a question for you. Remember that night I took you home from Danny's party four years ago? You were hung over, and worried about being too drunk to remember where you kept your pills. I took you by the drug store like a good brother for Plan B." I pause, getting a jumbled earful. My little sis can't believe I'm asking her about ancient history on the fly. "No, this isn't a damn game. Just answer me, sis. Answer this: do you remember the two chicks Danny had on his arm for awhile when he started that stupid band? Sugar-n-Spice or whatever the fuck they called themselves? Remember how pissed they were later that night?"

I pause again. Kendra's waist goes slack in my arms, frustration undoing her, fixing the same *I'm going to kill you* glare on my face. "Yeah, you remember. Now, say that again over speaker."

I tap another button on the phone. Jamie's voice explodes into the room through the receiver, louder than my rich neighbors tearing up the mountainside on their ATVs. "Huh? Knox, I'm not sure what you're doing, or why the hell this even matters."

"Just say what you said to me, Jamie. Please." I tap my

fingers on the counter, patience wearing thin with my sister's nosy questions.

"Okay, fine." Jamie sighs. "They were psycho. Practically ran you down the driveway with those golf clubs they jacked from Danny's father in the garage. Put a dent in your new jeep, I remember. You were pretty pissed that weekend, had me and mom over to help barbecue while you buffed it out. Seriously, what did you do to kick the hornet's nest?"

"You remember, Jamie." I hope she does. "Remember what they said? What they were screaming before we pulled away, before Danny came out and told them he'd personally throw them off his property if they didn't shut up?"

"Yeah. They said they didn't want your money. Left a mess of twenties all over the driveway to prove it, throwing it at us as we pulled away. They said you made them kiss before you decided their lips weren't good enough for a beej, and – oh! – they never do that for any man who decides to jerk them around." She pauses. "Ew. I forgot how gross they were. Did you *really* make them kiss?"

Kendra's green eyes still don't look too approving, but the hurt is gone. She knows I'm telling her the truth. "Thanks, Jamie. That'll do for now."

"Hey, idiot, what's really going on? You can't just call me up like that and –"

Click. I did, and I'm done. Hanging up, I set the phone down, turning to the only woman in this room whose opinion counts.

"I did some stupid, hurtful shit. No denying it. And I'm sorry for every bit of it – even the part where I made those drunken sluts kiss. Hope you'll find it in you to forgive me, Sunflower. I screwed up, and now I'm owning up."

Please. Inside, I'm begging. *Can't bear to watch our second spark flame out when it's barely been ignited.* She needs more. "I was screwed up after Sam, after Africa, after Victor," I say. "Asshole put me in handcuffs the first time, had me interrogated like I killed her, instead of the obvious fucking bum she skipped off to LA with. You were only eighteen. Too young. Too light. Too un-fucked for everything ahead if you'd hitched up with me then."

Truth be told, everything I'm still worried will poison her if I let her get too close. But now I'm ready to face the risk.

That ring on her finger, glittering in front of me, is far too real to be a mirage of wrong.

"Knox?" She whispers my name, coming closer, gently twining her arms around me. I've never had her hold me this tight.

"Yeah, Sunflower?"

"Shut the hell up and give me a kiss."

I do, smiling into it when I see the glow, the forgiveness in her eyes. Giving in and listening to every word she says has never tasted so good.

* * *

"You know we'll have to break the news to our families sooner or later, right?" Kendra leans in, head on my shoulder, watching Lizzie run around in the distance.

My little girl plays in a fountain under a huge canopy high overhead, the only kind of summer fun right for a day when it's hot as the sun's surface. I turn, twining my fingers with hers, loving how that warm gold band on her finger feels rubbing against mine. "We will. Ma doesn't know, so she'll be easy. Overjoyed, probably. Jamie..."

"Leave Jamers to me," she says, smiling up at me. "She's my best friend. I know it'll be a little shock at first. She might not be happy we hid this for so long, but she'll get over it. I want her front and center when we tie the knot."

Holy shit. My heartbeat picks up, drumming in my ribs, as soon as she says the last few words.

Marriage. I'm really going to do this. It's like watching the earth flip over right side up after so many years knocked on its ass. I never thought I'd see a light at the end of the tracks, but there it is, hot and bright and beautiful as the fireball hanging over Phoenix.

"Yeah, let's do your end first. That'll be easy. Your ma already thinks I'm such a 'nice young man,'" I remind her how it went down the day I came to propose, never imagining I'd ever really mean it.

"Oh, you'll have to try a bit harder than that. She loves the little girl, and thinks you're a good daddy, but they know about the crap that happened over the years. Jamie squawked too much the times she'd come by, and they follow the papers like frogs chase flies. She'll be a cakewalk compared to dad, though...he's very traditional. He'll want a date, a place, and a pastor before we discuss anything."

Shit. My future in-laws should be the least of my worries with everything else happening. But an angsty little voice in the back of my head wants to impress them. Convince her folks I'm not the dumpster fire who never got over his baby mama's disappearance and a lot of battle fatigue. I'm not so broken I won't give what's left in my soul to make their beautiful daughter the happiest woman alive.

"Let's not get ahead of ourselves. We can't talk dates until Wright gives up the chase. I'm not making plans, opening the gates for him to hurt us both if he isn't ready to shut up, and quit. We've got to cover our butts. So far, that freak you worked for isn't pressing any charges, but the story hit the local papers. Victor might've seen it. He'd love to have his lawyers reach out to Gannon, and see if he'll help strike gold."

"Information," she says, her smile fading. I hate having to see her consider the consequences. "He won't find anything. Gannon never named his assailant. I read the blogs, too."

"He's been a good boy and kept his lips shut. For now." My blood runs hot, imagining how I'll insert his moony face into his own sphincter, and make sure it never comes unstuck, if he ever breathes a word. "That may change anytime. I want something on record, Sunflower. Let's set up a meeting with my lawyer."

"Lawyer?"

I let her reluctantly sit up, snatching at my phone. "Call it insurance. Whatever it takes for cover in a court of law. The receptionist saw everything that happened at the party, if we can get her to talk to –"

"Lydia?" She wrinkles her nose. "Yeah, good luck with that. She'll put up with a lot from her employer, as long as he lets her slide without having to lift a finger. There isn't a moral bone in that girl's body. She won't flip and help us unless push comes to shove, and she knows Gannon won't keep signing her checks."

"Whatever." I have the backup plan in my head before

my man at the firm picks up. It involves a lot of money, the universal language that makes every greedy mouth on this planet open up and sing the song I write. "Yeah, Charlie? I need to see you downtown, stat. It's about my future wife..."

* * *

IT's a long day between the lawyer's office in Phoenix, shopping with Lizzie for new clothes, and running by an art store to pick up supplies. I've told Kendra she's getting a proper office in my house, the guestroom upstairs. It's a spacious room with Solarium windows, ferns, and its own private balcony overlooking the desert. Pristine view of the mountains and downtown Phoenix beyond.

Perfect for a creative. It's cute how she still doubts herself sometimes, always flushes a little when I talk about introducing her to household names Black Rhino has used for its wedding line over decades.

I want her to figure it out fast. Want her to start seeing herself, and the world, through my eyes.

Sunflower's star is too bright not to set the world on fire. I'll make her realize her own power. The elusive truth is, she was always too good to need a maggot like Eric Gannon.

Later, we wind down the day, watching a movie with Lizzie. I order pizza from our favorite place in Scottsdale, loaded with authentic Italian spice and lots of garlic. Just because I was born rich doesn't mean I turn my nose up at good, simple food.

My little girl is drifting off when it happens. Her face comes untucked from the blanket wrapped around her and Kendra. Lizzie looks at me, talking so clear and vivid at first I can't tell she's half-asleep.

"Mommy?" she whispers, rolling over in Sunflower's arms before we can do a double take. "Stay this time. Okay?"

Kendra freezes. Looks at me wide-eyed, fearful, like she doesn't know what to do.

"Go ahead and tell her, darling," I whisper, reaching over, running the tips of my fingers through peewee's hair. It's dark mahogany like mine, a match for the same blue depth and soul in her eyes, which flutter shut in her little face while she relaxes again.

"Of course, peanut," Kendra says, the corners of her eyes going moist. She leans forward, stamps a tiny kiss on my daughter's forehead, giving a smile that lights up the darkness in my private theater room. "I'll be here. Always."

I know what this is, and I'm not even scared. One of those rare moments sauntering through a man's bones, invading him with warmth and light. A confirmation smoke signal from the universe, like God himself reaching down, thwacking me across the forehead, and rumbling in my ear.

Here it is, dummy.

Everything you thought you'd never see. Remember that whole mysterious ways thing? Yeah.

You're welcome. Now, don't lose it. Cherish it with your life.

I reach over, clasping my woman's hand. She's worth the fight, and I know it, marveling at how fast my suffering makes sense when I open my eyes, looking over the two angels who've drifted into my life.

There's a weight on my chest through all the happiness, so fucking heavy it hurts.

It's up to me from here. *All of it.*

I will keep them safe. I will make them happy. I *will* marry this girl, and build my family piece by piece, strong as the diamonds set in that glorified promise ring on her hand.

It isn't real until I hear *I do,* and I've never wanted two words in my ear worse than this second.

"It's past her bedtime," I whisper, breaking the magic to help my woman up. She pushes my daughter into my arms, and we head upstairs together.

I give her sleepy little lips a few sips of water before we tuck her in. We only have to stand there quietly for a minute or two, at peace in our silence, watching my little lady drift off shortly after her head hits the pillow.

"Finally a good day," Kendra says, as soon as we're in the hall, Lizzie's door shut gently behind me.

"It's not over," I say, tasting the kiss that's been taunting me for hours. I've half a mind to swoop her up and carry her back downstairs, maybe use that theater room to play something more adult than live action fairy tales for Lizzie's sake. "We've missed so much, you and I. If she weren't there the whole time, you'd better believe I would've made up for the times we missed locking lips in front of a movie."

"Plenty of time left," she says, standing on her tip-toes, gazing into my eyes. I feel her hand graze my cheek, slipping through my five o'clock shadow, and *sweet fuck,* I'm a goner. "Easy, darling. The night is young. Before I get you out of that dress like I've been wanting all evening, there's something I want to show you first. Walk with me."

She follows me downstairs, questions in her eyes. Believe me, I wish I had answers, but all I can offer her is the same puzzle that's driven me insane on the nights when I was a much less happy man.

Kendra steps into my office, and I motion her into the seat across from my desk. Then I retrieve us a wine bottle from the cellar next door, pour it, and crack open the very last drawer in my desk. The box is always heavy. I think it's psychological. There's no earthly reason papers should ever feel this dense.

"This is everything," I say, ripping open the worn tab I've opened and sealed thousands of times. "Every scrap of information I have about why Sam disappeared. Most of it completely worthless."

"Holy crap," she whispers, pulling out the files gingerly, using the same care she'd give to a Medieval arti- fact. "You're telling me there's *nothing* in this, Knox? It looks like...wow, there must be five hundred pages!"

"Phone book sized minutia and dead ends. Hundreds and hundreds of pages to nowhere." I shut my yap, taking a pull off my wine glass, watching as she pages numbly through the secrets I've dumped in her lap. "She took off with the bum feeding her habit not long after Lizzie was born. By the time I got my discharge and came home from the war, she was gone for several months, disappeared without a trace in LA. Victor went over her dealer, Jake, with a fine-toothed fucking comb. Or he gave a good show of it. Then he decided to turn his full attention to me, the guy who took months out of his life looking for that careless bitch. Don't think she spent so much as a week in the hospital giving my little girl any attention before she freaked, had to get home to old habits, chase the high that took the edge off real life."

She looks up, lips askew, reaching for her wine with trembling fingers. "God. I can't imagine."

"Try. I want you to. Before, I thought I'd spend my life repeatedly burning our bridge to keep you away." I run my hands across the desk, taking hers, squeezing her fingers tight. This next part is very important.

"It all changed when you started wearing this," I run my finger against the ring, tempted when she blushes. *Dangerously* aware of the rising desire in my blood to shove these torture pages to the floor, and take her right here, spilling every pent up drop of my frustration deep in her supple cunt.

"Look, I don't want you sharing my crazy, but you need to understand it. Everything in this box is what's haunted me for years. Seeking closure, and never, ever finding it. If there's a piece that ties it all together, a smoking gun, I've never so much as smelled the damn gunpowder. All I have are loose ends, and the clock ticking down to the day when Lizzie figures out the piece of shit who birthed her is a ghost. It will happen, even if we're her family for years. I hope to God we will be. But she'll ask questions when she's good and ready. I need answers. I can't hide the truth from my daughter."

"Anything, Knox. I'm ready. I'm not scared." She closes her eyes, brings my hands to her lips, and lays sultry butterfly kisses over my knuckles. "I think...hell, I know I love you. Always have. I never really stopped since I was just a stupid kid with a crush, if you want to know the truth."

Do I ever. It's there when she looks me in the eye

again, bright and green and void, calling me to fill the hollow spaces she's carried around for years, deafened by the echoes.

"You already know I love you, too, Sunflower. I couldn't fucking stop, even when everything said try. I want you by my side, whether it's heaven or hell up ahead. Before tonight, this crap in front of us set my pulse more than I ever should've let it." There's thunder in my throat when we uncouple hands. I sweep the stack of documents off my desk in one fluid jerk, careful to make sure it hits the floor rather than painting my woman with splattered wine.

Not that I'd mind licking it off. Not even a little.

Next time we make eyes, I've got that bottle in my hand, forgetting the dregs left in my glass. I raise it to my lips and taste the sweetest sip I've had just shy of her full, plump lips. I stand, reach for Kendra's hand, and pass it to her. Watch the whole time while she mirrors me.

"Now kiss me, beautiful," I say, my palm circling behind her neck, melting her against me.

Her lips are unbearably sweet when they're soaked in wine. Unthinkably addicting.

We're incandescent. Clumsy in our loving. Enriched in the banquet of each other, gorging on this feast in hearts and souls, beyond ready to be tangled, messy, fused.

So. Damn. Ready.

The wine splashes her neck when I hoist her up in my arms, heading for the stairs. Another perfect signal from the universe. I stop to lick it off her skin before we head for the spa off the main floor.

Tonight, I want to light the flames low, bring her to the

outdoor shower stall with its glass and stone, and fuck her in front of the stars.

I want the entire universe to see what it's missing. What happens when a man denied this long learns to ignite the same way stars breathe life in the sky.

* * *

"GENTLY, Sunflower. Or – fuck! – hard, if that's really what you want to do!" With her mouth full of me, there's no going wrong.

My back arches against the cool stone wall, shower heads set to mist. It's like living a sex scene from the greatest movie in the world. There's no fade to black. Colors bleed from her naked skin, piercing the blue and orange light swirling around us.

Kendra's little face goes down, engulfing my cock, her palm pressed sweetly on my balls. There's a learning curve, yeah, but I can tell she's a natural. I swear I'll make my wife the hottest little cocksucker in the entire valley once she's learned the spots along my length that make me twitch.

Greedily, she's mine.

Completely mine.

Mine for fucking-ever.

My head rolls on my shoulders. I can't look down at her for more than brief glances while she strokes and sucks, better with every second, or I know I'll lose it like I'm back in high school.

She does terrible, marvelous things with those nymphette lips. My spinal cord catches fire from the torches hung around us, their gas flames gleaming in the night, giving every inch of her naked body a delicious sheen.

I wish I had a second cock to claim another orifice. But while I'm wishing for crazy things, I think I'll get my other wish – discovering what it's like to shoot off between those perky, perfect tits while she comes for me.

My hand slides into her hair, fisting it. I pull *hard* to get her attention, watching as she reluctantly takes my dick out of her mouth. "Stand up, Sunflower. Brought you a present before you're back on your knees."

She whimpers when I smack her little ass, two seconds before I pull her legs apart. She was so busy getting naked and on her knees she never noticed the silver ball behind my back. I hold it out, pushing it between her legs so she's able to look down and see, kissing at her shoulder.

"Knox, what's that?"

"Something better than the cheap little firecracker I stole from your room. This, darling, is straight up dynamite. Once it's in, get on your knees, and follow my lead." My fingers dip up, invading her pussy, pushing the perfect orb into her.

I know she's done when I use the tiny switch in my hand to turn it on. Her whole body jerks, nipples turned to mountain peaks. I help hold her down, surrounding my cock in her tits, and tell her what's next. "Push them together. Hold them there, and don't let go. I'll do the fucking rest. You come when I do."

She tries to suck me off and doesn't get very far. Flicking the switch, she's swept away as our new toy races to maximum speed, frigging her clit from the inside-out, brushing the spot in her pussy I'll take again later with my tongue.

Sunflower doesn't last long. Neither do I.

"Oh, hell. *Knox!*" My name has the honor of being the last thing on her lips before she arches, hands on her tits, squeezing my thrusting cock like a vice.

I come so fucking hard I can't even form words, roaring into the night.

* * *

"Turn the hell over. Show me that sweet ass, darling." My hands are on her lush cheeks, roaming like mad. I squeeze until she gives me a delectable moan.

Then I take her hands, pin them over her head, and flatten her against the spa's tile wall. The water spritz and moonlight calm my blood, keeps me from boiling over. I haven't gone soft since I shot off all over her just a few minutes ago.

Now, that dripping sweetness between her legs beckons like it's fucking enchanted.

Her shoulders are magnets for my mouth, pulling me to her skin. I can't stop kissing this woman.

Every second she's naked without my lips sealed on her flesh is a crime against nature.

Do I sound crazy? Obsessed? In lust?

Good. Because clearly it's all of the above, and there's a greater pulse drumming in my chest, too.

"Knox!" Kendra whimpers, sliding her hands against the wall, trying to stop her knees from shaking when my fingers search her steaming cunt. They drift inside her slowly, teasingly, telling her exactly what's coming when I'm done playing – but only after she's given me a few more Os.

NICOLE SNOW

If I'm mad, it's leaving her undone that keeps the last thread of my sanity intact. I don't just want her to come for me, come while every beautiful muscle in her body seizes, gives her up in total.

I *need* it.

Every ripple, every whimper, every moan. Every damn twitch in her eyes when she's lost in my rapture.

I'm on my knees. The toy is gone from her pussy, replaced with my thrusting fingers and hungry tongue. I pull her thighs apart, the better to lick deeper, sinking my tongue into her sweetness, savoring every quiver.

Fuck, she's sweet. Her cunt is thick honey dyed in pink and infused with ambrosia.

I'm as hungry as I am eager to see her come again.

She came for me twice with the remote control orb, both times mind blowing. And they're just a warm up when the night is this young, so dark and cool, calling to the primal beat in my pulse.

"Oh...oh...oh...*there!* Yes!" The little desert minx finds her groove when she's ridden my mouth long enough.

I crane my neck, reaching around to frig her clit while my tongue bathes in pink. Have I mentioned how much I *love* the very instant her moans become screams?

Kendra's spine arcs her body like a cat in heat. Those hips glued to my eyes undulate as I push her on faster, harder, breaking through whatever tentative barrier there is stopping this from being completely dirty from the very first second.

"Come for me, Sunflower. Come!" I urge her on, growling every word.

Her breath hitches. The tremors in her legs double.

Those silky thighs squeeze my fingers, urging me to flick her clit faster.

She comes in a silent scream, too overwhelmed by the lightning I'm pouring into her to make a sound. Her pussy takes me into a new world that's simple and overwhelming.

Hot.

Wet.

Divine.

I don't stop licking until her hurried breaths soften, her body rocks more gently, and she doesn't feel like her energy is melting into the supple moonlight and misty haze around us.

The pulse beating in my cock is making me blind by the time I stand up, still wiping my mouth, tasting her pussy. Normally, I'd hold her for a few soft minutes, give her a moment or two to recover.

Not tonight.

The electric urge in my dick won't wait. I take her arms in mine, make sure she's secure against the wall, and pull her soaked sweetness around every inch of me.

Goddamn, it's good. Can't imagine the day I'll ever miss the groan that rips from my throat every first thrust.

She isn't a virgin anymore, either. I'm able to fuck her like a proper lover now, fast and relentless, slowing my strokes only when I want to pull back to the hilt and slam into her again.

Her entire ass shakes when I do. Dear fuck, do I love it.

She calls my name a few more times. I slam another O through her body, gripping her hair as she stiffens, back arching, pussy convulsing around my cock as she loses it again.

It's a minute into her post-orgasmic bliss, and quickly working her to the next one, when I hear the words that light a fire in my ears. "Come in me, Knox. Please. I want it...I swear...oh, God...*please!*"

This isn't dirty talk.

I haven't had a chance to train her that way yet, and there's still too much of the innocence I love preventing her from moaning dark, nasty words in the night.

I know a primal voice when it speaks. Raw need grips her throat, instinctive lust channeling her tongue, fueling the fire in my balls to meltdown.

"You want this, Sunflower? Every damn drop?" Incredible how every word quickens the molten heat in my blood.

"Yes!"

"Then pull it out of me, woman." I'm snarling, head on her shoulder, teeth nipping at her earlobe. "Move your sweet pussy and work it the fuck out. Show me how damn bad you want it."

My hand smacks her ass. The other tangles deeper in her hair, giving it a vicious tug. I don't know what I've really done until her hips start beating a furious tempo against my thighs.

I let her set the pace, rocking backward, grinding her ass into my pubic bone while the grip on her hair gets tighter, tighter, tighter, and – *oh, fuck.*

I'm ten seconds from overload when I can't stop the greedy twitch at the base of my spine. My body moves like its possessed, crashing into hers, a war of thrusts as we collide. We're rocking, fucking, grunting over the edge.

She loses herself in another spastic release about a

second before I do. My fingers grip harder, and I give her bobbing, red asscheeks one more smack for good measure before my whole core becomes fire.

It rips up my spine and hits my brain before it dives low, lightning in my balls. It splits my senses. It makes me a raving lunatic for the next few minutes, more fiery seconds than I can count, each one stretched out an eternity as her pussy clenches, sucks, and wrings hot seed.

My cock explodes.

"Yeah, yeah, fuck! Kendra, *yeah*." It's sharp and incoherent, the only way good sex should be.

It flows out of me in steaming rivulets, deep into her. Before my cock jerks a third time, unleashing more fire, the hand that's not holding her hair like reigns slides around her waist, brushing her belly.

For a split second, I see that softness swollen with my kid. See her knocked up proper like it's heaven itself, and the harsh kiss I bury in her shoulder becomes a bite.

Hell yes.

I want her marked.

I want her owned.

I want her bred.

I want her *mine.*

Even when the vision fades, dulling like her scream in my ears, the enormity stays with me. I'm stuck on a single word, collapsing against the stone bench when I pull out of her, replenishing my lungs with sorely needed desert air.

How the hell didn't I see it before? Realize the heart-stopping power in that word and its promise?

Mine has a depth and volume bigger than the entire universe. *Mine* is another synonym for eternity.

"So amazing," she moans, still spilling what I've left in her when she slides into my lap, pushing her warm, rosy lips to mine.

I drink deep, even with my cock temporarily sated for the next five minutes. Staring into her green eyes, brighter every minute with love and light, there's a truth so strong it ripples through my bones.

Mine is now a sacrament, and it's all this precious Sunflower will ever be.

XI: IMPOSSIBLE POSSIBLE
(KENDRA)

*S*ometimes life takes such a sharp, crazy turn so far outside your ordinary experience, it moves the entire world. And not just the earth, but the moon, the stars, the sun above, and whole galaxies. The whole landscape I thought I knew shifts, merging with the endless sky.

It's been weeks since Knox confessed his love. The white knuckle diamonds on my finger are actually starting to make me feel like the future Mrs. Carlisle.

We're close to the end of the scorching summer and fierce monsoon, inching ever closer to Labor Day and the slow, but steady autumn balm that drifts across the valley.

Life goes on, different and better than before.

The smile on his face isn't so strange and alien anymore. Lizzie clings to me like a second shadow when he isn't around, showing me her best alongside the adorable little faults.

I'm working up the courage for the two big dinners

later this week, when we'll break the news to my parents, and then his mom and Jamie over the weekend.

I had to drop a million hints I want this done, whatever the danger that might or might not be out there still. We haven't had so much as an angry word or a death threat from Victor Wright. Knox's contacts at the company say he spends most of his days in Vegas, only flying back to the headquarters here in Phoenix for pressing matters.

Knox is talking to his lawyer, gearing up for a formal truce, something to formalize what we desperately hope is true: the creep has given up, and soon we'll be free to get on with our lives.

Even if he hasn't, we're not waiting. We have a hard wedding date in mind, sometime in November. I want it with my very soul. Want it in a way I never knew I could want anything.

In the meantime, until our families know the good news, I content myself with another unexpected consequence of falling in love.

I'm producing my best work. I've taken the glass slipper design Gannon tried to steal and owned it, reaching out to major fashion contacts in New York and Los Angeles. They love the design so much I haven't even had to lean on the Carlisle reputation.

There's nothing better than climbing the hills, peering at far off mountains yet to conquer. Oh, except for this new life as the soon-to-be Kendra Carlisle, where I've learned to kick ass harder, and there's always a spring in my step with a loving man and a delightful little girl. Family means more than any career coup.

I'm in the auxiliary workspace he's given me on his

property, listening to the radio. It's mid-day. Knox won't be home for a few more hours. He's downtown, drafting the inquiry to Victor with his lawyer, crafting the language as precisely as he says he needs to get a response.

The lovely studio on the third floor is where I do most of my work, but since it's a little cooler today, this converted garden shed lets me enjoy the lush outdoors around his estate.

It's also a delightful place to make sure Lizzie stays easily entertained while I put the finishing flourishes on my prototype glass shoes. I think I've finally found a solution for keeping feet equally comfortable in the valley's desert heat, or the cold in Minneapolis. A thin scrap of breathable thermal insulation I've installed this morning on the inside should, in theory, stop my poor toes from overheating or freezing to death.

But I won't know for sure until I take a walk. First, I slip into the shoes, and then walk over to the corner, where Lizzie is coloring with her finger on an app. She's filling in an orange tiger on her kiddie tablet.

"Ready for a walk and a fresh orange, peanut? You've been mighty busy over here all afternoon." I stoop down, rubbing her back.

She looks up at me, smacking her lips. "OJ? Yeahhh! Just lemme finish tiger, mommy."

I'm done when I hear those words. No matter how many times it happens, it still never fails to bring a wet heat to my eyes. Rifling my fingers through her hair, I sit, watching as she finishes her picture, filling in the tiger's black stripes. Only four years old, and her work ethic already mirrors mine.

She really *could* be my daughter.

Hell, as far as I'm concerned, she is. My stomach growls when the precious thing sits up, and grasps my hand. I'm looking forward to one of the fresh oranges off his tree myself. There's five different kinds to choose from, and I think I'll go for the biggest, sweetest ones today.

We take the grey stone path straight through the gardens. It's well kept and gorgeous, just like the man who owns it. A maze of desert brush, ferns, cacti, and palm trees in the distance. Citrus is the true star of this show, though, gently fanning our senses with its fragrance, stronger the closer we get.

We're halfway to the edge of the orange trees when I stop and look down at my feet. They're...amazingly cool. And in direct sunlight.

Holy crap. I did it.

I break into a smile, picking up the pace, knowing each bite of that orange is guaranteed to taste like sweet victory. I can't wait to tell Knox the news, and get another pair of these babies made. I'll send the new ones to an old college friend in Minnesota, Chelsea. There's no better proving ground for how my creation holds up in winter, and the many training grounds for hockey means she'll be able to get me a good report in the next week or two.

Then it's time to market the hell out of my hard work.

Lizzie skips ahead as far as I'll let her, holding my hand, humming in the sing-song way children do. I join her, trying to match the tune, laughing because I can't. It doesn't matter. I'm too busy wondering if I died sometime in the last few months and wound up in heaven without knowing it.

When we reach the oranges, Lizzie's eyes bug out. She

flies from my grip, running forward. I rush after her, following to where she stops and points at the huge, ripe fruits swaying overhead. "There, there!"

I can't remember the last day like this.

It's peaceful, marvelous, and perfect.

I reach up, retrieving two plump oranges. One for the little girl, and another for myself. Carefully opening the peel with the carving knife I left in my pocket from the studio, I hand Lizzie hers. Thumbing back the skin on mine, I lean low, inhaling its delicious promise.

I'm just about to take a bite when there's a loud rap on the gate next to us. Lizzie looks up, startled, orange juice dripping down her chin. I think it's an animal, at first, but no beast stands an even five feet at the gate, just a few inches shorter than me.

It's a woman. She's dressed in more white than I've ever seen outside a high end fashion show. It completely covers her; one long, layered dress complete with a wide ivory hat, broken only by a tuft of hair near her shoulders and the black pools of her sunglasses, obscuring her eyes.

"Who the scary lady?" Lizzie chirps, giving an anxious voice to the same question in my head.

What. The. Hell? Or who?

I'm on edge. It's probably nothing. Just a wandering neighbor from the other big houses in the hills, where money makes people eccentric. Or maybe some poor soul whose car broke down in the desert. Still, it takes several seconds to move my knees, surrounding the little girl's hand in a tighter grip.

"Easy, peanut. Let me do the talking, please," I whisper, hopefully out of earshot while we approach the intruder.

"Can I help you?" I ask, not liking how it's so hard to see her face.

"Important business call with Mr. Carlisle, actually. Forgive the interruption – no one answered when I rang the doorbell. I saw the car in the driveway and thought I'd take a quick walk to see if there's anyone home."

Why does this voice sound so familiar? I can't place it. I'm officially weirded out, but she seems harmless. Lizzie stirs at my side, clinging close to me, careful to remain well inside the palm tree's shade above.

Maybe it's truly business. I'm well aware the jewelry industry attracts some weirdos. She's well attired, at least, and not too twitchy.

"Miss, please," the woman says, fanning herself. The Coach purse at her side swings loosely on her shoulder. "It's Hades hot out here...and it's been a long walk."

"Of course," I say, deciding there's no clear threat. Just my mind playing tricks. "I'll meet you at the main gate in about five minutes. Give me a second to get her inside."

Nodding, the woman smiles, looking past me to the little girl. I grab Lizzie's hand again and lead her back through the gardens and into the house, her little hand sticky from the orange. I bring her to the family room and grab a bowl. Then I finish peeling her snack, and tell her to stay put on the sofa for a couple minutes while I meet the nice lady.

Please, God, don't let the nice part be wishful thinking. If it is, I won't let my trust get Lizzie in trouble, too. I tell myself I'm being paranoid. Surely, it's just business, like she says. Or else some annoying missionary from one of the weird, but harmless new age cults who sometimes cross over from California, trawling Phoenix's money for converts and big donations.

I wait by the door to the guard shack for several minutes. I see a white sedan with gold trim parked down the road, probably the woman's car, a basic luxury model well equipped for the heat.

It's unstaffed, like it usually is during the day. Knox says he's fine with just a night crew for security, considering the rugged terrain between here and the rest of Phoenix.

That's why it takes her awhile to reach the main gate. I'm already hitting the switch to open it when I see her. We take the shaded pathway up to the house, where I stop her outside the door, motioning to the shaded white bench on the porch.

"So, what's up? Is there a message you'd like to leave for Knox or...?"

The woman crosses her arms and frowns, refusing to sit next to me. "Not a message, per se."

What do you really want, lady? It's my turn to shoot her a sour look, waiting for her to get on with it.

She paces like a bird in front of me, releasing a slow, pent up sigh. "Incredible. You really don't recognize me, do you?"

I watch as she reaches up, taking off her oversized sunglasses, and then the wide-brimmed hat. There's a purple skunk stripe in her shiny black locks.

It takes a moment for my brain to catch up to what I'm seeing. Then nausea floods my system like poison and my knees start shaking. *Panic time.*

"Nah, I suppose you don't. We met like once at the bar, or maybe a mutual friend's house. Damn, I *really* wish

Knox were here for this. Oh, well." The grin on her face gets wider, more vicious. I'm about to vomit even before I hear the death sentence from her lips. "My name's Sam Wright. I'm here to bring my daughter home."

This is that part in a movie where time slows to a crawl, the reel goes screwy, and I hit my knees, fading to black from the shock. The first three happen in quick succession, but nothing could make me pass out when the next part of the disaster begins.

It starts with a tiny little voice whispering excitedly through the screen. "Mommy, I'm scared!"

"There you are, precious." Sam may be dressed in white, but she moves like a raven. I watch her swoop in, numb to my own senses, fighting to struggle to my feet while the invader bitch grabs the door. "Come to mama!"

"No! No, no, no, no, *no...*" My vision goes red. My throat splits in two. My tongue is a dagger, desperate for blood.

I catch myself on the brink. Jesus. I *can't* scare Lizzie when the last thread in my brain finally snaps.

Rushing forward, I stop just short of tackling the psycho bitch. If she didn't have her dirty hands on *my* little girl already, on the priceless little person Knox trusted me with, I'd do terrible things.

But Lizzie is in her arms, confusion and sadness exploding across her tiny face.

"Let her go, leave, and I won't have to call the police," I say, making her the only offer she'll get.

"You're a feisty one, aren't you? My, I see some things haven't changed with Knox's taste in women –"

"We're *nothing* alike," I growl. I put my soul into those words.

"Yeah, whatever. If you say so, bitch." Sam goes back to ignoring me, bouncing the increasingly nervous looking little girl in her arms. "Listen, before you do anything stupid, do us both a favor: reach into my purse. Should be unzipped. There's a nice folded paper there that should clear this up, assuming you don't want me to do the tattling down at the Phoenix P.D."

I don't know what she's talking about. My fingers plunge into her purse. I don't have to sift around to find the paper. It unfurls neatly in my fingers.

My eyes skim the words. Each phrase sticking in my brain is lethal.

Arizona district court. By order of Judge Nancy H. Willingston...

Full custody of Elizabeth Jayne Carlisle be turned over...

The rightful mother and guardian, Samantha Victoria Wright...

Until such time as proper visitation rights are determined in a court of law...

Fuck time. It's broken, shattered beyond repair, and it's completely run out for me.

My knees hit the ground so hard it chatters my teeth before I see the evil witch turn her back, and start down the path toward the gate. My foot twists unevenly under me, banging something hard. Glass shards scrape concrete.

So much for being durable. I've chipped my left slipper. The next time I beat my foot into the pavement, I feel the force of glass breaking, coming to pieces like an eggshell wrapped around my toes. Safety glass shouldn't cut, but they do. The abrasions skip my skin completely and go to my heart, tearing me apart from the inside-out.

Before I hear Lizzie cry, I'm sobbing helplessly, sorrow and rage blistering my cheeks because I know if I make a single move, it'll probably be the wrong one, and we'll lose her forever.

Before I hear the white car's engine and see it flash by as it descends the mountain, I try to contemplate how I'll even explain what just happened to Knox.

I can't.

There are no words.

I'm numb. Scared. Alone.

How is it even possible to have everything I thought I'd won ripped away from me in a matter of minutes?

* * *

OF COURSE, he's not answering his phone. I only send twenty desperate texts and leave five crying voicemails before I breakdown and get a hold of his lawyer.

I tell Charlie what happened. He's no nonsense, all brass tacks. I try to give him details, a physical description, read the words on that awful fucking page, but I can't.

Words won't come.

I'm too blinded by tears to see them clearly. My voice is certainly too broken to repeat them. I tell him, for the love of God, to make sure he reaches Knox. I need him home.

It's an agonizing wait. The better part of an hour before his truck roars into the spacious garage, a loud bang sounding before he kills the engine. He's probably in such a rush to find out how wrecked our lives are that he isn't driving safely.

I'm more scared than ever. If this is bad enough to break his ten year combat discipline, what the hell will it do to *me?*

Worse, it's barely begun.

"Goddamn. Fuck. Kendra?!" His entrance tells me I'm not alone in my inability to form complete sentences. It's a small comfort when he steps forward, swoops me against his shoulder, and crushes the air out of my lungs in the sternest embrace ever. "I came as soon as I heard. Are you okay?"

I nod, shaking my head against his chest. His grip eases once he's satisfied I'm telling the truth.

"We'll find our way out of this, Sunflower. Don't worry. Need you to sit and tell me everything."

I nod, more functional than I've been for the past hour with his love. I just might survive the interrogation next.

We sit near his unlit fireplace, a frigid glass of water trembling in my hand, while I very calmly try going over the facts.

Yes, she showed up out of nowhere.

Yes, she put her dirty hands on our little girl, took her through the gate, and strapped her into the booster seat she had waiting in that car.

No – *Jesus, no* – I couldn't do anything.

I couldn't and I wanted to. I'd have given my life to stop that woman, if only she didn't have the key to paralysis.

Knox snatches the court order from my hands and reads it at least three times, until he's satisfied it's authentic.

"After all this time," he says, shaking his head, running stiff fingers over his face. "I can't believe I didn't see it.

The countless detectives, long nights searching, weekends lost in LA combing through homeless shelters...all for fucking nothing. She wasn't dead. She's been out there this whole time, waiting to screw me over and take Lizzie."

"We don't know that," I say, leaning forward, grasping his hand. I rub his thick, calloused palms, trying to be comforting. "She could've shown up on a whim. Maybe Wright knew where she was the entire time. Could've had her stuffed away in some clinic. Maybe he had her fixed and cleaned up just in time to get to us the only way he could. Maybe –"

"Stop. What's the point? All the what-ifs in the world aren't bringing her back. The time for asking how ended the second she stepped on this property and got what she wanted. Nothing left to do but stop her. I need to talk to Charlie."

That bitter lump is in my throat again. Slowly, I nod, clinging to his hand. I don't want to let go. I'm terrified where we'll fall if I do. "Do you want me with?"

"Yeah," he whispers, quiet and introspective. Then his eyes flick to mine, bright as crystal sky. "You know I do, darling. You're part of this family. Always will be, no matter what."

He drags my hand to his lips. The kiss he plants on my skin dashes the darkness inside me, if only for a few scarce seconds. "Let me grab my purse."

On our way out, he pauses for a second near the door, kicking the shattered pile of my slipper gently with his toe. "Shit. You mean you lost –"

"It's not important," I say, hiding my tears. "I can

always make more shoes. I can't sculpt another Lizzie." He nods, and we're off.

It's a long, congested drive downtown. We ride on in silence, listening to soft rock piping through his speakers for comfort. I don't know why this feels so heavy, so dangerous, like a boulder hanging overhead, ready to crush us.

Lizzie's absence is suffocating. I try not to cry, to be strong for him, but the small, caring looks he gives me when we're stopped at each intersection leaves tiny cuts on my heart.

I can only take so many before I snap.

But as bad as this is, it's no time for panic.

I take deep breaths, wiping my tears, losing more than I'd like when Knox grabs my hand and whispers. "This'll be over soon. I never let the things that really matter get away. *Never.*"

I know what time it really is. It's the moment I realize how spectacular love is when hearts pace to tragedy. Every beat, every second, every glance more alive and scary and beautiful than every day of life before it.

More real than the evil anyone could ever do.

Whatever happens next, I promise I won't break. I'll be strong for him, for myself, for the family I'm not letting go. Damn it, we *will* bring her home.

XII: DIAMOND CUT (KNOX)

"*D*a-da, it hurts!" *Lizzie squirms, tears in her little eyes as I blot her scrapped knee with antiseptic, before I rip the bandage from its wrapper. "Why, da, why?"*

"Life, peewee. Mistakes happen, and sometimes they hurt. You didn't do anything wrong. You didn't see the rock that was there when you tripped. Daddy should have held on tighter. You wouldn't have taken such a tumble."

It fucks me up inside to see her in any pain. Sure, it's normal kid stuff, but every time she looks at me, I see the hundreds of kids I've encountered over the years who weren't so lucky to get away with a boo-boo and a Band-Aid.

That Afghan boy clutching his ma's leg, watching us patrol his village with huge, scared eyes. The market where his old man just got torched by a terrorist fuckwit's bomb still on fire.

The little girl on crutches in that town I couldn't pronounce next to prime mining country. Her father, the warlord my crew had to negotiate with for shipping access, insisted she'd broken both legs in a terrible landslide last rainy season.

But I heard how he slapped around her older brother later

that night, how he pressed him to the wall, and might not have stopped if I hadn't shown up when I did. He was in a drug-fueled rage, the shit in the syringes on the dirty bed all he cared to buy with his loot, besides the guns. He never saw me coming when I grabbed him around the neck, pushed the needle in his chest, and emptied its contents directly into his heart.

The kid never said a word when he saw his body. Neither did the girl. Their eyes before we left were all the thanks I needed.

Wright chewed me out when I got back home for letting a 'top notch supplier' die, when I could've sent a medic for his 'overdose.'

I told him to get fucked.

"Da-da, it hurts!" Lizzie whines again, whimpering when I wrap the bandage tight around her knee, giving it a butterfly pat with my fingers.

"Know it does, sweetheart, but you're okay. The knee will heal. We'll both look closer next time we're at the park, and make sure this never happens again."

"But...but da...you can't see. Can't always look. Not always ever." Her little brow ripples confusion.

Technically, she's right. Bless her little soul.

I can't keep my eyes on her twenty-four hours a day. Hell, I'm lucky to have twelve hours outside work.

I won't be able to stop the next dozen mistakes her toddler legs bring her to. Not when she's with other kids, or when she's older and heading off to school. Not when she becomes a young woman and starts hanging out with the boys who come sniffing around her.

But damn it, I'll try. I'll try like every dad who ever found that brute, unconditional love like a blow to the gut the first

NICOLE SNOW

time he held his infant daughter, and he locked eyes with his proudest creation.

She is my soul, my flesh, my life.

I will protect her. I will teach her right from wrong. I will suffer the blame when her face bleeds tears, whether it's over a spilled juice box, or finding out her mother was a screwed up junkie when she's fifteen years older, and we sit down for the inevitable talk.

"*Lizzie, love, there are times when I can't always be around, when one of us slips up and somebody gets hurt one way or another,*" *I say, pausing to kiss her forehead.* "*But I want you to know...whatever happens, you've got daddy's love. Long as you're with me, you'll never hurt long. Love always heals. I'll always do my best to keep you smiling.*"

"*Ever, da-ddy?*" *She smiles, knowing the answer before it's out of my lips.* "*Ever?*"

"*Forever, baby girl. No real harm will ever come as long as I'm around. Nobody's taking you away.*"

* * *

How the fuck was it six months ago?

My legs are numb when I park the truck and we step onto the asphalt outside the high rise with Charlie's firm. Everything concrete is still steaming from sunset.

It's surreal.

One minute, it's just a normal day. I'm looking forward to coming home to my family, hashing out how we'll break the wedding plans over the next week to both sides.

Then I'm on the darkest, coldest ride of my life, gripping the wheel so tight my fingers hurt. It's all I can do not to explode as I flashback to six months ago, when

198

Lizzie slid on gravel in that park, and I swore my love for the thousandth time since she was born.

I'd always be there with love, presence, and strength, I said. Everything a man musters to shield his sweetest innocent from the world.

Except this time, I wasn't. I couldn't be. The bitch showed up without me anywhere, and I wonder if it's for the best because it bought us some time.

I'd certainly be in a cell right now if it was me she'd found, and not Kendra.

I'm gripping Sunflower's hand as we step inside. A vent spews the air conditioning on us full blast as we ride the elevator.

Every minute I'm breaking my promise to my little girl stabs deeper at my soul. Turns my blood dark and toxic.

Lizzie, I'm sorry. I can't let it end like this. Can't let Victor and that disappearing freak who's her mom in name-only take away my sun.

Charlie waits for us in his office. He sits up as soon as we enter, a tall man, his eyes on fire when he looks from me, and then to the woman at my side. "Oh. I thought you'd be alone, Knox," he says.

Kendra's fingers tighten on mine. "Is my presence here a problem?"

Charlie looks at me. His dark eyes glow like the answer to her question might be yes. *What the fuck?*

I don't understand, and I damn sure don't like it.

"Charlie, what's wrong?" My voice booms, more venom than I intend creeping into my tone.

My lawyer clears his throat uncomfortably. He lifts his eyebrows for a second, like he's bracing for an asteroid to come crashing through his window overlooking Phoenix. Then, he turns, still not giving an answer, and retrieves a few papers from the far side of his desk.

"Forgive me. I think you'd better see this for yourself. Last page, to be specific. Take a second, flip through it, and..." *Try not to shoot the messenger,* is what I think he wants to stay. "Take a moment to digest, please. I'll be out here if you need me. I'll do my best to formulate a response once you see what we're up against."

He doesn't even ask permission to leave. Just gets up and scurries off, leaving Kendra and I alone with the mystery package.

"Go ahead. We'd better read it." Kendra squeezes my hand, speaking softly, her voice making the ice glazing my back a whole lot colder.

There's no point delaying another second. What's one more ugly shock after a day full of them?

I snatch at the papers and begin flipping through them. Trying to get it over with.

First page is an identical copy of the custody order left on my doorstep. The next have headers from two local psychologists – men I've never seen – both affirming, under penalty of perjury, that the 'corroborating information' attached is serious and informative enough to make a diagnosis in absentia.

I see everything laid out real neat. Like a shopping list for psychosis.

Anger issues. Depression. Unmanaged war trauma.

Verdict: *unfit* for primary custody.

Particularly when there's two perfectly good guardians waiting in the eyes of Victor's lackeys. Her mother and grandfather will do the job I can't.

"Bullshit," I hiss, clenching my teeth. Kendra strokes my arm softly, but it isn't helping.

My heartbeat roars in my ears as I flip to the last page. Whatever it is, I know it's bound to piss me off. It's got to be horrific if it's made Charlie jump ship, abandoning his office like he's anticipating I'll turn over his desk, break chairs, smash the twenty foot square barrier between this building's innards and the evening sky.

It's...an ambush.

What's on that page is Kendra's handwriting. Or, rather, a photocopy of a note she's written, judging by how the ink doesn't smudge underneath my numb finger, hot and clammy in its fury.

Each word knocks a new piece of my heart out.

YOU'VE ORDERED *a statement regarding Knox Carlisle's fitness for custody. My assessment is as follows, in full compliance with the law, under advice of my own attorney:*

Knox Carlisle wants to be a good father, deep down inside. He tries.

But there are times when I worry. Love isn't always enough to cover serious deficits.

Frankly, after living with him for several weeks, I think he lacks the emotional capacity to tend his daughter's needs.

Knox can be intimidating. Self-centered. Angry and violent.

I don't know if this is due to the war or what he does overseas in the diamond business. Maybe it's the lingering mystery over Samantha Wright's disappearance that's made him cold and indifferent. Maybe it's work-related stress. Maybe he was born this way.

It's not my place to say. That's your job.

Let me stress that I don't think this is permanent. He can change. He loves his little girl, and it's not impossible one day he'll be able to deliver the emotional discipline she deserves.

This statement is not meant to be anything except my personal observations, recorded and certified by my counsel, in compliance with the law.

I DON'T WANT to believe it's true. The handwritten date above is just a few weeks ago, not long after Gannon opened the gates of hell, and we started making peace.

Timely betrayal. Backstabbing just when I trusted her.

When I turn toward her, shoving her hand away, and we finally lock eyes, I don't know who the fuck I even am.

The old Knox never would've been this blind. He'd have seen it coming.

Loving this woman just cost me my little girl.

"Knox?" Kendra calls my name, panic rising in her voice.

I stand up, pacing the room to the window, running my fingers through my hair. For a second, I contemplate ripping it out. It's not like there's another way to relieve the insanity boiling in my skull every second my back is turned, palm against the glass, knowing she's rammed the knife through my heart.

I can't believe she concealed it this long as well as she did.

"Jesus Christ. You don't really think I...I mean...I don't know what this is." She's trembling, holding it in her hand. "Knox, I swear, on everything I'll ever love – I did *not* write this. Please, you have to –"

"I don't have to do shit." Even I'm surprised how

bitterly cold it sounds. My tongue hurts like it's frosted over.

I march past her, ignoring the hot, vicious tears rolling down her cheeks, making a zig-zag for the door. I find Charlie on the balcony just outside, a cigarette hanging from his lips. It falls out the second I grab him by his lapels.

"Whoa, Knox, calm down!"

"Why didn't you tell me, you useless fuck? What am I paying you for?" I'm shaking him like a rabid dog with a squirrel and I don't want to stop.

"Easy. *Easy!*" Words fly out between his chattering teeth while I fling him around. "Whoa, whoa, holy shit. Knox, please, you're gonna kill me!"

He isn't wrong. I don't throw him against the wall for another few seconds, not until I'm ready to drop the question burning acid through my soul. "Is it her fucking handwriting? Huh?! Did you send this to forensics?"

"Knox!" I stop just short of squeezing his throat. His eyes are huge, and he slumps in my arms, choosing his next words very carefully. I give him a few seconds to gather his breath. "Everything happened so fast. I only got the package here this afternoon. When I called you, and left the voicemail, you didn't get back to me for another hour. By then, you knew what was going on yourself, after Samantha –"

"Yeah, yeah, we both know what happened. Get to the goddamned point. Was it her handwriting?"

His eyes pinch shut, as if he's bracing for an imminent collision. "I fished out her Gannon statement from a few weeks ago and compared the handwriting. Look, Godzilla, I'm no specialist, but...it sure looks the same."

Fuck.

I let his feet hit the ground, sucking in my own cheeks, instinct clenching my jaw. I taste blood.

"I'm sorry. I didn't have a clue how to break the news with her standing right in front of me. I hate that it had to go down this way, my man. Really, really sorry." He stiffens to full height, brushing off his jacket in quick, nervous sweeps. "Next time, let's learn to keep our hands to ourselves. Okay, buddy? Or else I'm doubling your retainer."

I don't care. I've heard enough. I start walking to the elevator.

She's waiting for me next to it, tapping her foot impatiently, sniffing back tears. It's incredible how fast my empathy is obliterated. I don't even acknowledge her presence as my fist crashes into the button on the wall.

"It's not true, Knox. I didn't write a single word. Can't you see the truth?" She's staring through me. I never glance her way, just gaze dumbly at the silver door, wondering how long it'll take to melt a neat hole through it. "Goddammit, say something!"

She snaps first. Grabbing my shoulders, Kendra digs her nails in so hard it should hurt.

If only I could feel anything.

My turn to whip around, pinching her arms, flattening her against the wall. She's breathing the same quick, fierce way that used to turn me on. Incredible how there's no desire to do anything except never lay eyes on this two-timing bitch again.

She'll know my suffering. I brand my hate into those vivid green eyes where I thought I'd find my forever before this afternoon. *How the hell could I ever be so stupid?*

"I loved you, Kendra. First like a sister, then like my own flesh and blood." Past-tense chokes me. "Go home. Stay away from Jamie and ma's place for awhile. I'll have a moving company drop your shit off in a few weeks."

Sadness drowns her eyes. "Knox...you're insane. If you'll just *work* with me, give us a chance to figure out what *really* happened."

So much desperation. Damn if I don't want to believe her. But I'm done being blinded by comforting lies, including the biggest one of all called 'love.'

"Stop fucking talking," I growl. "Charlie told me everything. It's your handwriting."

"Screw Charlie! And yeah, I *know* it is, Knox. I don't deny it. What I can't figure out is *how*. I'm telling you, and believe me, I get how crazy this sounds, but I didn't fucking write it!" She's screaming. So loud my lawyer's receptionist shoots a worried look down the hall, one hand on her phone. "Do you think I'd *ever* do anything to hurt you? Or Lizzie? Why in God's name would I?"

Fear.

Distress.

A love that was two weeks too late to blossom in her heart, and maybe truly came after she'd twisted the knife. She wanted her revenge for that night at Danny's house, maybe, and sat on it for fucking years.

None of it matters anymore.

I can't let this get worse. I need to save Lizzie. There's no time for a run-in with security.

"Give me a sixty second head start, and I'll be gone. Call an Uber or a cab home." The elevator chimes and the doors slide open. I step inside, turn, and look through the tears in her eyes one last time. "I'm sorry, Kendra."

"No! No, you're not," she whimpers, wiping her face, considering whether or not she wants to jump inside before the doors slam shut. "If you ever cared, there'd be no apologizing. You'd stay."

"Wrong," I say, adjusting my tie. "I'm sorry for your sake, Kendra. You'll have to live with what you've done for the rest of your life. I'm also fucking sorry for myself. I'm the guy who has to come up with a story after Lizzie's back, and explain why she doesn't have a mommy again."

Her eyes drop. So do mine.

The door closes and I feel the lurch as it drops down the skyscraper.

Next stop is the darkest pit of hell.

XIII: HOW? (KENDRA)

I didn't know there were so many ways to make a woman's heart scorched earth. Not before I lost everything in less than two hours, and I had to flatten myself against the wall just to breathe, completely hollowed out.

She doesn't have a mommy again. His last words echo in my mind, over and over, a monstrous taunt bent on breaking the last thread holding my sanity together if I don't start moving *now*.

Thankfully, the elevator chimes. I step in, grab the banister, and let it carry me to the ground floor. I say a silent prayer for him to be gone, out of the parking garage and away from this place. If I see his car while I'm waiting on the curb, I might step in front of it.

He's already *killed* me emotionally.

A minute later, I'm at the end of the block, watching my ride criss-cross its way through Phoenix. I don't even look at the name when I see the Incoming Call, thinking it's probably my driver.

"Hello?" What I really mean is, *please, God, can it just be over?*

"Traitor! Did you really think I'd never find out?" Jamie's shrill voice stabs at my ear. "You were dating my brother the *whole* time and hiding it. Marrying him! What. The. Hell. Kendra? I thought we were friends."

I see it now. The last domino to fall today is my oldest, closest friendship. If I hadn't just lost everything else in my life, maybe I'd give a damn.

"Jamers –" I sigh. "Look, it's not what you think. And I'm pretty sure it's over. The engagement is off." My eyes are on my ring when I say it. Just looking at it brings waves of nausea, regret, heartache.

Where is that stupid Uber? "Listen, I can't talk right now." I mean it.

"No, don't fucking bother. No need. If you're planning to elope with another dumb story, don't bother hiding it from me. It's mom who's really crushed."

My phone makes its familiar clicking sound as she hangs up. It takes two more minutes before my ride pulls up on the curb.

Plenty of time to hold in an internal scream.

* * *

IT'S BEEN at least an entire day since I fell back to earth. So far from the asshole's majestic estate, lovely finishes, sprawling bed, and irresistible kisses. A chasm separates my cluttered old bedroom studio from the beautiful garden shed surrounded by citrus and sunflowers. I swear a lifetime has passed since I heard his little girl's laughter.

208

My little girl. The only one who ever called me mommy.

I'm tearing up when I hear the hushed voices outside. My parents know to leave me alone, let me recover, give me privacy while they talk quietly about 'something troubling me' that has to do with my best friend and that 'nice young man.'

If only they knew the truth.

The Nice Young Man is Mr. Hyde when he thinks I've done wrong. He's a quick-to-shoot, heartless, wounded asshole.

Yet still, somehow, the asshole I loved.

I bury my face in the pillows again. That's where it stays until the knock. "Honey?" Mom's voice, an octave higher than it usually is with concern. "I brought you some dinner."

The door creaks as she pushes it open a crack. Probably just checking to be sure I'm alive. "Leave it on my dresser, please. Thanks."

She does, and slips out quietly. There's a lot we don't see eye-to-eye on, but kicking me when I'm down has never been her style. My parents are also introverts, just like me, and I'm lucky they understand how important it is to try healing alone.

Assuming there's any coming back from this. I don't know that there is.

Frankly, I don't know anything. Nothing changed since the grim discovery.

I've only had a few hours without a pounding headache to contemplate how someone duplicated my handwriting perfectly, framing me for a crime I'd never commit in a trillion years. Unless I was drugged and hypnotized to write it and forgot – an angle I've honestly considered – then someone with a PhD in foul play sprung their trap flawlessly.

That evening, I'm sitting by the tiny pool in my parent's backyard. The moon glows overhead, but it's not a healing energy. It's swollen on my pain, glowing with my loss, hanging high in the glossy night sky. Mysterious and unreachable as the pieces of my life just pulverized.

This shouldn't be so hard. I had my new life no more than a few weeks. That ring I've stuffed into a dark corner in my drawer didn't feel real until this month.

Why does it feel like we were already a family for years? Why am I sitting here staring at the soft, cool waters, knees tucked under my palms, sweating because I'm going through withdrawals.

I don't want to live without him, or that precious little girl.

"How?" I mutter to myself, biting my lip. This is the first time since it all blew to hell that I've been able to focus.

I can't figure it out. I don't know where to begin. I wrack my brain for possibilities, anyone who would've had the skills and motive to ruin my life in the cruelest way possible.

Wright had to be involved. Sam's reappearance was coordinated with my fake statement to the court and the snap custody decision. Several articles I've read say there's nothing normal about this. Victor clearly leaned on his connections and wealth to ram through a decision, a real shock when the legal system typically moves at a crawl.

I remember sitting down with Charlie the first time. He looked on while his secretary dictated everything I said about Gannon, word for word, from the moment I took the internship until he went berserk.

It's a cold, creeping realization when it comes. My jaw drops, and I whisper two words. "Gannon. *Crap.*"

I bolt up. I don't know how, but the artist is involved. He's the only one with the talent to string together words I never said. I remember reading about last year's exhibition, when he created a letter-white bridal gown covered in ink, love lines he duplicated by hand, lifted from the famous romance notes between Napoleon Bonaparte and Josephine.

There's no time to contemplate more. I don't know how he intercepted my statement, or how he got it out of Charlie's office, but right now it doesn't matter.

I need evidence.

I'm halfway to my car, planning to drive downtown into Phoenix, when I realize how utterly alone I am. I freeze, one hand on my car door, drawing deep breaths in the cool night.

I shouldn't do this alone. If I run into Gannon, it's game over, and waiting for him to call the police to haul me out in handcuffs would be getting off lightly.

He's violent and insane. If I go to the studio, and he corners me alone...

I don't want to think what would happen. If he's truly capable of framing me with false words, then I have no doubt he's perfectly able to hide a body, too, if rage makes him do the unthinkable.

I'm sighing as I take out my phone. Searching my

contacts, I find the number, and press call, then wait for her to pick up.

It rings four times. Just when I think I'm getting voice-mail, Jamie's angry voice snaps on the line. "What do you want?"

"To apologize, Jamers. I know I hurt you, but I really didn't mean it. This thing between me and Knox...it wasn't real at first. Our relationship was a fraud. A strictly business relationship." I hesitate, remembering not to call it an engagement. I don't know what the hell happens with us next, if there's still an *us* to happen. "It was just a ploy to make sure he kept Lizzie when that asshole started threatening him. I played girlfriend, fiancée, loving mommy for a few weeks...and, well, things happened. It wasn't just play anymore. That ring he gave me meant something the longer I wore it. We were planning to tie the knot for real, and I was going to tell you when –"

"Girl, just stop. I don't need your whole life's story. I pieced together enough from the announcements and my idiot brother shrugging off my calls. I'm *pissed* that you thought you had to hide it."

"We didn't have a choice," I say quietly. "It wasn't meant to last. A few months, until the end of summer at the latest. Then we were supposed to go our separate ways. Technically, I guess we are."

"That's where I want answers. *What* the hell's really going on? Knox is absolutely crazy over something. He won't tell me or mom."

Shit. How do I tell my best friend her lovely little niece is gone? And she might never be coming home if we fail, if we can't find what we need, and fix this.

"It's a long story. I'd start at the beginning, but you've known more about Sam longer than me, so let's skip ahead. She's back."

I tell her everything that's happened this summer, from the day he made that insane proposal to my internship ending abruptly with that crazy thief. Right to the day Sam showed up at Knox's place, and stole our baby girl away from us.

I lose twenty more minutes to the story, the grief, the endless curses and threats that gurgle from her throat when she tells me all the ways she'll end the Wrights in graphic detail. She's so much like Knox at his scariest it almost makes me smile, how much the need to shoot first and kick ass is part of the Carlisle bloodline.

"I did *nothing*, Jamie. I swear. You've seen the times I sat with you and Lizzie and your mom. Even when Knox was a complete asshole to me, and I tried to forget him all those years, I never had a grudge. I never saw a bad father. They made up everything, and somehow got it to Knox's lawyer, and then to him when he was hurt, not thinking straight..."

Holy hell. Stop a sec. Am I forgiving the man who crushed my beating heart in front of me?

The good news, when it's finally over, is that I'm no longer her enemy.

Unfortunately, we've lost twenty more precious minutes.

"Can I come over now?" I whisper, holding my breath as the question I've been waiting for slips out.

"Duh. We'll knock some sense into my stupid brother later. Right now, we have a peanut to save."

* * *

I'M NOT ALONE ANYMORE. Thank God.

It almost feels like old times when I'm in the car with Jamers, zooming into downtown Phoenix, the city's lights pulsing with hope. Teenagers scrape the sidewalks skateboarding, lending the night a rowdy soundtrack.

Everything is dark, exciting, and alive.

Then I remember how everything is still on the line, and I shudder.

My brain tries to freeze, but I won't let it. The stakes are just too high. I'll fix this mess, clear my name, and save Lizzie. After that, I'll slap my man across the face, and find out whether he wants to continue being an asshole, or get on with the life I think we're meant to have.

"There it is. Next turn. Should be an empty space in the alley," I say, pointing.

Jamers hums to herself, switching the radio off, while she pulls into the gap. The engine dies, leaving an eerie silence. No other cars around. The absence and the late hour makes me hopeful we've beat Gannon.

Now for my other worry – the code on the rear door. I'm holding my breath while Jamie walks with me, stands at my side, and watches me input numbers from memory.

I can't exhale until I hear the *thunk*, and the light flashes green. Another miracle.

I'm grateful the egomaniac puts himself above trivial housekeeping, and Lydia the receptionist never goes above and beyond her pay grade. "Come on," I say, leading us inside.

It's very dim. Like stepping into an underground tunnel. I expect to see the old exhibits and experimental dresses hanging off the mannequins with an extra creepy vibe.

Instead, it's weirdly empty. Boxes sit in the corner, stacked to the ceiling, too much like a move in motion.

He's planning to skip town soon.

There can only be two reasons. His humiliation and hurt by Knox was either too great...or he thinks he's gotten his revenge, and he's planning to get out while the going is good.

"What are we looking for?" Jamers whispers impatiently, her eyes darting around the room.

"His office." I see the door half-shut, praying it hasn't been picked as clean as the studio. "If there's anything here, it'll be in the files. Lydia was always really slow to organize anything on paper. He'll tend to his art first, too, and leave the less important stuff to linger until the very end."

Jamie nods, more sure than I am. Of course, I have no clue when *the end* is supposed to be. He could be moving in a few more days, for all I know.

I push into his office and flick the switch for the lights. Loud fluorescent lamps hum to life, temporarily blinding me. It's messier than I remember.

Jamie walks past me and rips open a drawer, dumping out its contents on the ground. I'm standing there, deafened by the noise it makes, hand briefly covering my mouth. "Holy shit, keep it down. We're supposed to stay quiet."

"We're alone and we're wasting time every second we're not digging. Help me, Kendra." She drops to her knees, sifting through the mess on the floor, scowling when she sees the contents.

She isn't wrong. I'm technically breaking and entering, doing things that are all kinds of illegal. Why get timid now?

Lizzie's smiling little face throbs in my head while I walk across the room, and open another drawer. I'm doing this for her. Nobody else. Not even the gorgeous ass who won't keep his piercing blue eyes out of my head at the worst times.

Rage, frustration, and fear are a potent cocktail. I put them to work, demolishing three more drawers in the next few minutes, hitting the floor and emptying the files while Jamie swears across the room.

So far, it's useless. We have a mountain of old tax returns and licensing documents from the city. A commendation letter from Gannon's old school. Worn notebooks with his ideas – who knows how many are original?

Even a file full of faded nudes on Polaroid and a few blank videotapes labeled PRIVATE. I wrinkle my nose, doubting he's kept them all these years just for his muse.

Half an hour later, the room is a total mess. It's like the aftermath of a raccoon raid, junk scattered everywhere, and we're still empty handed.

"God damn," Jamie says, wiping the sweat off her forehead using the back of her hand. "Is there anywhere else he'd keep the incriminating stuff? We've ransacked everything here!"

She leans against a stack of boxes in the corner, letting the drawer she's just yanked from his computer desk hit the floor. Metal goes everywhere, mostly paperclips. My eyes scan past her, to the top of the brown packages. They're a worst case scenario waiting to unfold.

"All these boxes," I say sadly, squeezing my hands, one after the other. They're already dry and sore from the rapid fire digging we've wasted our time on. "They're our only hope."

Jamers does a slow turn, backing off the stack she's leaning on, hands balling into fists as she looks the ten foot stack up and down. "You mean...shit! Fuck. We don't have time for this. It'll take all night to go through a tenth of what's here."

"We'd better get started," I say, words heavy in my throat, the darkness pooling in my belly heavier by the second.

She looks at me like I can't be serious. But I am. More than ever, knowing this is our last shot.

I walk past her, step just outside the office, and pull the first box I see next to me, fishing out my keychain. It has a tiny folding sharp edge attached I use to cut the tape.

Jamers swears again, angry and incomprehensible. Part of me regrets bringing her here. She's lost focus. We might have another hour or two tops, before we risk late night police patrols or a visit from security making the rounds, assuming Gannon hired a service.

It isn't enough time to find anything. I'm losing it when she walks out a second later, stopping next to me, stretching with her hands above her head. "What about the violins?"

I don't know what she's talking about until I look where she's pointing. There, up against the wall, is a neat stack of violin cases, at least half a dozen.

"Odd. Never saw those in the studio before..." My heartbeat fumbles. I did my research on Eric Gannon before I interned for him.

He's done plenty in art and fashion, but music was never part of his resume.

I walk toward them, hand out, ready to lift the top case. It's possible the violins are just pieces of an unfinished project, something from his more eccentric days, when he...

Scratch that thought. Something inside rattles. Not like an instrument should that's a good fit for its case. Jamie gives me a wide-eyed look, noticing the questions swirling in my eyes. "Kendra, what the hell? Do we need to bust them open?"

Before I can say anything, or flick the smudged silver holding the case shut, my best friend yanks it from my hands, pops the clasps, and gives the case a furious kick.

We gasp as it hits the floor, spilling the contents. My heart thumps loud in my ears as I crouch, running my hand through the mess where the non-existent violin should be.

Papers. Tools. Something that looks like a grid, one molded for duplicating letters like a pro when it's held over a page.

Jackpot? I'm not sure it is until I hold up the pages with messy ink scrawled across them. It's a jumble of words. Random phrases I recognize, lines I gave Charlie when I tried to defend myself from Gannon, and then the hellish words I read just yesterday.

My statement.

Emotional discipline.

Angry and violent.

Cold and indifferent.

"Son of a..." Jamie trails off, whistling through her

teeth. She doesn't understand what we've found, but she knows it's important.

"Yeah. My handwriting, copied from the note I gave Charlie after psycho attacked. It's almost like a cipher without the code. He used it to make the fraud...and it looks like he's had a lot of practice."

Thumbing through the pages, I see he practiced words many times. Sometimes crafting new ones from my letters, over and over again until they looked just right, until he had enough for his soul killing lie.

"Um, what are we still waiting for?" Jamie stands up, rushes to the tall stack of cases, and begins pulling them apart. There's plenty more damning evidence where the first came from.

I find copies of my original statement with Charlie. A torn note with a header from Black Rhino, desk of Victor Wright, nothing on it except what looks like his signature and a number.

Eight hundred thousand.

Is this the payoff? The bribe? The extra incentive Victor used to get Gannon involved, assuming revenge against me and Knox wasn't motivation enough?

I'm shaking. It's not everyday a miracle comes, even a little one. This is like an angel appearing in front of us, glowing hand pointed to exactly the right spot, and saying a single word in their best James Earl Jones voice: *Look.*

How lucky can I be? How stupid would I be to squander it?

I have to keep going. My hands move furiously, documenting everything, snapping pictures, laying it out and kicking it with my shoe, capturing as much as we possibly can in case everything disappears tomorrow.

There's also stuff tucked in the last few boxes I think is just junk. A makeup kit, dye, directions to a lonely spot in the Sonoran desert, where I'd guess he's involved with some other bad juju.

Hopefully nothing that has to do with this. There's also a passport, and tucked behind it in a flimsy cardboard box, a cash wad, at least fifty thousand dollars, which Jamers pries apart, stuffing a few crisp thousand in bills into her pocket.

"Whoa, what *are* you doing?" I grab her shoulders, spinning her around.

"Payback for our pain and suffering. No way does he get to keep a single dollar after what he pulled. I'm not letting that asshole leave the country before he's paid with everything here."

"Jamers, no. We're already tampering with evidence. Let the police sort what's here tonight, and we get going, we'll actually report it soon." I give her a sharp look, glancing at my phone. It's low on battery and late, well past midnight. "We have to get going."

"Fine," she says reluctantly, fishing the money out of her pants, tossing it around like confetti. "I don't really care if it winds up buying some Fed new rims for his cruiser. If this crap gets Lizzie back safely, we've done our job."

She steps aside, still throwing handfuls across the room, leaving a total mess.

I let myself smile. If we're quick, and we get out now, the odds of this story having a happy ending are improving. Showering cash is a fitting way to end this.

If it weren't for human greed, this wouldn't be happening. Gannon and Wright wouldn't need to play these games, destroy our lives, and do God knows what to the fragile psyche of that poor little girl.

"You good?" I ask, throwing a hand on her shoulder that says, *you'd better be.* "We need to go."

"Yeah, I've had my fun," she says, rubbing her eyes. A low giggle escapes her lips. I haven't seen blue eyes burn to electric since the last happy night with Knox, and the memory tugs on my heart.

I turn, ready to lead her out, but the lightning is all wrong. It's darker where the door to the alley should be.

It takes me several seconds to realize it's a shadow, a silhouette, a man blocking our path. His arms are crossed, and he looks pissed.

Jamie whimpers first, covering her mouth with both hands from the shock. I'm too numb, my heart in my ears, pondering why our miracle luck couldn't last for just one more minute.

"This is how you thought you'd get to me, Ms. Sawyer?" Gannon's low, vicious voice fills the room a second before he steps into the icy light. His face is colder, a white bridge across the nose Knox broke. "I'm disappointed. I expected more hissing, more screams, a gun to a knife fight, perhaps..."

"Kendra!" Jamie sputters my name, and holds her hand up as he creeps forward, closer and closer, twisting something sharp and deadly in his hands. It's a switch-blade. "Step aside, creep. Leave us the fuck – oh, Jesus!"

Alone. I close my eyes for a split second longer than I should, finishing the sentence. I don't want to open them again.

Because when I do, I know I'll see Gannon throwing

her against the wall, his hand on her throat, the shiny blade in the other.

Because I know there's no help coming, and no one even knows we're here.

Because when I have to look at what I've done, what's left of my heart is in ruins. I gave my best, and it wasn't good enough. It just let us into a living nightmare.

XIV: GOODBYE MIRAGE (KNOX)

Eight Hours Earlier

I WAKE up in a snarling fit, furious and unrefreshed. My nap put me out for all of two hours, leaving a sick, restless feeling like I haven't had since the power naps between Taliban ambushes. Or the shut-eye we barely got in Sierra Leone, trading night shifts, planning for the next round of criminal fucks we'd have to meet to secure our cargo.

I'm as rested as I'll ever be in this empty bed. I run my hand along Kendra's spot next to me.

Fuck. That word is a black hole in the pit of my gut.

Pure regret. I saw her eyes tearing up again while I got on the elevator, right after I told her we were over.

She betrayed me. I hurt her. We died with a whimper.

It doesn't seem real, but the images that won't stop flashing in my skull say otherwise.

Our loss sticks deep, a poison dart I just can't extract

from the darkest chambers of my heart.

Why, why, why the fuck did it have to happen? Why did she screw me over?

Too many questions, and no answers.

My less rational side still isn't certain she did. It doesn't want to believe she'd turn on me, joining the assholes trying to steal my little girl. But Charlie showed me the truth. I read the statement myself, saw her handwriting with my own eyes. I'd be a total fool to listen to my heart.

Love won't bring Lizzie back. Neither will forgiveness.

I need decisions. Stone cold logic. Nothing less.

There are life and death consequences ahead, equally as heavy as the combat zones I've spent half my life in. If I want to bring my little girl home and cut the cancer from my company, I need info. Then I need solutions.

There's a lot I don't need, too.

Don't have time to cry in the corner over the bruises Sunflower left under my skin. I damn sure don't have time to miss her, nor should I after the rat-fuck trap she led me into.

So many unknowns. So little mercy.

I have to find Sam, or Victor, and find out exactly what I'm dealing with. Need to find out where my daughter is even more. I have to sit up, clear my head, and focus.

Nothing's more important. Time to get to work.

* * *

JAMIE RINGS MY PHONE NON-STOP, leaving several angry voicemails. I listen to them when I'm in my truck, heading for outer Scottsdale.

She doesn't know about Lizzie missing yet, thank God, which means mom doesn't know either.

"Knox, call back. We want answers. You can't hide it anymore." Jamie pauses, sighs, and her voice drops lower. "Look, let's cut the crap, okay? You've been messed in the head for years. That's what worries me. You're my brother, as much as I wonder what I've done to deserve it sometimes. I'm scared you're making a reckless, crazy decision. I'm worried for Kendra, too. So is ma. I'd be crazy to stand by while you mess up my best friend while saying diddly about your engagement. Remember the insane crap dad did before his...you know. Call me. I can't let the same thing happen to you."

Hearing her mention my old man's final days makes me clench the steering wheel tighter. I grit my teeth. Comparing the mid-life crisis he had before his ticker exploded to my very real dilemma is apples to fucking oranges.

I remember how much he pissed me off sneaking around. Came home to his end a kid, barely out of boot-camp, and left with no more illusions in my eyes. It hits me like yesterday. Everything.

The late hours away from our house. The letters from some woman named Judy he tucked into that Cuban cigar box in his office, where mom would never look. I wouldn't have found them myself if I hadn't stumbled home drunk one night from Danny's place after the funeral, and decided I shouldn't let his Cubans go to waste.

I kept the letters after he died. Threw them into the old ammo box my grandfather left, where I still have the coins from Carson City he gave me as a kid, plus a few old photos.

Sunflower must be in half of them. Growing older, prettier, more irresistible in slow motion.

From the time she was just my bratty little sister's shadow, chasing kids with Supersoakers, to when I started to look at her like I knew I shouldn't. She blossomed into a young woman right before my life changed forever.

I've never opened those letters. Never had the will. If dad was a cheat living a double-life, then I don't want, don't *need* the fucking proof.

Don't want to know I staked my life on a lie when I gave his eulogy. Swore I'd be a good man, do right by my family, live in his footsteps and make him proud.

I've done that in spite of who he was.

When all this is over, I'm finding that damn box and burning it.

I don't ever need to read those letters. I definitely don't need to see more photos, including the ones with an older Sunflower holding Lizzie. I added those just a couple weeks ago, after our evening trip to Camelback.

We stayed until just past sunset, swapping Lizzie back and forth when she was too tired to walk, hiking to the peak. First real family outing.

Second time we saw those stars together since we were young and innocent and in denial. I thought they'd shine over our love forever.

Last night, they never looked so dull and dead, hanging over Phoenix like antique silver meant to be forgotten.

Yes, asshole. You need to forget a lot of things.

And I do, forcing my brain into combat mode. I need

to stop a greater loss before it happens, before I lose my little girl forever.

I'm on the street I haven't traveled in a couple weeks, straight through Black Rhino's gates, when I really start focusing. It takes less than a minute to notice the black vehicles. More here than usual, and a quick drive around the back streets tells me they're parked near every entrance.

Heightened security. I don't see Victor's chopper parked on top of the tower's helipad. It's no comfort.

Wherever he is, he's far from oblivious. He knows my first, second, and third instinct will be to get to him or Sam. But it won't happen here.

I reach for my phone, inputting the address to his private road. He lives further out from the developed areas than I do in the best hills, just outside the valley. His neighbors miles away are tycoons and movie stars looking for a quiet escape from the West Coast hustle.

I haven't visited his place since two Christmases ago, when we tried to put on a brave face for Lizzie's second visit ever with Santa. It takes a half hour to drive out there, and another to find a hidden place in the rocks to park my truck.

Grabbing my binoculars, I peer between boulders, assessing the security situation and looking for weak points, imagining the places inside his sprawling mansion where my daughter might be.

He's light on bodyguards, just like me. Five minutes before I stop moving, a black SUV trawls up the road, pulls through his gate, and drives onto the backroads criss-crossing his property. He's got a patrol, but it's so sparse, he knows he rarely needs it.

NICOLE SNOW

It's easy to evade for a man with my skills. Getting through the gate, a little harder.

When I'm on his property, inside the perimeter, I take the path through his gardens. Everything is mausoleum white and overgrown, including the fountain. I stop behind it, listening to a cleaning lady whistling while she sweeps his patio.

It's hard as fuck resisting the urge to break past her. But I do, counting the minutes, hoping I'll find my way inside the house without running into the wrong person.

I don't know how long Sam's been back, or what her state of mind is. If she's just come from rehab, odds are good she's there, too. Probably resting, getting help from his household staff, and maybe private doctors.

How do I brace myself to see a ghost? I don't know, but I will.

A late summer monsoon breaks through the sky just after I hear the woman disappear, closing the French doors behind her. I crouch in the rain, counting the minutes I always discipline myself to wait in these situations, a grace period to minimize undesirable encounters.

I'm lucky I remembered to bring my tactical jacket, despite the heat. It keeps me dry, repelling most of the water.

Ten more seconds. When I hit zero, I run, staying low to the ground as I reach the door and cup my hands over my eyes, peering inside.

No one in the hall.

It's a flimsy door. I think it'll be easy to break the lock, but I don't even need to. Fate throws me a bone. I realize it's unlocked as soon as I twist the handle, giving easy access.

I'm in, wracking my brain to remember the basic layout of the house.

There's a hall, a bathroom, a study and several guest bedrooms, I think. Also, the sun room with the old piano, where that lady he hired played us Christmas carols. It's the only place Lizzie would remember, and possibly find comfort in.

I'm almost there, when a soft murmur behind the door in the adjacent room catches my ear. It's a low voice, so hushed I can't make out any words. Someone talking softly, simply, rhythmically like they would to someone barely conscious, or maybe an animal, or a child.

My kid. Son of a bitch.

I press my ear against the wood, straining to hear more. The voice isn't much clearer, its words indistinct. It sounds more like a song. A story being read from a book, perhaps. I wait as long as I can stand, assuring myself there's only one person in there with her. Not with much confidence.

Please, God, do me this favor. Let there be one.

I hated Victor and his wretched daughter before. Now, I want to send them to the darkest corners of hell for what I have to do next, scaring my little girl.

It's a small mercy I don't have to kick down the door. I throw it open, stepping inside, and see my little angel sitting cross-legged on the floor, a coloring book in her hand. She looks up excitedly for a second when she sees me, her tiny lips moving.

"Daddyyyyy!" She stands, wide-eyed, and comes running as fast as her stubby legs can take her.

I haven't forgotten the danger we're in. But damn if I

don't allow myself this, scoop her up, and press her tight to my chest, kissing her forehead.

She's alone. For now. The voice in the room was Pebbles the fucking Dinosaur, singing a song about rainbows on the TV mounted in the corner.

I couldn't be more relieved. Too bad it doesn't last long. There's no way she's been alone for long.

Whoever's looking after her probably just stepped out for a smoke, a drink of water, or a bathroom break, maybe.

I haven't thought this far ahead, as crazy as it sounds. Didn't think I'd get to her this easy.

As much as every instinct in my bones is howling *go, go, go*, I can't just carry her out of here with a court order hanging over us. Not if I want to avoid a frenzied trip across the Mexican border next, and a very messy attempt to start a new life elsewhere, with fake names and a lot of suppressed memories.

No, damn it, it's too easy. I can't scar my little girl like that.

And if I'm being brutally honest, I can't walk away from everything else that should be mine.

Not Black Rhino. Not ma and Jamie.

Not Sunflower, as bad as I've salted the earth where we were supposed to water our future, and watch it come alive.

"How you been, peewee? Missed you like crazy." *Who the hell were you with?* I want to say, but I can't just bark questions like she's an adult. "Are you with grandpa? Maybe Sam? Anybody?"

She shakes her head when I run through the list, smiling. I'm grateful she doesn't understand any of this. She can't hear my heart slamming my ribs like an engine spooling up to a hundred miles an hour, and I'm glad.

She shakes her little head. "Just her, daddy. Her."

I think this is the first time I don't find her cuteness vague. In fact, it's a little creepy.

Too bad. I calm her with a soft bounce in my arms, then head into the hall, wondering how long it'll take us to encounter someone in this house.

A door opens on the other side of the level. Slowly, haltingly, I move toward it, squeezing my baby girl tighter, pressing her face to my chest. Servant lady stumbles out of what looks like the laundry room a second later.

Instant screaming.

I hear a hodge-podge of English and Spanish flying from her lips. I can't make out a single word, but the tone sounds like a plea for mercy. I lift my hand, careful to keep Lizzie close to my chest, shielding her as much as possible from this sideshow.

"Easy, lady, I'm not here to hurt anyone. I just need to talk to your boss. Where's Victor? Sam?"

"Ms. Wright?" she clucks, turning around, her soft brown skin nearly drained of its color. On second thought, it doesn't sound like a question. "This man..."

The woman stops, retreating behind the door. I hear a heavy sigh inside the laundry room, a chair scraping as somebody gets up, and footsteps that send my heart higher in my throat.

A second later, she's in front of me. Samantha Wright, my biggest mistake, the ghost who tortured me for four fucking years.

"Knox?" she says, looking me up and down like she's

struggling just as much as I am with what's in front of her. "You're faster than I thought."

That's when I notice it. Something's off.

Maybe it's the soft, almost restrained tone in her voice. But it's her appearance, too. She's Sam on the surface, but she isn't the same rebel who called to my drunken, stupid body like a siren when we conceived Lizzie in the bar. She's also not the haggard looking woman chained to her addiction I saw in the photos from LA.

More than anything, it's the hair that's changed. It's jet black, bangs cut short, just like I remember, but the color...it's the wrong shade of purple.

She's either had serious plastic surgery, or something a thousand times more fucked up than I imagined is happening. "Lizzie, listen to daddy. I want you to put your hands over your ears and cover them until I say we're good. Okay?"

"K." My little girl knows not to mess around. She presses her tiny hands as tightly as she can to her head. I pull her closer, forming a protective shield with my body before I step up to the stranger in front of us.

Fake Sam looks scared now. She backs against the wall when I'm still a few feet away, her cheeks twitching. "Hey, hey, let's not get crazy here. Not in front of Lizzie. We had to do it. I'm really sorry you're not taking this well, but you didn't leave us much choice. We –"

"Shut up. It's my turn for question time," I growl, reaching for her head with one hand. She whimpers when I grab her hair, ball it in a fist, and don't stop pulling until I know there's no escape. "You're not Sam. You just look like her. Who the fucking *hell* are you?"

She stops cringing and looks at me, licking her lips.

Whatever twisted secret she's holding in, I want it out in the open. *Now.*

Preferably before I have to separate the purple stripe from her scalp.

"*Vete! Vete!* Police on their way, Ms. Wright!" Servant Lady reappears, a defiant look in her eyes. She shoos me with her hand, standing in the doorway behind Fake Sam, as if I'm just one more pesky desert lizard invading the house.

I share another look with Fake Sam. Even her eyes glow unnaturally, glistening with tears, or maybe because they're fake contacts. I can't tell. I just pull the hair bunched in my fingers harder, stumbling backward when it comes out in a fistful.

Far easier than any natural hair should. It's a wig. Underneath, it's all dirty blonde, fading pink tips at the ends. Servant Lady screams, pointing at the mess in my hands, and then at the imposter in front of her.

It takes me several seconds to remember where I've seen her before. It's Lydia. Pinkie the Hedgehog, Gannon's lazy assistant. Apparently, she lives a double life as an undercover merc, or Victor recruited the psycho artist I pummeled to double-team me hard.

"Forget it, Juanita," Lydia says, staggering back and grabbing at her arm. "Tell them not to come. We're hosed."

Servant Lady looks bewildered, terrified.

That makes two of us. Difference is, I don't go numb. If there's any chance at all she'll do as she's told in this blind stupor, and Fake Sam wants to work with me, I'll jump on it and count my blessings later.

Slowly, I crouch down, letting Lizzie touch the floor. I hold her little hand while I reach into the tactical pack strapped to my left leg. I fumble with the zipper and reach inside, holding up eight thousand dollars in crisp hundreds. I've filled the small space to capacity.

"Take it, lady. It's yours, if you'll call 9-11 back and just tell them there's been a huge mistake." I don't wait for her to comply before I look at Lydia. "And you, Pinkie, we need to talk. I want to know why you're running around calling yourself Sam, dressed just like her. Cooperate, and we both stay out of trouble."

Lydia flips her natural hair, hands on her hips, rolling her eyes. "Please, Mr. Moneybags. You'll have to do better than that if you want my help. Bidding starts at double whatever you're giving her."

I grit my teeth. Juanita steps out behind her, tentatively, and snatches the money from my hand. I watch her retreat back into the laundry room, phone pressed to her ear, listening quietly as she mumbles something about a false alarm.

"Fine," I rumble, standing up. I smooth a hand through Lizzie's hair, gently ruffling it, trying to keep her calm. "Let's talk. But the second you scare my little girl, rattle her worse than she already is by this crap, it's a different game. You won't like the ending."

* * *

HALF AN HOUR LATER, we're sitting in the sun room again, Lizzie safely in the corner with her kid's show, and hopefully out of earshot, too. I'm sitting across from the gumsmacking receptionist, watching as she twirls a green line of goo out of her mouth around her finger, and pops it back in.

She chews extra loudly and glares. It's the dumbest intimidation tactic I've ever seen, or else she's just that bored with the sky falling around her.

How did this woman ever pull it off for a single second?

"Twenty thousand dollars. More off the books if you testify. That's my final offer, and I'm losing my patience."

"Really? Guess it's gonna be a long evening, then. You don't hear boo until I'm fifty thousand richer."

"Cut the shit, Pixie. We both know this is ending at thirty five. I'll round it up to forty because I'm a nice person. Forty thousand, cold cash, plus a really nice trip to Vegas, all expenses paid for."

She frowns. "But I've always wanted to see Cancun."

"Fine. Mexico," I growl, regretting my volume when I see Lizzie turn toward us for a second, questions in her innocent eyes.

There's nothing I want more than to keep them that way. That's why I agree to this money-grubbing bitch's demands.

She smiles, flashing her pearly whites. "Awesome. I'm super glad we could hash it out. That rich idiot, Gannon, only paid me ten even for the acting stunt. Severance, he called it."

"Where's Samantha Wright? The real one?"

She sniffs once, her smile fading. "Dead. Do you really think I'd be here right now if they had the real deal?"

I always knew it. Still feels like a bullet in my gut, certain and final in its impact. "You know that for a fact? How? How did she die?"

"Well, I saw the files. Gannon gave me plenty, even showed me a few old tapes he got from Victor Wright. Tried to learn her mannerisms so I could do the job perfectly. I had a little acting experience in college, and I'm not *that* rusty."

You did a piss poor job. I keep my comments to myself, leaning back in my chair, never warming the coldness in my eyes.

"Sad to say, there wasn't much to work with. Those tapes...ugh. They let me watch so I'd know how to act. Wasn't much to see. The woman was dying. Total junkie, stuck in some expensive rehab place, talking out of her head while her organs shut down. They had her so doped up all she did was call for some guy named Jake. Never mentioned the kid, or you, or anybody else. Not even once."

What little sympathy I had a few seconds ago melts. Addiction is a demon, but fuck, she couldn't muster a goodbye for Lizzie one damn time?

Kendra's smiling face fills my mind. I see her clear as day, the only woman I ever loved, who ever gave a shit about my own flesh and blood. Only one Lizzie ever called mommy without breaking me in two.

Then she betrayed me. Or I believe she did, and I treated her worse than a stain on my rug.

"Hey, does that help? You're looking kinda out of it. I mean, Gannon said Mr. Wright told him you thought she was gone for years. He stressed I had to be on-point, and the appearance had to be just right to be believable. I thought he did amazing work with the makeup. Only second guessed himself about a million times and had me sit for hours while he worked. Guess it was hopeless, considering how you knew her, and saw through it from the get-go. You were right."

I wish I still lived in a world where being right counted.

"What about Kendra?" I ask, head-on into the next question burning me alive. "How'd they get to her? What the fuck was it – an offer? A threat?"

My hands grip the cherry wood arms of the chair so hard it hurts. Any tighter, and I'll break them, or snap my own fingers first.

"Huh?" Lydia blinks a few times, cocking her head. "They didn't *do* anything. Thought you'd figured that part out since you saw through the disguise so quick."

"What do you mean?"

"Your lawyer, whatever his face...he was sloppy when he took down that statement about what happened when Kendra quit. And holy shit, that was the *best* way to go out I've ever seen. Except for how he went ballistic on her after, I mean." She narrows her eyes, giving me a look like she can't believe she has to explain everything. "Gannon called him in a rage a few days after you busted up his face, and he could talk again. I thought you knew?"

I don't know shit. Just regret not pitching Charlie off his balcony, thirty floors to the steaming Phoenix pavement, when I had the chance. My eyes go to Lizzie, the only thing in this room that gives me some peace.

Shaking my head, I lean forward, a warning in my eyes. "Get to the damn point. This isn't cocktail hour."

"Well, Gannon was pretty pissed, like I said. I heard the whole thing. He was screaming in his office, making all kinds of threats, some your guy should've recorded if he was any use. That was about a day before I think his beating hit the local news, and your buddy, Wright, got in touch. Your lawyer told him to back off, that he had solid evidence against him if he didn't. My boss is too stupid to know when to quit. He must've pressed your lawyer's buttons because he got Kendra's statement faxed over. That's how he had her handwriting to work with when he came up with those stupid grids, and spent a week hunched on the floor like a monkey, practicing his letters over and over again like he was back in grade school, making me help check for similarities...hey, are you okay?"

On the surface, I'm a rock. A stern, immovable boulder, timeless in my anger, looking through her at my beautiful daughter because if I look anywhere else, I'll explode.

Inside, it's volcanic.

Rage at my stupidity, falling for this obvious shit I should've seen coming after two wars, and three tours in hellholes chasing blood diamonds.

Pain at my loss, and pain without mercy, knowing I deserve every end of the finger pointing for making what they tried to pull a thousand times worse.

Agony. Fiery, sharp, and fatal.

A snake named remorse bites my heart, injecting truth venom, making me feel every rotten thing I did to my woman, my love, my beautiful almost bride. And all because I got so twisted up in the games these fucking liars played, I became one myself.

I'm on my feet, standing, pacing the room. I don't say anything before I walk over, lift my little girl high in my arms, and hear her laugh.

It's the only way I remember how to smile, even if it's empty and full of pain.

"Yo, are we done, or...?" Lydia shifts her chair around

to face me, brow furrowed, wondering if I've lost my mind.

"No. You'll do what you're paid for, and right now I need a babysitter."

"Um, what? That's not what we agreed –"

"Two thousand dollars to shut up, stay close, and watch my kid. Should be on the house for how you've torched my life, and Kendra's too, but there might be something left to save. Lucky you. Shake your ass," I growl, shooting her a sharp look. "We're getting out of here and visiting asshole's studio. I need evidence. You'll help me find it to nail his coffin shut. Then you're coming along while I visit my girl and explain everything."

* * *

I CAN'T GET my sister on the line, and I don't know why. We swing by ma's place anyway before we head downtown. That's where I learn my sister went out this evening.

With Sunflower. And she hasn't been back for hours.

Shit. Ignoring the dirty looks ma gives Lydia, I tell her she's a substitute babysitter, and now I need to get her home. I'll find out if Jamie needs a ride on the way. Lizzie is already asleep by the time I pass her to grandma.

When we're back in my truck, the bubblegum mercenary isn't even staring at her phone. She's looking down at her fidgeting hands, face pale, too afraid to look me in the eye. Can't blame her when my rage might cause spontaneous combustion across a room.

"I'm really sorry about this. I didn't expect anyone else would get involved, you know."

"Quit apologizing. I'm not changing our terms or my mind. If Jamie and Kendra are all right, you walk with the payment we agreed to." *And if they're not...*

I roll over the nightmarish options in my head. I see myself digging a lonely grave out in the desert, and there's not a shred of remorse. It's too kind a fate for the self-serving creature next to me, and it isn't a tenth of what I'll do to Victor and Gannon if they've hurt my family, my wife.

No. Fuck this anger, this static in my head. It isn't helping. I force myself to grip the wheel, a road bound meditation, eyes locked on the highway, heading into Phoenix.

I'm somewhere else. Inside the stormy landscape where possibilities multiply, a thin roll of the dice is all it takes to determine which thrive, and which die. I'm between Schrodinger's cat and cosmic miracles, where everything is uncertain, dread building in my heart.

I reach through the darkness for an anchor, the lone emotion blazing like a beacon in my heart, throbbing for the same people over and over again.

Kendra. Lizzie. Jamie. Ma.

Kendra.

"Oh, Jesus – he's here!" Lydia gasps, covering her mouth, pointing to the black car parked at the end of the narrow alley as we near the studio.

Unsurprising, and irrelevant.

I know what I have to do.

"Hey, hey, what the fuck are you doing?" she hisses as I park the truck, reaching behind me for the tactical gear in its steel case. Her scared eyes double their darkness when she sees me pull the nine, check to make sure it's locked and loaded, and stuff it into the holster near my belt. "Deal's off. I can't be a part of this, buddy. I totally did *not* sign up to be an accessory to murder and –"

"Shut up." I grab her wrist, twisting it into a helpless position, waiting until I see the look that recognizes I'm not fucking around. "You'll stay behind me. I'll keep you safe. You know the place better than anybody else. I want to go in through the front. He won't expect it."

"You know what happens if he catches us, right?"

My look hardens. "And you know what happens if he's hurt my sis and the woman I'm marrying, yeah? He's not alone in there."

She looks past me, noticing the other vehicle in the lot, behind the artist's black car. The lump scraping her throat as she swallows is loud and audible. "God. Okay, okay, if we have to..."

"Make it fast. Stay behind me. If you've still got a key or something, I want you to have it ready by the time we're at the door."

For once in her life, the hedgehog listens. She even beats me to the entrance by a pace or two, hands over her face, looking through the glass. By all appearances, its empty in the waiting area, her old desk bare except for a few wires hanging out.

"We were closing up and moving out this weekend," she whispers, fumbling her code into the keypad next to the door. "Bastard didn't even offer real severance outside this stupid acting gig. Said what I'd made on this job was more than enough."

I'm grateful Gannon is such a snake I've turned his little pet. But if he's as big a viper as I think he is, the same as Victor, I should also be very afraid, knowing he's in there with Kendra and Jamie.

My turn to swallow worry, pain, bitter optimism. That last emotion, I cling to when the door opens, and I blow past her, storming into the building. I haven't charged in with my gun drawn since Africa.

It's alien here in Phoenix, brushing past the receptionist's desk, slowing when I get to the studio's door. I give myself two whole seconds, listening for voices, any obvious hints at what I'm walking into.

There's nothing. It's eerily quiet, except for something that sounds like a fan running. My hand hits the door before my brain consciously realizes it's someone breathing.

Heavy. Strained. Helpless.

I'm in, eyes adjusting to the darkness, ears tuned to the most sinister words I've heard outside a bad action movie. Only, this evil fuckery is right in front of me. "A pity you're so clueless. If you had any idea how rich your gorgeous, alabaster skin is going to make me on the black market once it's picked from your bones and cured, you'd simply –"

"Knox!" Two women scream my name in unison.

"Asshole!" I slam into him like a freight train, knocking him away from the table he's leaning over.

I hear something heavy and metallic hit the floor, see it slide across the room, silvery and sharp in the dull light. He's lost the knife he was holding. I've also lost my gun, knocked out of my hand in the struggle with this prick.

I can't see where it went, and there isn't time to sweep my hands over the floor looking. Not if I want to keep the edge.

Fine. Let's do this the old fashioned way.

My fists take over, slamming into his putrid face, hell-bent on erasing him from this world.

Screams surround me. The artist is faster than he looks, and greasy, too. It's hard to get a hold around his throat, so I just keep punching. His hands go everywhere, desperate and weaker than mine, but he's frantic. Completely drunk on adrenaline, which makes Johnny Average a beast.

I look around, searching for a weakness. But I'm in too big a rage, too distracted when I look up, watching Sunflower's green eyes go bright with a plea, her face turned toward me from the table.

"Your side!" she yells, a split second before another voice behind me starts screaming the same thing.

"Knox, holy shit, behind you!" That voice belongs to my sister.

And it's the last thing I hear before the resounding gunshot. Hellfire cuts through my guts, rips through several organs, draining my life shockingly fast.

Gannon's eyelids flutter hatefully under me. He's getting stronger by the nano-second, and I'm getting weaker, trying like hell to hit him one more time.

But I can't.

I'm shot. I'm paralyzed. I'm losing a lot of fucking blood.

I collapse on top of him, a lifeless weight, vaguely noticing how he struggles to get his hands between us to pry me off. More screaming, so much more, but I can't tell from who.

I can't make out anything.

I'm dying.

XV: PARADISE HAS A PULSE
(KENDRA)

Three Days Later

"HE'S COMING out of it, Ms. Sawyer. Any second now." The nurse taps her finger lightly against the IV hooked to his arm, frowning when his vitals don't improve on the monitor.

"It's Carlisle soon," *So I hope.* It comes out more harshly than I'd like. Lizzie squirms in my arms, roused from her nap. Outrageous optimism will do that, I guess...assuming it's not delusion.

I have no idea what Knox will say when he wakes up.

Our last earthly talk before the studio had him confused, betrayed. I saw his love become hate in his eyes. Lights became chasms.

Then he saved my life. All of us here, really. The sleepy little girl on my lap, the best friend holding the old woman's hand, both of them blotting at their eyes.

We're staring at the same man. He's never looked more powerful with his eyes shut, elysian chest rising and falling, his hospital gown slightly ruffled from pulling on it in his sleep.

He's a dreaming irony. Somehow, he's become the center of the universe in this bed, the rock tethering so many lives, stronger than he ever was in his camo, his battle hardened bloodlust, his eyes like burning stars.

He saved your life, idiot. It runs through my mind with a thousand other emotions, none I can catch for long enough to define, outside the gratitude in the very air filling this room.

His lips move first. He's trying to say his first words in days. I lean in, hugging Lizzie tighter, napalm in my eyes. They're the hot, blinding tears I promised myself a dozen times wouldn't come when we reached this moment.

So much for that.

It's a bigger challenge trying to stop myself from blubbering like a baby when the throat I just want to kiss starts moving, struggling to add words to twitching lips. "Sun...Sunflower. Oh, Christ. Where the...where the hell am I?"

He winces, sitting up, scanning the room. It's dead silent, except for the door closing as his nurse steps out, giving us some privacy. Knox takes us in one at a time.

"Easy," I whisper, leaning in.

"I didn't...die?" he whispers, glancing at the source of his pain under the sheet, the long stitches running through his abdomen.

"Hardly, Mr. Drama King." Jamie's words are little sister sarcasm, but her tone is fluid honey. "You're alive. In Phoenix. On planet earth. Lucky us."

He shoots her a scornful look. Then she stands, leans over me, and pecks him on the forehead. "No, idiot. I'm serious about the last part – *lucky us.* Welcome back, Knox."

His mother moves in for a quick kiss, too, whispering a few indistinct words to her baby boy. I'm bouncing Lizzie gently, trying to wake the little girl from her nap as much as I am distracting myself. I can't breakdown in front of him.

I promised I'd be strong, present, here for him when he shows me what he needs. My heart also drums a furious beat through my bones, uncertainty its music.

I don't know what happens next.

I don't know how he feels.

I don't know how we forget the wreck the last time we spoke.

Or how we love again.

"Sunflower..." He whispers my nickname again, eyes fixed on me, flitting briefly to the little girl when Jamers and Mrs. Carlisle give us some space. "How?"

I pause, staring at the others, soft smiles shining on their faces.

It's time, just like we discussed.

"Let's give you kids some time alone," his mother says, brushing her granddaughter's hair over her ear before she turns, heading for the door. Jamie winks, as if to say *good luck,* and then she's gone, too.

"Daddy? You're okay, okay?" Lizzie slides forward in my arms, tapping him gently on the shoulder.

That gets a smile from both of us. It's the first we share since our own little hell, and then the big one Gannon and Wright created.

"I'm breathing and in one piece...or near enough. Thanks for reminding me to count my blessings, peewee." He reaches out, ruffling the little girl's hair. She wraps her tiny hands around his finger while Knox looks at me. "Thought I'd lost you and my own life. What happened?"

My smile withers. I hate having to re-live the most heart-stopping moments of my life, but I'm able to because, deep down, they're over. "You lost a lot of blood. I saw his hand going for the gun and cried out, tried to warn you."

"Too little, too late," he says, nodding.

"You were...hurt." I pause, staring at Lizzie's curious face. I pull her in close, careful to cover her ears. It isn't more than a few seconds before she's drifting off again, sleepy and content. "He pulled the trigger before we could do anything. I was in no shape to fight. He punched Jamie in the face, held me down on that table, whispered those horrible things. If you hadn't gotten there when you did..."

"Lucky timing. Thought my luck ran out as soon as I felt that bullet slice through me. How the hell am I still alive? And you, Sunflower?"

"He cracked when he saw the blood. I don't know if he was delusional, confused from you hitting him, or what...but you went down hard. Trapped him. He tried to push you off and got his hands bloody. Then he started screaming, thrashing, shooting wildly into the ceiling until there was nothing left to fire. Lydia rushed in when she heard his gun clicking."

Knox snorts, shaking his head. "Saved by a fucking hedgehog? Life has a sicker sense of humor than I thought."

"Well...not quite." I close my eyes briefly, re-living the

last time I saw Eric Gannon. "Lydia rushed in, holding a big black rock she pulled from the junk in the corner. One of his old Zen explorations pieces. She was about to bash his head in, put him out cold, but he started screaming again. He got out from under you, running for the door."

Knox's face tenses. "Don't tell me. He got away?"

"No. He ran straight into your friend, Wright, who must've known he was a loose cannon. He showed up surrounded by guys in black body armor, half a dozen, maybe. They looked like a SWAT team."

"Fuck," Knox growls, lowering his eyes. When he brings them back to me, they're alive again. Conscious with a fire that's still willing to kill, if need be, to make this right.

I'm grateful he won't have to.

"The rest of it was just a blur, honestly. They grabbed Gannon, restrained him. He never had a chance against so many. Then they noticed Jamers, pointing her finger and screaming, telling them to get an ambulance out here, stat. The men, I can only think they recognized you."

"My old acquisitions crew," Knox says, finally understanding. "Christ. They'd be the only ones he could trust, if he meant to put down a rabid dog and not say anything about it."

"He never had a chance. They turned on him as soon as they saw you bleeding out. He screamed all kinds of threats when one of them refused to drop his phone. I saw your eyes open when they put Victor Wright in handcuffs, too, and held him there while we waited for the police. I hoped you saw, but I guess you didn't, or maybe you don't remember."

"Thought it was as dream, darling," he says quietly,

running his fingers over mine. "Some sort of hallucination before I left this world, my mind seeing what I wanted to happen, what I needed to save you from, before it went bad."

"You *did* save us, Knox. Does it really matter who finished it? Without you, God only knows where it would've went. Nowhere good. Look at us," I say, a tremor in my voice, grasping his hand. It's so warm, just like the little girl in my grip. "Everybody's here. Alive. Safe. Happy." *Or soon to be,* I mentally add, bracing for what happens next, now that the how is over.

Next, he'll want whys. And those damn whys are what always matter most.

"I was wrong about you, Kendra," he says, grasping my hand more firmly, bringing it to his chest. "Walked straight into their trap, willing to believe the lies I should've seen through from the very first second."

I look away. It's too much. If I hold his eyes, I *will* start crying again, and I really don't want to wake up Lizzie when she's sleeping so peacefully. "Forget it. It's not like you could've known. Obviously, we're not happy over it, but people make mistakes."

"No. The shit I laid on you was unforgivable. What I said, what I feared, thinking you've pried into my heart with a dagger in the back...that wasn't Victor, or Gannon, or even a simple misunderstanding under ugly fucking circumstances. Sunflower, look at me."

I do. His eyes are so bright, catching the mid-day sun seeping in through the open blinds. They're clearer, vaster, more beautiful than the pristine Arizona sky behind the glass.

"Real talk: it was never their scheme. That was just a

catalyst. I got nasty because I was scared." His confession doesn't come easy. His grip tightens on my hand, and he brings it to his lips, giving my skin the world's slowest kiss. There's no stopping those tears now. "I couldn't believe we were real. All this time, letting you in over the crazy weeks since this thing started, and it still wasn't good enough. Thought I was destined to be alone, and maybe it'd be better that way, too. Didn't know I still had it in me to love, and love like we did the best summer I ever lived. I was sure we'd lost that years ago, after that night on Camelback, when life got dark, death marching me through the worst shit a man can live."

"Knox, you're too hard on yourself. It's okay. We can go on. Move past it and –"

"Sunflower, I love your lips moving more than the sunrise itself, but I'm not done." He kisses me again, priming every nerve.

I swear to almighty God it's his energy in my veins, his pulse in my body, his soul in my eyes when I wipe the tears rolling down my cheeks, shift Lizzie against my shoulder, and lean in for the next part. "Tell me," I whisper, our faces less than a foot apart.

"That bullet in my guts changed everything. I'm not afraid anymore. Rescuing my little girl reminded me we're not saved unless I let go, and start believing in us. Not just when you're up against me, sweet as honey, prettier and sexier than any woman I'll see in the next ten lifetimes. Not when you're wearing that ring, or when I've got my fingers in your hair, bringing you in for a kiss I never want to end.

"Sunflower, I've learned to believe. Convinced myself we're alive in every breath I take. Whenever you're stuck in this brain, which is pretty much a constant, I see a reason to make my lungs work, and enjoy it. I see that dorky half-grown kid I started to love before she was a woman I couldn't resist. I see the stars we'll always share, bright as they were that night on Camelback, when this insanity started without us even knowing. Facing losing you was worse than death, Kendra."

Worse? How much more can a human heart possibly take?

I don't know, but I keep listening, resting my forehead on his. He grabs my wrist, pulls me lower, pushes his lips as close to my ear as he can get. "Worse because I know, just fucking *know*, that there's no clear line where the us begins. Not anymore. Maybe not ever. I think you know that, too, darling. And if I'm wrong, and you don't know? Too bad. I want you to be my wife. I want to spend every day knowing you're as much a part of my life as that angel you're holding, and you always will be. You're the only one who ever could be her ma, and the only one I'll ever marry with a vow worth more than any ring."

There are no words. I think he's stolen mine. I'm hollowed out, hanging on to him so hard my hand shakes, dripping every echo he said through my soul, as surely as the rivulets steaming down my cheeks keep coming.

He takes his free hand, lifts it up, and brushes the streams over my ear, until he's cleared them. "Did I ever say stop looking at me, Sunflower?"

"No, but I'm done," I say weakly, listening as Lizzie smacks her lips on my shoulder and mumbles in her sleep. "I can't look at you anymore. Kiss me, Knox, before she wakes up."

And he does.

And I kiss back.

And I remember why I've stuck with him through our agony like never, ever before.

* * *

Three Weeks Later

"IT'S BEAUTIFUL, HONEY." Mom holds my hand lightly, turning it over to see the ring. The diamonds catch the morning light, scattering it back across Scottsdale's breakfast hour. "Honestly, I'd expect nothing less from a jewelry tycoon."

I smile. "I'd have corrected you a few weeks ago. But it's his company now, completely, we're all better off. I'm grateful."

That's an understatement. I can't believe sometimes the insanity is really over, or near enough.

Victor Wright goes to trial next week. Gannon won't be far behind him, assuming my old boss doesn't just spend the rest of his days in a high security psych ward.

"Just between us, you're *certain* about this, yes?" She gives me a sideways glance, sipping her prickly pear infused tea. "It's tremendous work becoming a wife. Double when it involves a little girl."

"I've never been more sure about anything, mom. You've met him, and Lizzie, too. Even dad said he liked them after dinner."

"He does. Your father's just concerned, dear, the same as me. We want you happy and safe, without walking into something you're not fully prepared –"

"Hold on." I raise my hand, pushing an invisible barrier between us. "You think I'm not? Really? After we've lived a thriller movie? After I told you how he saved me from that psycho, t*wice,* and I almost lost him? After I caught hell from my best friend, who's *finally* about to pass her last semester, by the way?" Jamie and me are about to be sisters-in-law, and we're actually happy about it.

Mom sets her tea down. "Kendra, that's wonderful. You two had a wild road to love. There's no denying it. I'm not questioning your love, or your devotion, or your happiness."

No? I wonder. *Then why the second guessing? Jesus, mom, the wedding is less than a month away.*

October, the month that seems to stretch on the longest in Arizona, will be the starting line for our eternity. It couldn't be more perfect.

"I don't get it." I shrug. "What are you asking then?"

"You've found your happiness and the love of your life. Now, I just want to know you'll keep them."

I open my mouth to fire back, but I close it again with the first unsaid word stuck on my tongue.

There's nothing more infuriating than when your mother is right.

XVI: LONGEST DAYS (KNOX)

Two Weeks Later

I CAN'T REMEMBER the last time I ever smiled looking at this asshole. It must've been for a Christmas photo years ago, when we sat for his photographer, Lizzie in my arms, fake plastic smiles plastered to our faces.

The smile today is entirely real.

"Mr. Foreman, if you'll please, kindly read this court the jury's verdict." The Judge watches, perched like a hawk draped in black on his high bench, staring at the skinny man in the jury block who stands, holding a piece of paper.

"Your Honor, we find Victor Philips Wright guilty on all counts: first degree criminal conspiracy to commit murder, first degree conspiracy of fraud, first degree child endangerment, first degree..."

The words melt together the longer I listen. It's

euphoria to my ears, and it gives me the strength to keep my eyes locked on the asshole in his rat pit. Remarkably, he stares back the whole time, his jaw clenched, grinding his teeth as it sinks in that, yes, he's going away forever.

Bye-bye, mansion.

Bye-bye, billionaire net worth.

Bye-bye, granddaughter you never gave a single shit about.

Bye-bye, chances to ever fuck with me or my family ever again.

It's quiet. The foreman finishes reading the long list of crimes ensuring he'll stay locked up until the sun goes cold.

I just wish a monster like him could understand. If he knew the pain he'd caused, if he ever regretted the kids who got caught in the crossfire while we chased diamonds through those petty warlord fiefdoms, if he was sorry for scaring Lizzie, or ripping away the woman I loved, or maybe had remorse for stuffing his own daughter away to die anonymously in a dirty fucking hospital far beneath his means...I might not feel this way.

Oh, but I do, and it's the sickest happiness I've ever known. It's the last shot of vengeance tonic I'll savor before I walk out of here and return to a normal life, where I've learned to smile at things that are a thousand times more healthy.

I hear the judge's gavel slap the wood. Then the cameras clicking as the media hounds leap to their feet, chasing their photo ops. It's the most high profile criminal case the valley is likely to see for the next decade, maybe longer.

I just sit back while the bailiff helps him up with two

more guards at his side, leading him to the exit. When he gets to me, he stops, refusing to move until they prod him.

Look me in the eye, asshole. It's the last time.

"You're as guilty as I am, Carlisle. You'll never be a good man, no matter how many times you sit there high and mighty, trying to convince yourself it's true. Go to hell."

"Move along," the bailiff growls, giving him a shove.

Victor twists his head over his shoulder before he moves, eyes locked on me as long as humanly possible, like he's trying to make a curse stick.

There's time to mouth a one sentence reply before he's through the door.

"Here's your guilt, heartless fuck." I bang on my chest, just once, sending a shock through the organ that's taken the biggest beating, and hasn't quit on me yet. That's the true difference between us. "Already faced mine, and won. Now, I get to watch you rot."

* * *

Much as I tell myself it's over, I can't get the dirty, spell-bound look that evil bastard gave me out of my head.

It wasn't a lie. I've faced my own demons and conquered, except for one.

Later, when I'm home, I figure out how. I have dinner like usual with Sunflower and my baby girl. It's steak, asparagus, and the best goddamned garlic potatoes this side of the Superstition mountains tonight. We all do the cooking. I even let Lizzie help do the fun part, mashing up the potatoes.

We talk about the wedding, watch a movie, and put Lizzie down to sleep.

I'm starting to feel human again. Finding it easier to move like I never had hot lead tearing through my guts. The wound is healing nicely, and my sore abs are finally able to keep up with the need in my balls, which hasn't slowed since the day I got out of the hospital, and started sharing a bed with the woman I love.

I'm not the only one who's missed hard, frequent sex, and eager to make up for lost time. Sunflower can't keep her hands off me. She's got her fingers on my chest, nails on my back, teeth on my lips as soon as we're in the hall, my little girl's door shut behind us.

I take her hand and squeeze, reaching for her lips with the other. I lay my finger across her lips. "Easy, darling. Before we fuck ourselves to Neptune and back, there's something I want to show you. Come on."

Curiosity puts a hold on her lust. She follows me as I lead us downstairs, past my office, into the extra storage room beyond. I haven't touched the box tucked in the corner for weeks.

Before tonight, I only added to it. Never so much as held the paper inside between my fingers for years. I reach in, seeking the letters with a dead man's hand-writing.

"What's this?" she whispers, the anticipation building in her fingers on mine.

"These belonged to my old man. Secrets he left behind. Probably dirty ones, judging by how he did them. I've avoided it for too long, but now I want the truth. Hell, I need it," I growl, staring into her eyes, jade green as unsettled as the blue in mine. "I can't go on not knowing, darling. Everything I'm doing is a reset, wiping the slate clean, so we can start our life the only way we ought to."

I kiss her hand. She nods, urging me on. My thumb slides over the seal. It's addressed to Judy, the bitch I think is dad's mistress when he went through his mid-life crisis.

"Never showed these to ma. Never opened them. Too busy running from whatever's inside," I say, slicing the edge with my pocket knife. "She can't know what's in here. Me, on the other hand...it's time. Can't go through life wondering how bad he was, how fucked up I have the potential to be at my core. If he was screwing around behind ma's back, I need to know. I'll do what it takes to avoid his mistakes, even if they're ugly as hell."

I stop. My eyes scan the very first sentence, and that's all it takes to drive home how wrong I've been.

JUDY,

YOU'VE GOT to stop him. We've wasted too much time trying to catch him red-handed. No more chasing the circumstantial.

I can't let him do another diamond run. He's enriching killers for our product.

I've told him over and over, there are better ways. Costlier, but cleaner ways to get our product, and easier ways to make up what we lose on acquisitions in better marketing.

He doesn't listen. And he's about to go behind my back, breaking my veto as full partner.

We can't let him.

Can't leave this mess for my son someday. Can't let him

come after me, or my family, because I think he knows we're after him, closing in.

You know how many nights I've sat up, wired, wondering how far he'll go to get his way?

Victor doesn't even look after his own daughter. She's a troubled kid, going down a bad path, and I'm scared as hell she'll never have the heart for this business, should he ever step aside.

Not in her condition. Maybe not ever.

Go to the Feds. I'll fax you the secret ledger he keeps for funding his raiders. Hurry, Judy, before it's too late.

"KNOX?" Kendra's angelic hand curves, tracing my neck with her fingers.

It's the only thing that keeps the pressure in my skull from causing an explosion. My heart hasn't slammed against my ribs like this since the night Gannon shot me.

"Knox, are you okay? Talk to me!" She squeezes me harder, bringing her lips to my skin.

Without saying anything, I drop the letter and turn, pulling my beacon back to this world into my arms. "I was wrong, Sunflower. So wrong it aches like it fucking should at its best and worse. So wrong for so damn long, and I've never been happier."

"I was worried," she whispers, smiling when our lips brush.

"I still am," I say, sifting fingers through her hair, fisting those gold locks like precious silk. Her eyes question mine, seeking a way to help.

We kiss for a good minute. My hands move, gripping her skin, sliding to her ass. They jerk her against me, fitting her hips snug against mine, my cock hard and ready in my trousers.

"Down," I tell her. "Hit the floor and spread 'em."

I couldn't be more serious. There's a storm rolling through my bones I barely understand, but I know weathering it involves her tight cunt wringing my balls dry. There's no time to go upstairs.

Fuck the bed tonight, the spa, or even the kitchen counter.

There's a thousand words I have no language to say. I just need it out of me, the same way I need to be inside her this very second.

The low growl in my throat slips out when I push my fingers under her belt. She gasps when I pop the clasp, the zipper, and rip them down her legs. Her lush little ass falls out under me as we go down, her on all fours, wet spot calling every inch of me through her panties.

My pants disappear easy, and so does the last scrap of fabric hiding her sweet pink. Kendra moans, panties twisted around her knees.

"You know what this means? Why I'm having my way here and *now?*" I push inside her on the last word. Her back arches and a shrill cry spills out of her. Music to my ears.

Her pleasure is the only answer I get. Only one I need. Kissing her neck, right above the shoulders, I thrust harder, bringing her to me, fist tangled in her hair.

"This is it, Sunflower. The only fucking therapy I'll ever need. I should've had you years ago, put our first kid inside you, made you this promise." She sinks across my cock, swallowing it up to the hilt. My free hand brushes her side, traces her arm, and stops to bundle my fingers in hers. Another gasp. Another moan. Another wicked pull of my lips, becoming a carnal smile. "I *will* wife you as hard as this fuck, darling. I'll burn like the blood in your finger under my ring. I'll let the past die, knowing our future's as loud and precious as your heart strumming in your chest this second. No more bullshit. No more lies. No more secrets. Let's do forever, Sunflower, because that's all we've ever had."

It's a strange time to have an epiphany when I'm crashing into the woman I love, grunting each time her ass connects with my skin, turning to embers as the fire in my balls reaches to my throat.

But I'd be a fool to ignore it.

I'd be mad to second guess.

I'd be blind, deaf, and dumb all at once to ignore the spark kindling my heart.

Because it's not really a spark. It's a starscape lighting up the blackness inside me, melting it, shining on the path to my forever like never before.

She's whimpering, shaking at the knees, a beautiful mess under me whispering the same mantra.

Yes, yes, yes!

Knox!

Please!

"Come for me already," I whisper in her ear, slowing my strokes so she can hear me loud and clear, even as I'm pumping her harder. Her divine ass ripples from the power I'm giving every thrust. "Come like you were meant to since we found our stars."

I don't try to hold back when her fingers pinch mine, her knees quake harder, and the drawn out mewl in her throat becomes steady, shrill ecstasy. I'm her willing prisoner.

I'm growling when I hitch forward again, hold myself deep, and feel my spine ignite. Come floods out in vicious bursts, into my forever, so swift it steals my breath.

Even when I can't breathe, when I'm balls deep and out of my mind, I'm happier than I've ever been because I'm with her.

With her.

Around her.

In her.

Forever, unbelievably, hers.

* * *

MY BIOGRAPHY HAS A DOZEN PARTS. Soldier, father, son, brother, lover, and even fool.

It's *man* that never sat right with me until the last few weeks flash by like a monsoon.

Now, there's no question.

I'm whole. Complete. Crazier than I've ever been in all the best ways.

I walk out of that room holding dad's letters in one hand, and Sunflower slung over my shoulder with the other.

We head upstairs. I take her three more times that night, exhausting our pent up lust in my bed, the same mattress I can't wait to wear down once she's finally my wife.

In the morning, I read the rest of his letters. All six. The last was written just a couple weeks before dad's heart attack, when life got real, and I started to fear finding out who he really was.

There's no more doubt.

My old man never cheated on ma. He never put a black mark on this family, or on me.

He tried sparing us a lot of blood, sweat, and tears.

He thought he had Black Rhino's CFO on his side. But Judy Winds cracked and couldn't carry their plan through after he dropped dead.

The woman wasn't strong like him. She confessed everything to Victor not long after dad died. He gave her a fat severance and accepted her resignation.

A little detective work in the corporate records tells me everything. It also says she died a footnote in Albuquerque a few years into retirement, just a couple years ago.

If I had a regretful bone in my body, I'd wonder why cowardice and bad luck fucked things up for years. I'd dwell on it, wish like hell it'd happened differently, sparing us the misery.

But I don't. Not anymore. It's time to put the past to bed.

I march the letters outside and tuck them in the fire pit next to my citrus trees, except for one. The old lighter I still carry gives its flame. It's habit, keeping it in my pocket from when I used to smoke.

I haven't had a cig in years. It's a thousand times more satisfying watching dead worlds burn.

The breeze ruffles the last letter in my hand. Kendra saw plenty when I pulled them out in front of her, but this one is for two sets of eyes only.

It's two pages. There's a brief note from Judy,

promising she'll keep the enclosed safe, in the event 'something terrible' happens. Then on the next page, a confession.

SON,

WHAT DO I EVEN SAY? *You're grown up, finding yourself, and you're a bigger hero than I'll ever be by heading off to boot camp soon.*

I don't have a crystal ball. No magic words to pass down from the Carlisles who came before. No litany of wisdom because I'm not that arrogant.

I just have the truth, and here it is: some very serious affairs with Black Rhino are coming to a head soon. I don't know what will happen.

If I wind up in jail, or dead, or even worse, here's what I want you to do in one simple word.

Live.

By your terms. By your passion. Find the love of your life and have a few kids. Spend more time with them than the days I got with you and Jamie.

Forget the money. There's always more somewhere and it's never worth it if it makes you dirty.

Honor me by having a good life, and making sure your sister has the same.

Live. With love always.

I READ his words over and over before I slip it back in its envelope, and keep it safe for Jamie.

The irony should gut me, thinking my father left me with a lot of doubts, when all he's left is his very best.

No. I take it like a man standing next to the fire.

I'm still smiling the very second Kendra comes out, Lizzie hanging on her hand, both of them laughing over some lighthearted chatter I missed.

I don't know what dad's words would've meant if I'd read them a year ago.

Instead, I've been living his advice without knowing it, renewed in every heartbeat, every breath, every time I lay eyes on my family, and know they're a finer treasure than any I ever asked for.

This is my life on this rock. And for the first time in ages, I love it.

Cinderella, Prince Charming, and the Fairy-fucking-Godmother combined never had it this good.

XVII: UNDER SUN AND STARS
(KENDRA)

One Month Later

TOMORROW, it's Paris.

Tonight, it's Sedona.

We watch the red October sunset slip low in the sky over the tinted mountains, a beacon reminding me how much time has passed. Twenty-four hours since I officially became the latest Mrs. Carlisle.

"Pretty far from the casita, aren't we?" I say, rubbing his arm. He flashes a grin as he shifts gears, bringing us higher into the mountains, away from the cozy and luxurious vacation house he owns below.

"Not high enough yet by half, Sunflower. Don't tell me you're still dog tired from yesterday?"

My fingers squeeze his bicep. Hard, needy, and mine. "I'm human, Knox. You only kept me up all night and insisted we take off by noon for the helicopter ride up here."

We spent hours before we landed touring the awesome canyons and mountain vistas. If Earth wears a diamond ring like the one on my finger, it's here, perched between Phoenix and Flagstaff in a splendor merging fine stones with crystal skies. Raw beauty layered purple, red, and blue in endless combinations.

"A man's entitled to his wedding night. Best fuck I ever had since our first, darling. And that's hard to pin down with so many good ones in between. Even harder to believe...hell, I'm still *hard* myself."

"Honeymoon isn't over, ass. Are we really going to do it on two continents in just as many days?"

He nods. Completely serious.

"Do I joke about life and death, Sunflower?"

Nope. That's totally not his caveman style. Of course, he shows his tenderness when he thinks I'm not looking, too.

Like when we went to Jamie's graduation just before the wedding. He practically broke his little sister in a bear hug, lifting her up in his arms, and telling her, *you finally did it, sis. I'm fucking proud.*

If she was any other woman, I'd be jealous.

His heart shined through again when we handed Lizzie off to her grandmas after the reception. Yes, *both* of them.

She's spending time with Mrs. Carlisle, mom, and her new grandpa while we're gone for the next week. My parents looked like they couldn't wait to have a little girl running around the house again. They only told about a million stories from my childhood antics in front of everyone.

Knox laughed, teased me with his eyes, but he couldn't keep them off his baby girl for long. She hasn't been away from him for so long since the trip to Africa he's sworn will be his last with a gun and a mission. Next time, he says, it'll be charity.

I get him. It's scary to let go, even just for a vacation, but he did it for us. He did it to go beyond the vows, and make sure our families become one, stitched together in our messy, happy love.

"Last warning, darling," he says, squeezing my hand as the truck rolls on. "By the time we get up this mountain, you better have those lips ready."

Dear God. I don't know whether I'm supposed to be shocked by his bossy business or turned on, but there's a definite rush of heat between my thighs. I snuggle in, holding his arm tighter, each curl of my hand bringing more memories.

Every time I can't believe I'm a married woman, I re-live the ceremony. I see it all on repeat. I want to cry again.

Mom, dad, Jamie, and my new mother-in-law, smiling while I walked down the aisle, thankful for the paper thin veil obscuring my tears.

Promising myself I'd be strong. Naturally, I cracked like a baby, sniffling through the first part of the cere-mony. I caught myself when it counted, thankfully, and held it together while we swapped vows.

Lizzie grinning up at us as grandma helped her lift the pillow holding our rings. I had a feeling she'd love the ritual, the excitement, and of course the fairy tale trappings of the wedding, but I didn't know she'd *understand* it.

When I looked into her eyes, I knew. And so did she.

To love. To cherish. To have and to hold.

I do. And so does he.

Infinity times over.

Our vows were one of those surreal, beautiful moments that swell to a crescendo before I'm even able to tell where the music is coming from. And once I realize it's always been in our hearts, we're man and wife, and it's time to kiss the bride.

I'll never forget how my husband's lips tasted the first time they conquered mine. Familiar, but different than when they were a mere lover's kiss.

Sweeter. Sexier. Stronger. Emotional steroids.

Our kiss lived a storm, a flood, and a blooming desert oasis in sixty seconds flat.

Frantic and hopeful as our own joined pulse.

Timeless, maybe, when my tongue folded against his, and our forever yawned to heaven.

Endless. Really and truly because that's the vow I took. Not just the words I muttered in front of our pastor and everyone I care about, but the promise in every breath, every pulse, every glance completely high on us.

When I open my eyes and happy reminiscing scatters like butterflies, his truck stops. I feel his lips connect with my forehead, and he takes my hand, giving it a gentle pinch. "We're here. Just in time for champagne and sky."

I don't quite follow what he means until I look up, popping the door. It's hard not to trip all over myself, especially when my jaw is almost dragging on the ground.

"You...you did this for us? Or hired someone?"

"All me, Sunflower. Set it up with a guy to rent the top of this mountain and make sure it's ours as long as we want. The rest, no. No damn way I'd ever let another man touch something this personal."

Heart, meet knees. I don't snap out of my stupor until he takes my hand, leading me forward.

What looks like a beautiful white pagoda sits safely near the cliff. Next to it, a cooler, full of ice, champagne, caviar, and fancy cheeses. I see them all when he throws a simple cloth over the small wire table, and retrieves a bottle with two crystal glasses.

Any other woman would be ruined by the stunning romantic view. We're just in time to see the night sky descend over the red sun waving farewell. But for me, it's the flowers.

They're everywhere. Sunflowers line the walking path and form the inner circle around our little sanctuary.

Tall. Yellow. Vivid.

Brighter than the dying sun.

"Amazing," I whisper, probably for the fifth time. We share a smile, and I try to communicate the emotions beyond simple words blowing through my soul.

"Wrong. You'll see something truly amazing in another hour when our stars come, and we're living everything we should've had from the first damn word." He silences me before I can answer with a kiss.

My hands slide down his back, tracing his muscles, falling against the soft plush cushion under the bench. I've had two sips of champagne since we clinked glasses, and I'm done. His kisses are so much better, so deliciously addicting.

"A whole hour? What in the world will we do to pass

the time?" I whisper, sticking my tongue out through my teeth.

Hot breath quickens against my throat. Knox kisses me there while his hand slips to the curve of my hip, leaving no doubt what's on the agenda all night.

"Magic, Cinderella," he rumbles. His voice fades, swallowed in my moan, and the sweet pressure of his lips on my skin. "Wish you'd brought those fancy slippers with. One day, I *will* fuck you while they're on your ankles. Always wondered what they'd feel like digging into my skin."

I shudder. The taboo thought gives me plenty reason to smile. It's not just imagining his piston thrusts between my thighs while I scream, sinking the glass heels into his muscular legs. It's the fact that without him, they'd be trapped in a patent lawsuit between me and Gannon, rather than getting ready for their first big European fashion show.

That's the other reason we've picked Paris for our honeymoon. The city of lights drips romance and history in every street, and when he learned I'd been tapped by a big name brand overseas for their fall show, he insisted.

Now, though, his lips are demanding something else. Knox growls when he catches my skirt, tossing it high over my waist, and his mouth grazes my legs.

My hands reach over my head, find the edge of the bench, and brace. I need all the leverage I can get to withstand the tsunami when his tongue flicks higher, crawling up my thighs, a movement away from my pulsing center.

I'm not the only one in for a wicked surprise. He groans, tongue arching over my slick pussy lips, a satisfied rumble caught in his throat. "Good girl. No panties."

NICOLE SNOW

"Just like you asked. What kind of woman would I be to deny my husband a simple request?" I smile, looking down as his fingers pinch my thighs, a marvelously feral glint in his sky blue eyes. It's incredible how brilliant the sunset makes them glow.

"You'd be the girl who doesn't get to come on my face two times before I fuck you at the top of the world."

Sweet mercy.

Ecstasy holds every inch of me hostage as he pins me down, spreads me open, pushing his face between my folds. When I'm tossing my head back, squirming, trying to remember my own name, I'm in awe. It's incredible how his familiar tongue still feels strange and wonderful.

Knox's mouth was always the beginning and the end.

He licks me, faster and harder as my pleasure builds. He knows my body's rhythm, how to touch every nerve to make our song. It's the same mouth he used to tease me, torture me, awaken me going back a decade.

And now it belongs to my husband.

Now, it's inside me, just like his words are seared in my brain.

Now, it's a reminder he owns everything, starting with the bead beneath his tongue.

My clit throbs against his licks. They cut fierce circles around it, a circuit of pure sex, feeding the fireball building in my belly.

His mouth is too occupied to speak, but I hear his commands every time his fingers sink into my thighs. *Give it the fuck up for me, Kendra.*

Come.

My first orgasm is a scream. My body seizes, hips

272

thrusting, frantically trying to catch his mouth, greedy and ready for more, more, *more.*

I can't fathom how long I ride his face. It's darker, the sun's last pale orange stripe retreating over the mountains, and somehow he's pulled off my skirt in the commotion. I'm straddling his chest, slick and panting, hands gliding over his tattoos while I open his shirt. He's popped the buttons for me.

Reaching for his cock, I feel it through his trousers, and moan. I *need* him in me.

Knox grabs my hand, a smirk on his lips. The blue flames in his eyes melt mine several times over.

"Did I say fuck me yet, darling? You owe this tongue another O. Pay your dues." He helps drag me naked up his chest, until I'm positioned over his face. Then his hands circle to my ass, catching hold, pulling me into the white hot fire blinding me on the first lick.

This pressure, this angle, this otherworldly tongue takes me prisoner. And I'm a willing captive. So damn ready there's no doubt this is ending in a seething mess.

I whimper when he pulls my legs shut around his head. His tongue feels bigger somehow underneath, sweeping my entire pussy. He shoves it inside me and fucks my walls hard, equally rough and sensual. Harbinger of the hard-on I know is tenting behind me while I moan, rocking my hips on his face.

And Knox rocks me, too. Straight to my very core. I'm doused in fire and dipped in his muscular valley again. He holds me down when I try to squirm away, unrelenting when I pause for even a second, overwhelmed by the building tension.

"Knox..." I whine his name, a split second before my

knees shake, and my pussy pinches tight around his tongue. "Knox! Holy hell."

He growls his reply. Wordless, predictable, unbearably hot.

You better fucking come.

When his mouth finds my clit, there's no question. No choice. It's submission at its finest; a low, sweeping, wild surrender to the lightning he's brought to my depths.

Another suck.

Another soft kiss of his teeth, holding on, dragging me deeper.

Another lick, smothering my hostage clit over and over and *over.*

That's exactly what I am.

Over. Done. Ended.

I come apart quaking, screaming, hands splayed and trembling on his chest. He holds me up to nirvana. The pressure building inside me isn't just fire.

It's wet, so wet. I'm squirting all over him, and I have a second of self-conscious shame.

But it only quickens his tongue. The animal heat of his thirst deepens, and he drinks my lust, my passion, my coming undone.

I throw my head to the newborn night sky and let out a silent scream. It's too intense. I can't even make a sound.

It's a full body release on his tongue. I think I black out, deep in the zone, and don't come back until softer kisses touch my inner thigh. His hands are in mine, locked at the fingers.

"What?" I whisper, smiling, staring down into his blue-eyed mystery.

"Admiring the view. It'd be a crime not to. You're more

beautiful every time you come for me, Sunflower. Fuck, you taste good, even though it just makes me hungrier."

His tongue sweeps across his lips. There's still a chill halfway up my spine when his arms wrap around my waist, lifting me like I'm nothing, and we shift positions.

Knox moves between my legs, pushing his bare cock against my pussy. I'm in heat again the instant he's in, as if I haven't just come twice on his tongue.

"You ready, wife?" His eyes are deadly serious. He rolls his hips, sliding his cock to my entrance, agonizingly close.

I can't even move. There are no words, so I grip my lip with my bottom teeth, and nod. His fingers climb behind my head, finding their place in my hair. Taking hold, he watches me open my eyes, and stare into the brightest two stars in his face. His eyes stand out among the brilliance blooming in the sky high above his head.

I loved our wedding night, but this is better. I'm about to have my husband at the edge of eternity.

"Can't hear you, darling," he whispers, running his lips down my neck, taking one nipple in his mouth.

He doesn't let go until my moan becomes a plea. "Please. Knox, fuck, *please.*"

One word.

One thrust.

One madness.

Every rock hard inch of him sinks into me. My hips come home against his, and my legs wrap tight, ankles nesting the backs of his thighs.

There's no more room for words. Just firm, sweet silence, the sounds of us colliding as the universe blurs around us, beauty lost in two hearts overflowing.

His mouth takes mine while his cock owns me from the inside out.

Tongues frolic, muscles pinch, pleasure rampages a conduit through us.

He devours every moan. I take every kiss, every grunt, every scorching sound spilling out of him into my soul.

"Fuck, fuck, fuck," he groans, hips hammering mine, thrusts coming faster. He fills me so full his pubic bone crashes across my clit, igniting a devilish friction.

I don't last long. My fingers grapple at his shoulders, rolling down his back. Teeth clenching, eyes rolling, body blazing, it's done.

Coming!

Release rips me in two. I think I'd be gone forever if I didn't feel his heat behind me, full and intense.

Knox sinks in as far as he can go. Pleasure squeezes from his throat in feral bursts. His grunts are thunder breaking the night.

"Sunflower!" My name is the last thing on his lips before the molten flood.

He breaks inside me.

Seed. Smoke. Fire.

My pussy finds a new climax I didn't know was possible.

Somewhere on earth, I'm a clawing, mewling, shaking mess. Locked to my lover, my husband, my one. Sealed to forever, as sure as the night sky brightening around us.

But I'm not just on a beautiful Sedona mountaintop anymore, lovingly prepared for our first real coupling as man and wife.

I'm deeper in his soul, the one and only spirit meant for me, so familiar I don't lose myself in his sky blue beauty and tragic strength. When I come out of the trance, I've got my hand on his cheek, loving how his stubble prickles my palm.

He pulls out with a reluctant sigh, and stays on top. He rests between my legs, as if he's shielding me from the night.

"Love you, hubby," I whisper, bringing my lips to his for a recovery kiss.

So many layers in his lips. So many ways to taste love.

When we break away, he's smiling, brushing loose hair over my ear. "Love you, too, Sunflower. But you're looking the wrong way."

I don't know what he means. Gently, he tilts my face, until we're both staring over the mountaintops.

The night sky glows. Vast and full, stars bleeding from the hilt, their soft light splashes across the sunflowers surrounding us. It's a heavenly ring brought to earth, and just for us.

"They're still there. They never left us. That goes double for me, Kendra. I'll love you like my wife deserves longer than those mountains stand," he says, voice lower by the gravity of his promise.

"Longer than our stars shine? Because that's how long, how much I was planning to love you," I whisper hopefully, touching my forehead to kiss. God, his heat is precious.

"Forever, darling, and that's a long damn time. Rest. Catch your breath. We've got a private jet waiting at the airport tomorrow, and night's young. We're not even close to done yet."

He's as true as his word. We're a tangled mess of scarce

words, many glances, and furious explosions until our stars begin to hide from the sun.

The next morning, I'm groggy. My legs feel like they've been soaked in bourbon and lit on fire. It's a drag just climbing in his truck and heading for the airport. I pass out with my head on his shoulder once we're on the plane, on our way to a quick fueling stop somewhere on the east coast, and then onto Paris.

I never dreamed this kind of happiness meant being undone.

Oh, but I'm learning.

I'm loving it.

And nothing will ever wipe this fairy tale smile off my face.

THANKS!

Want more Nicole Snow? Sign up for my newsletter to hear about new releases, exclusive subscriber giveaways, and more fun stuff!

JOIN THE NICOLE SNOW NEWSLETTER! - http://eepurl.com/HwFW1

Thank you so much for buying this ebook. I hope my romances will sweeten your days with pleasure, drama, and all the feels! I tell the stories you want to hear.

If you liked this book, please consider leaving a review and checking out my other romance tales.

Got a comment on my work? Email me at

THANKS!

nicole@nicolesnowbooks.com. I love hearing from my fans!

Nicole Snow

More Intense Romance by Nicole Snow

LOVE SCARS: BAD BOY'S BRIDE

MERCILESS LOVE: A DARK ROMANCE

RECKLESSLY HIS: A BAD BOY MAFIA ROMANCE

STEPBROTHER CHARMING: A BILLIONAIRE BAD BOY ROMANCE

STEPBROTHER UNSEALED: A BAD BOY MILITARY ROMANCE

PRINCE WITH BENEFITS: A BILLIONAIRE ROYAL ROMANCE

MARRY ME AGAIN: A BILLIONAIRE SECOND CHANCE ROMANCE

Prairie Devils MC Books

OUTLAW KIND OF LOVE

NOMAD KIND OF LOVE

SAVAGE KIND OF LOVE

WICKED KIND OF LOVE

BITTER KIND OF LOVE

Grizzlies MC Books

OUTLAW'S KISS

OUTLAW'S OBSESSION

OUTLAW'S BRIDE

OUTLAW'S VOW

Deadly Pistols MC Books

NEVER LOVE AN OUTLAW

NEVER KISS AN OUTLAW

NEVER HAVE AN OUTLAW'S BABY

NEVER WED AN OUTLAW

Baby Fever Books

BABY FEVER BRIDE

BABY FEVER PROMISE

BABY FEVER SECRETS

Only Pretend Books

FIANCÉ ON PAPER

SEXY SAMPLES: FIANCÉ ON PAPER

I: Look Who's Back (Maddie)

Something in his makeup made him an utter bastard, but I owed him my life.

It's my heart I refused to give up without a fight. If only I'd known from the very start Calvin Randolph never backs down.

Not in love. Not in business. Not in any corner of his battered existence.

I'll never understand it.

Maybe he's missing the gene that stops a normal man from sinking his hands into the earth and ripping it to messy, screaming shreds until he gets his way.

Perhaps defeat just never made sense in his head.

Or possibly it's because this was just meant to be. There's a natural mischief in every heart that loves bringing together what's complicated, dangerous, and totally incompatible in a blinding impact.

Oh, but I still wish I'd *known*, before our blind collision became love.

We would have prevented so much suffering.

* * *

I'm in no mood to pull a jet black envelope out of my mailbox. Not after an exhausting day dealing with corporate legalese and a language barrier that's like a migraine prescription. Especially when said legalese is a hodge-podge of English and Mandarin bullet points outlining bewildering trade concepts that make me want to pop aspirin like Junior Mints.

But the coal colored envelope isn't what ends me. It's a single word, the one and only scrawled on the front in bright pink, without so much as a return address or a stamp to accompany it.

DOLL.

No one's called me that in years. Seven, to be precise.

I have to steady myself against the mailbox when my heartbeat goes into my ears. For a second I'm afraid I'll faint.

It's incredible how the only man who'd ever call me a name I haven't heard since high school still has a freakish ability to reduce me to a knee-shaking, cement lunged mess so many years later.

My fingernail slides across the seal, digs in, and splits it open. I tear gingerly, like I'm expecting a snake or a tarantula to jump out. There isn't enough room for creepy crawlies, I suppose, though I wonder about the hard lump in the corner, rubbing it against my palm.

The constant noise in the hall of my cramped Beijing flat has faded from a roar to a whisper. It's hard to focus on the slim white note I pluck out when I'm trying to remember how to breathe. There's no mistaking the handwriting.

They're his words. I'd recognize them anywhere, even after so long.

Blunt, mysterious, and taunting as ever. He keeps it short and sweet – assuming there's anything sweet about reaching down inside me, and yanking out a dozen painful memories at once.

It's been too long.
  You still owe me that favor, doll, and I'm cashing in.
  Marry me.

-Cal

"Marry me?" I read it again, shaking my head.

If this is a joke, it isn't funny. And I already know it isn't. Cal wouldn't break a seven year silence for a stupid laugh. It's serious, and it's a brand new kind of terrifying.

My eyes trace his three insane sentences four times before my knees give out.

I go down hard, banging my legs on the scuffed tile, dropping the envelope. The object anchored in the corner bounces out with a clatter as loud as a crashing symbol, leaving a haunting echo in my ears.

I look down and mentally start planning my goodbyes. It's a gold ring with a huge rock in the middle, set into a flourish designed to mimic a small rose. I don't need to try it on to know it's probably my size.

I flip the note over in my hands before I lose it. There's a number scrawled on the backside in the same firm, demanding script. CALL ME, says the two words next to it in bold, as if it's the most natural thing in the world to ask for a mail order bride in less than ten words.

As if it hasn't stopped my heart several times over.

I can't believe he's back.

I can't believe he's found me here, on the other side of the Earth, and decided to drag me back to the hell we both left behind.

I really, *really* can't believe what he's asking me to do.

But it's my fault, isn't it? I'm the one who said I'd do *anything*, if he ever needed it.

Without him, I wouldn't have my dream career working trade contracts in China for a prestigious Seattle company. I'd be lucky serving tables with the criminal stain on my record if he hadn't stepped in, and saved me when it seemed hopeless.

There's a lot I don't know.

Like why he's gone emergency bride hunting, for one. Or what he's been doing since the last dark day I saw him, crying while they hauled him off in handcuffs. I don't even know what kind of devils are in the details if I actually agree to this madness – and it's not like I have a choice.

Small town guilt will gnaw at my soul forever if I turn him down.

Oh, but he'll catch up with me again soon, and let me know exactly what new hell awaits. That much, I'm certain.

It won't be long before I'm face-to-face again with the sharp blue eyes that used to make my blood run hot. Twisted up in knots like a gullible seventeen year old with a bad crush and a blind spot for bad people before I know what's hit me. And yes, revisiting every horrible thing that happened at Maynard Academy in ways I haven't since my therapist discharged me with flying colors.

He's right about one thing, the only thing that matters in any of this: I owe him. Big time.

All the unknowns in the world are worthless stacked up against this simple truth.

So I'll wait, I'll shrivel up inside, and I'll chew on the same nagging question some more.

Jesus, Cal. What the hell have you gotten yourself into?

* * *

Seven Years Ago

The beautiful boy with the constant entourage ignored me until my seventh day at the new school.

How my parents thought I'd ever fit into this place, I don't know. They just saw the school's shiny academic track record and absorbed its prestige from Seattle socialites several leagues higher than we'd ever be. A fast track scholarship I won in an essay contest sealed the deal. My old English teacher in Everett submitted it behind my back when I was ready to throw it in the trash, and the rest is history.

Who could blame them for leaping at the chance? They want the absolute best for me. I'm ready to make my family proud, even if it means trading a huge piece of my seventeen year old social life for the best education several states over.

It's not like Maynard Academy has a welcome wagon. The other kids keep their awkward distance since the first day I show up on the seating charts next to them. Almost like they smell the stink of my missing trust fund, or the Mercedes that didn't materialize as soon as I got my license.

I still take the bus. And I'm not sure my parents could ever afford a trust lawyer on their seventy thousand combined income, raising two girls. Their struggle to keep up rent and bills reminds me how lucky I am to get a scholarship to this place.

Turns out the benefactor behind the money at Sterner Corp shares my love for John Steinbeck.

Ever since we moved down to south Seattle, uprooting lives and careers just for this special chance, I'm in another world.

If the black lacquered study desks, the library with the crystal chandeliers and the skylights, or the marble fountain out front hadn't tipped me off the first week, the natural pecking order here certainly does.

My face is stuck in a German textbook when he comes up to me. He doesn't bother with introductions, just pushes his fingers into my book, and rips it out of my hands.

"Do you ever speak?" His voice is smooth as ice, a rogue smirk tugging at his lips.

"Hey!" I stand up, dropping the rest of my small book stack on the floor, arms folded. "I don't know, don't *you* have any manners?"

"There's never been much point," he tells me, sizing me up with his sky blue eyes.

I hate it, but he isn't wrong. It took all of three days

here to notice how everyone hangs on his every word. There are always a couple grinning jocks and puppy-eyed cheerleaders at his shoulder. I think the teachers would love to knock 'Mr. Randolph' down a few marks, if only he didn't keep acing all his tests.

He's too good a student and too big a dick to be worth the trouble.

I've seen the summary sheets tacked to the boards. Every time, every class, Calvin Randolph ranks infuriatingly high. I've heard the gossip going around, too. Just because I like to keep my nose buried in my books doesn't mean I'm deaf.

He's a straight A jerk with money, good looks, and brains behind his predictable God complex.

"Seen you around, Maddie, and you haven't said shit. That's a first for me, being ignored like I'm not worth your time." Oh, he also has a filthy mouth, which makes it doubly ridiculous every woman in our class would kill to have it on hers. "I'd love to know why. Everybody, new or old, wants on my good side if they want off Scourge's bad."

For such cool, calming eyes, they burn like the sun. My cheeks go red, flustered and hot when I jerk my eyes off his. "I don't know who that is," I say. "It's only been a week."

"Interesting. Thought a girl who goes for the librarian look would be a lot more observant than that." I stick out my hand, going for my language book, but he jerks it away like I'm a helpless kitten. His smirk blooms into a cruel smile. "It's okay if you're a slow learner, doll. I'd have my eyes glued to this boring crap all the time too if I didn't have a photographic memory."

He's so full of it he's overflowing.

"Give it back," I snap, looking around to see if there are any teachers walking by. I'm not sure I'd have the courage to ask them to step in. This school isn't any different from an ordinary high school when it comes to attitudes, despite the family income level. Nobody wants to be the class runt who goes crying for help, and suffers the outcast consequences.

"Cal, I'm not playing around. I need to get to class."

The second to last bell of the day sounds over the speaker, adding its emphasis to my words. He clucks his tongue once, his strong jaw tightening. "So, you do know my name."

"What do you *want?*" I whine, trying to keep it together. "I don't have time for games."

I try to snatch my book again. Too slow. He lifts it higher, far above my head. I'm barely up to the neck attached to his broad, vast shoulders. He towers over me, one more way his body tells me how small I am next to him. Even physiology rubs in his superiority.

"I want you to crack a damned smile first," he says, laying a patronizing hand on my shoulder. "Show me something human. I've seen two expressions on your face since the day you showed up, doll. Tell me there's more."

"What happens on my face is *my* business, jerk. Not yours." By some miracle, he relents, letting my German book swing down with my hand the next time I grab it. I stumble a few steps back toward the bench to collect my mess of things.

I've got maybe sixty seconds to make it to class before the next bell if I don't want a tardy slip.

"Jerk? You're adorable." He steps closer, swallowing me

in his shadow. A few of the kids racing down the halls slow, watching the tension unfolding between us. "On second thought, fuck the smile. I'd love to see those lips say something nasty a whole lot more than I'd like them right-side up. Fact that you're blushing at the mere suggestion tells me I'm on the right track, doll."

His tone is creeping me out. I stuff a few loose books into my backpack, sling it over my shoulder, and start moving down the hall. Sighing, I decide to waste a few more precious seconds asking him the only question that really interests me.

"Why do you keep calling me that – 'doll?'"

"Christ, do I have to explain *everything?*" His smirk is back, and I decide I don't like it, no matter how much light it adds to his gorgeous face. "Button nose, brown eyes, chestnut hair that looks like it's never seen a real salon. You don't fit the Maynard mold. Must be smart if you made it here in the first place without money, but I can't say I'm impressed. Brains don't matter here. It's my job to make sure you find out how this school works the easy way. You don't want hard."

Hard? I have to stop my brain from going into the gutter, especially when he's looking at me like that. I'm also confused. *What in God's name is he talking about?*

I don't remember being so insulted, and never by a man who uses his good looks like a concealed weapon. "I'm perfectly capable of figuring it out myself. Thanks very much, ass," I yell back over my shoulder, moving my feet to put as much distance between us as quickly as I can.

"Thanks for giving me exactly what I want," he growls back, hands on his hips, his strong arms bulging at his sides. They look more like they belong to a weight lifter in his twenties than a boy who's just a year older than me.

The last class of the day, chemistry, is just a blur. It's one of the few I don't share with Cal this semester, thank God.

He's the lucky one, though. Not me. If I had to sit with his smug, searing blue eyes locked on me for more than another minute, I think I'd rush to find the easiest recipe for a test tube stink bomb that would teach him not to stick his nose where it doesn't belong.

* * *

Okay, so, maybe he's not the biggest dickweed at Maynard after all. It's a couple more weeks before I find out why everyone dreads Scourge. He's gone for my first weeks thanks to a long suspension. Meanwhile, I've aced my language studies, made a few loose friends, and even settled into a study routine blissfully free from Cal's attention.

That changes when the human storm blows in.

There's a commotion in front of our lockers at noon, near lunch, when the kid in the leather jacket rolls in late. He wears mostly black, just like every other coward in a tough guy shell since time began. Chains hang off his sleeves, looking like they were designed for whipping anyone in his path. I don't understand how he gets away with it at first, seeing how it violates every part of the school dress code.

He's every bad school bully stereotype rolled in a cliché. Shaggy dark hair with a black widow red stripe running through the middle, piercings out the wazoo, and a sour scowl dominating his face that makes Cal's smirk look downright angelic. He also has tattoos peaking out his neckline and crawling along his wrists. Screaming skulls, shooting fire, blood dipped daggers – the scary trifecta for a troubled young man trying his best to look hard.

I've also wondered why there's never anyone using the locker on my left side. I wrongly concluded it might be a spare.

Oh, sweet Jesus, if only I'd been so lucky.

Alex "Scourge" Palkovich Jr. shows me he means business without uttering a word. The boys and girls in front of him who don't clear a path fast enough get pushed out of his way. I get my first shot of panic when he's still ten feet away, after everybody between us slams their lockers shut and scurries across the hall.

"You." He points. I freeze in my tracks. "Where the fuck's Hugo? You his new girl, or what?"

"Hugo?" I don't know that name.

The psycho has his hands on my shoulders, shaking me like a ragdoll, before I'm able to remember why it sounds so familiar.

I inherited my locker from another student. There's a worn label stuck inside my locker with that name. *Hugo.*

"Don't play dumb with me," he snarls.

"Jeez, look, I don't know him. Honest. I'm not who you're looking –"

"Shut up! Stop covering for his fucking ass, little girl. He put me out for three weeks when his sorry ass got caught smoking what I sold. Nobody does business and then fucks me over, understand? No one!"

My nerves are on needles. His nostrils flare, and the

muscular fingers digging into my arms are starting to hurt. "Sorry, I'm new here. I don't think I can help you," I try to tell him, cool as I can manage. "I really don't know Hugo."

He sucks in a long, ragged breath and then shoves me away. He pushes me hard. My shoulder impacts the locker with an *oomph*, and I'm left leaning against it, wide-eyed and staring at the mess of a boy fuming next to me.

Scourge twists the knob on his locker for the combo, nearly rips the door off when he opens it, and slams it with a deafening bang after staring inside for a few breathless seconds. He looks at me. "Consider this your only warning. I find out you lied to me, I'll spend coin getting even, bitch. Already had two suspensions this year. Not afraid of a third, and you look like you're dying for someone to pull up that skirt and throw you against the nearest wall, teach you some fucking respect."

I can't breathe. I can't think. I can't stop my thumping heart from making me light-headed.

"Maddie, come on," Chelle says, tugging at my arm. "Get away from him."

I let her numbly lead me away to the school cafeteria. As soon as we've grabbed lunch and sat down, I start asking questions. It's the best way not to breakdown and cry after one of the scariest encounters of my life.

"What's his deal? Why do they let him stay?" I can't stop thinking how Cal used that name – doll –

as if I'm the misfit at this school. My chicken tenders and chocolate milk comfort me with the slightly-better-than-average charm school cafeteria food has. The academy's selection is nothing amazing, but it's filling and just tasty enough.

"Special protection. Principal Ross wants to run for school council next year, haven't you heard?" Chelle smiles sadly. I shake my head. "Well, guess whose father just happens to be a major shaker in Seattle politics? Ever heard of Alex Palkovich Sr., the councilman?"

"Oh, God." I wrinkle my nose. "You mean *he's* Scourge's dad? He used to show up for fundraisers and inspirational speeches at my dad's company."

"Yep, the apple falls pretty far from the tree this time. It's banged up and rotten."

"Who does he think he's convincing, anyway? I mean, the scary ink, the piercings, the punk bomber jacket...amazing he doesn't get called out for breaking dress code." I look down at my own soft blue blouse and plaid skirt, frowning.

Chelle just laughs. "Girl, you've got a lot to learn about how backs are scratched at Maynard. He's gotten in trouble tons of times. Scourge never gets suspended unless he's done *really* bad. Hugo got caught by his pastor smoking the roaches he bought off that kid. Gave up his source pretty quick, and they had to do something this time because the police were involved."

"Yeah, Hugo, I keep hearing that name. Where the heck is he?"

"You don't get on Scourge's bad side and get away without catching hell," Chelle says, wagging a finger. "Hugo's folks were smart. They pulled him out and transferred to Jackson High the next county over. Heard he *begged* them for it. It's not as good, of course, but it's better than spending the rest of his high school career waiting for the knife in his back."

I'm worried she means it literally. Could it be *that* bad?

I knew this boy was bad news, but I didn't know he was a total loon.

"And what's with the name? Scourge?"

Chelle opens her mouth to answer, but another voice cuts her off behind me. "Scourge of God, doll. It's from one of those dumb death metal bands he listens to. He only says it about ten times a week to remind us what hot shit he thinks he is. And don't you know he's got an Uncle in the *fucking Grizzlies?*"

When I spin my chair around, Cal stands there with a twinkle in his blue eyes, his hair tossed in a subtle, delicious mess. He's just come from gym, still wearing his black lacrosse shorts and grey jersey with the school's royal crested M.

"I wasn't asking you." I turn, pointing my nose in the air. I'm not in any mood for his games after what just went down.

"Heard you had a little run in with our pal. Move over, Emily." He takes her seat without even acknowledging the blonde sophomore next to me who looks like she's just been kissed because he remembers her name.

"I thought the Grizzlies cleaned up their act. That's what mom says, anyway. She used to ride with them sometimes in her wilder days, before she settled down with dad." I'm frowning, trying to figure out why he's decided to give me his precious attention today if it's not for his own amusement.

"They did. The uncle he makes sure everybody knows about has been in jail for years. One of the turds they flushed before the club started making money off clubs and bars from what I hear."

"Always so eloquent," Chelle says, sticking her tongue out.

"Did I invite you to this conversation?" he asks, scorning her with a glance, before turning back to me. "Shame about your mom, though. Good times are under-rated. Sure hope the wild streak is hereditary. You look like you could use some fun and take your mind off this crap, doll."

I'm blushing, and I hate it. Especially because it's all too easy to imagine the good times he has in mind.

There's no hope. I'm more like every other girl in my class than I care to admit: smitten, shaken, and yes, completely fascinated by this tactless jerk with an angel's looks. He's bad, thoughtless, and more than a little annoy-ing. But he's safe in a way Scourge isn't, despite how easy his teasing becomes insults.

He also gives everyone on his side a certain amount of protection from what I've gathered. Hugo never got close to Cal, and he became easy prey.

"Seriously, don't be scared of him, doll. *Do* stay out of his way. Tried to warn you when you got here. I can help."

Great. So he's come to impress me by playing hero. No thanks.

I'm also done being a doormat for anyone today. Walking out and giving him the cold shoulder feels like an easy way to replenish the self-esteem I've hemorrhaged with the bully.

"Tell me if you change your mind, doll. We'll work something out." His eyes aren't moving when they lock on, and the flush invading my skin just keeps growing.

I have to get out of here.

It's my turn to do the eye roll. Without saying

anything, I pick my tray up, and pause just long enough to share another look with him before the blood rushes to my cheeks. "I'm old enough to take care of myself, thanks. If I ever need your advice, Cal, I'll ask."

He doesn't say a word. But he watches me the entire time as I throw my trash away, drop the tray off, and head out for my evening classes. I resist the urge to turn around until the very end.

Of course, I do. How could I resist?

I'm just in time to see Chelle kick him under the table. He gives her a dirty look, stands, and heads back to his crew of jocks across the cafeteria.

Like I need this weirdo treating me like a damsel in distress, I think to myself, smiling for reasons I can't pin down as I head off to Pre-Calc.

I wish I'd taken more time then to appreciate the smiles we shared, however small. Months later, after the train wreck everyone took to calling 'the incident,' it's a miracle I ever learned to fake smile again.

GET FIANCÉ ON PAPER AT YOUR FAVORITE RETAILER!

Printed in Great Britain
by Amazon